Where The Winds Blow

by

Philip Rennett

Book 3 of the Path Finder Series

First published in Great Britain in 2025
by Pea Arr Books

ISBN: 978-1-7385747-2-8

Cover design by
Daniel Greenhalgh
cargocollective.com/danielgreenhalgh

Where The Winds Blow is a work of fiction.
Names, characters, places, and incidents either are the product
of the author's imagination or are used fictitiously.
Any resemblance to actual persons, living or dead,
events or locales, is entirely coincidental.

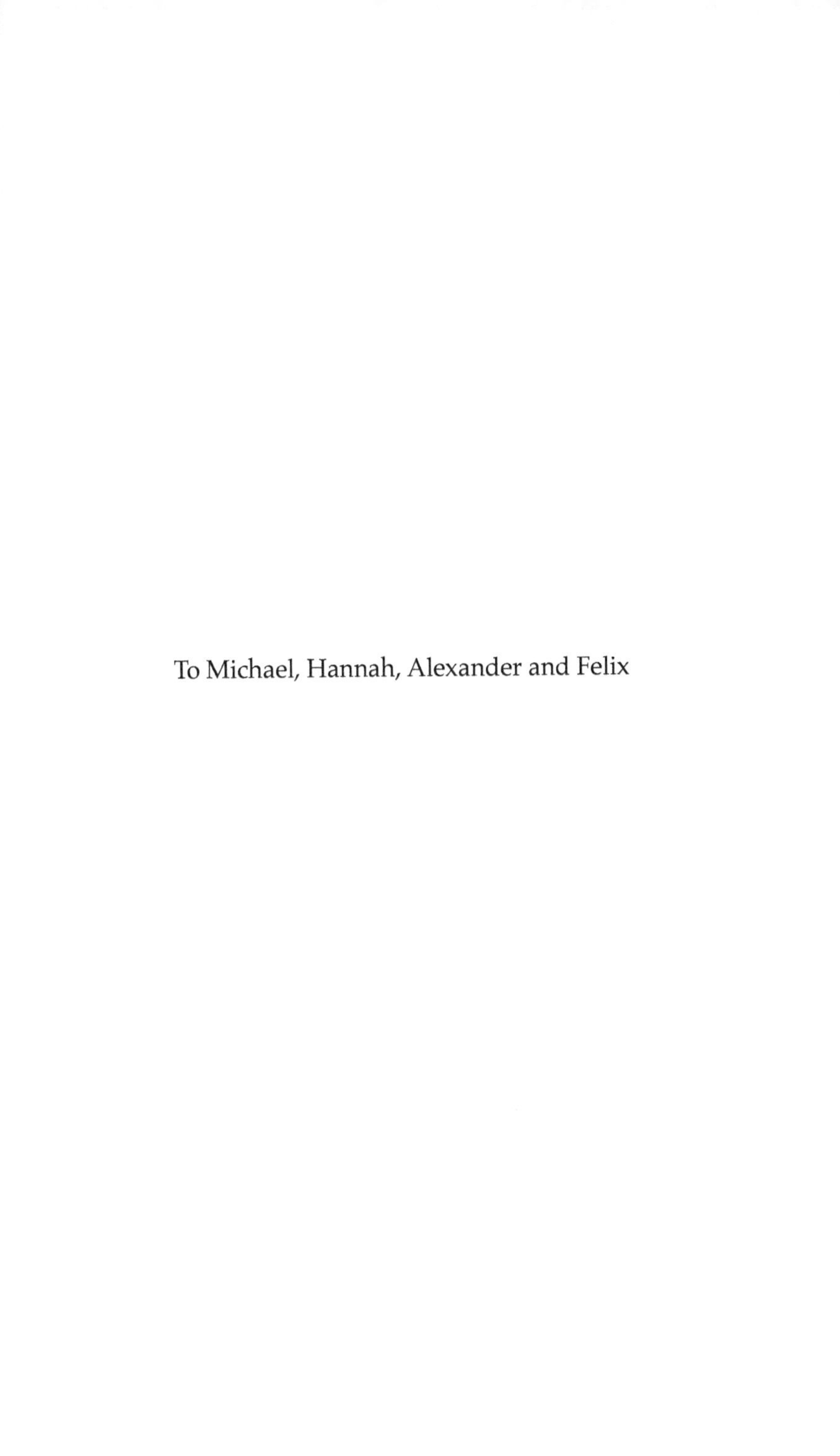

To Michael, Hannah, Alexander and Felix

Prologue

Six weeks after his mother's death and three days after her funeral, the most feared man in Ireland walked quietly through the graveyard at St Patrick's church in Clonbrinny. He came to a halt at the newest patch of disturbed soil, the edges of the large grave still soft and crumbling.

The sun made a tentative appearance through the clouds, saw who was below, thought better of it, and disappeared again. For fifteen minutes, Declan Kelly, the cause of genuine nightmares for gangsters, politicians and police alike, stood and stared at the mound of earth, daring it to twitch. Not a word or a gesture, even when his brother Connor and their best friend and minder Brendan joined him. Not when nine of the funeral mourners made their way up from the hotel and shuffled around, like reluctant witnesses to a road accident.

It was only when Father Aidan stepped out from the church porch and coughed politely that Declan stirred. He turned from the grave, where his mother now rested in peace alongside his father, two brothers and a sister, and looked surprised to see the group behind him.

He walked between them, shaking hands and giving hugs to all, including the priest, then led the party into the darkness of the church and headed towards the pulpit.

"Thank you all for coming to the funeral and for waiting to meet up," Declan said, as if this was some mildly inconvenient brunch reschedule. The group filtered into the front two pews with all the enthusiasm of a jury about to hear closing arguments in a tax fraud case.

Nobody would admit it aloud, not even under duress, but the 72-hour delay between the funeral and now had been a godsend, but not long enough. Some had used the time to recover from a wake that nobody could remember and were now almost sober. Others had finally regained control of their bodily functions, but only just. As an ensemble, they looked like the most unlikely identity parade in police history.

Only two people in the lineup felt fine. Former Downing Street chief of staff Martin Barnwell and his wife Mavis were first-time visitors to the area and had been on their best behaviour. The accounts of recent events from locals eager to share had either limited their alcohol intake or been sufficiently sobering to speed up the recovery process.

As *Path Finder's* high-profile financial backer, Greek billionaire *Isaac Dele*mos felt sick with anxiety as he waited to learn if the project... vision... call it what you will... would deliver enough to justify his investment and commitment. There was only so much damage to his global reputation that he was prepared to take.

"As you know," continued Declan, waving towards Connor, "We've been busy the last few weeks and not just with the funeral."

He reeled off the number of subscribers to *Path Finder*, the funds they had generated and reports on the reaction of individuals, political groups, governments and non-governmental organisations to the launch of the concept.

"The systems are working well and coping with the volume of applications to join," added Connor, blushing as he spoke. "There have been several attempts to break in, but every hacker has departed with a bloody nose. Word is getting around that it's not worth the effort. The government agencies keep trying, bless them. We use our ICARUS online defence system to infiltrate every attempt but - as per our agreement - are keeping quiet and doing nothing to monitor or take control of those systems."

Andy Blackwell, Mindy Abbott and Martin Barnwell all nodded at the same time. The last thing they wanted was to be viewed as a threat.

The more those organisations saw them as harmless and left them alone, the more chance they had of getting *Path Finder* off the ground.

"However, we are compiling a database of individual subscribers of interest - people who we feel are a threat, a potentially important ally or both. We'll give you access to it, so you can make up your own minds."

Declan nodded his thanks to Connor and then continued. The brothers had cancelled bookings at their famously exclusive Peace Castle on Ireland's west coast for the next six months. The impressive facility, together with its own airfield, was now reserved for *Path Finder* meetings and conferences. If something of a lower profile was required, then The Fallen Hero - host of the recent wake for Clodagh - would be the host.

Orla, the hotel's owner, nodded enthusiastically while new boyfriend and retired police sergeant Stuart Morris squeezed her hand.

The Hero may be a run-of-the-mill hotel and bar in a run-of-the-mill town, but recent events had proven once again that Clonbrinny was a fortress, fiercely protected by its people.

With this in mind, Declan had unexpected news.

"We held a meeting yesterday at our Dublin offices with… let's just say… the criminal elite," he began.

"It all went surprisingly well, given that two of them had been shooting at each other just a week earlier in the city centre. Anyway, long story short, Clonbrinny is safe. Nobody will touch us, guaranteed. In return, we won't use ICARUS or the offensive version, DEDALUS, against them."

Connor could barely contain himself, partly because a protected Clonbrinny had been the dream of his now-dead father and partly because he knew what was coming next.

"Tell them the rest, Dec."

His elder brother looked at the expectant and curious faces in the pews and rested his gaze on the UK's former prime minister. Andy stared back at the scarred face, hoping his expression didn't signal the discomfort he felt.

Declan laughed, and the sound bounced around the centuries-old walls - possibly the first time they had heard such a noise.

"This is crazy, isn't it?" he asked. "A former UK prime minister, formidable political operators, a famous billionaire and an Irish 'criminal overlord' are investing serious resources and risking their reputations on something we have yet to define. Something that attracts tens of thousands of new supporters each day, even though they have as much idea as we do over what it actually is. Andy... Martin... Mindy... it's been six weeks, we've done next to nothing and *still* the people show faith in us; in *Path Finder*."

Andy shifted uncomfortably, while Martin leaned back and folded his arms, watching Declan carefully.

"Do you know what's even crazier? The men and women we met yesterday? They've all bought into the idea. They turned up with a list of commitments they are already implementing. Car theft: they're only targeting high-end, petrol cars and are leaving hybrids and electrics alone. In fact, they're posting notes on the windscreen explaining why the vehicle's been left and thanking the owners for being green.

Drugs: they're reviewing their supply chains to see if they can source fair trade products and import them using the most environmentally friendly manner. Protection: businesses will get a 50% discount on their tariff if they install solar panels or donate 25% of the proposed tariff to rainforest charities."

"You'll be telling us next they're demanding kidnap ransoms in carbon credits," Mavis Barnwell said, shaking her head.

"Not quite, but they're going to offer ethically sourced snacks, wellbeing sessions and zero-waste toiletries to their hostages. The point is, as silly as these ideas sound, they're implementing them. Some will have an impact; some won't..."

"But, whatever their reasons, they're not messing about searching for a perfect solution," mused *Path Finder's* founder.

"And now we have the systems, meeting locations and support in place," said the founder's fiancée, "Neither should we."

Red Adair

The two months following the kick up the backside in St Patricks had been swan-like: not much happening on the surface, but plenty of kicking going on underneath.

The rear garden of the terraced house next door to the recently married Simon and Pippa Pope was very different now the new neighbours had settled in. However, 'neighbours' and 'settled in' didn't quite reflect the entire story.

The occupants were usually at their London home, or flying around the world to talk at conferences or with influential organisations, using their political nous to collect thoughts and opinions on *Path Finder* without actually saying what it was. Philosophy, global movement, religion, pretentious twaddle, naïve idealism - the identity of *Path Finder* had yet to be clearly defined and attracted a broad range of opinion in the meantime.

Many had their own ideas, but the thoughts of the people who counted - *Path Finder*'s founders - remained unknown and would do so for a while yet. Until the end of the evening's barbecue, at the very least.

The small mid-terraced house on a quiet country lane at the edge of a Midlands village was a welcome, secret escape from all the hoo-hah.

Its back garden was narrow but unusually long, bordered on each side by a six-foot-high wooden and concrete fence, with plates of armoured steel hidden within each wooden panel. A thick gorse hedge at the far end hid the property from prying eyes and deterred currently non-existent intruders. The immaculate lawn turf was bedding in nicely after being laid a couple of months earlier.

Immediately outside the back of the house was a large patio area, recently paved with slabs and easily accommodating a large wooden table, eight comfortable chairs, and a barbecue. Fairy lights, hanging limply between potted olive trees, flickered intermittently. They seemed to struggle to stay lit and failed to add charm to the evening.

Near the back door, the brand new barbecue grill smoked away as new neighbour, former prime minister and aspiring grill master Andy Blackwell hovered around it, flipping the food with panache, but with little of the required culinary skill.

Standing nearby, three men silently studied their host's cooking antics with a mixture of amusement, curiosity and alarm.

Inside the large kitchen diner, the chef's fiancée and *Path Finder*'s chief executive blithely ignored the impending culinary disaster. Along with Pippa, Dave Westlake's Irish partner, Siobhan and Siobhan's mother Orla, Mindy Abbott focussed on her alcohol intake just in case it could help to repel the potential salmonella.

Strategically positioned CCTV cameras covered the scene and beyond, feeding images to a monitoring station in the third and final property in the row, acquired with admirable speed by Greek billionaire Isaac Delemos. This housed a well-armed, very capable security team and the high-level communications services required by the Popes' new neighbours.

Oblivious to the cooking disaster, but attracted by the enticing, slightly charred aromas from the patio, two off-lead greyhounds stood still, side-by-side on the lawn, focussing solely on Blackwell's antics.

Fred, who was deep, glossy black with a small patch of white on his chest, and Ginger, a pale fawn-colored greyhound, were patient animals. However, the dogs' experience of barbecues in their garden next door meant even they eventually realised something was seriously amiss. With a wealth of meaty treats at serious risk, the time for polite etiquette had passed. Both turned slightly, stared hard at Simon and barked.

Andy laughed. "Patience, you two. Not long now."

"Oh, they're not panicking about getting something to eat," smiled Simon Pope, raising his hand to cease the clamour. "They're worried it won't be edible."

"And if those two are worried about it being edible, we should all be concerned," offered the tall figure of Dave Westlake, with all the diplomacy of a brick smashing through a window. "Come and have a drink, Andy. Leave that catastrophe to an expert."

Blackwell frowned, then sighed, his countenance illuminated and threatened by the wild flames licking higher from the grill, but partly shrouded by the clouds of smoke making his eyes run. The barbecue should have been perfect. It featured expensive meat, gourmet sauces and rubs, instructions from a Michelin chef, and several alarm clocks for precision.

"I used to run a country, you know," he reminded them as he removed his chef's apron and gave it to his next-door neighbour. "It was much easier than this."

He wandered indoors to grab a beer and give the good news to Mindy and the others hiding with the alcohol in the kitchen.

Pope - now known as Red Adair - assumed his position behind the potential health threat and reviewed the situation.

"We have exploding sausages, bulging burgers, rank ribs and salmonella time bombs in the shape of chicken breasts," he reported. "The vegetables are virtually charcoal."

Retired police sergeant Stuart Morris whistled softly. "Time to call the Chinese takeaway?" he suggested.

Pope surveyed the carnage, looked at the items on the nearby table and took a swig from his bottle of Monk's Perm. "Not while there's still hope," he murmured, before issuing his orders. "Get me a spray bottle of water ASAP and ask Mindy to turn on the oven. If there's a meat thermometer hiding somewhere, find it."

Even before the water arrived, Simon had removed all the food from the grill and placed it on a couple of large plates. Clouds of steam hid the patio from view for a time as the water spray quenched the inferno.

As the heat calmed, Pope wrapped the ribs in foil after adding a splash of his own beer, then placed them in the kitchen oven to braise. He grabbed a clean spatula and smashed the burger bulges to help them cook inside. Unfortunately, help came too late to rescue the veg. The former prime minister of the UK had to prepare some more, making thicker slices and watching them carefully while they cooked. How the mighty can fall.

The hosts and other guests looked on, amazed and impressed. All apart from Dave Westlake.

I've seen this man before, he thought. *In any emergency, and if there's no time to think about it, he's as cool as a cucumber. Calm, decisive and ruthlessly well organised.* The previous circumstances had been slightly different, involving an ambush, explosions, confusion and likely death in a small Afghan town, but today's warehouseman had kept all the acumen of yesterday's padre.

The Policy Boards

Three hours after the dramatic and successful rescue of the barbecue feast, five of the eight participants relaxed on the patio, having the conversation that only exists in the early hours when tipsy partygoers can't decide whether to call it a night or to continue putting the world to rights.

Fred and Ginger had already gone. Having worked out there was no more food left to eat and it wouldn't be too long before their breakfast, the dogs had slipped through the fence gate and were fast asleep on their beds in the Popes' kitchen.

The Popes themselves were in their new neighbours' kitchen, trying to help with the clear up alongside Mindy. Here, the conversation avoided the current patio topic of whether it was possible to barbecue a deckchair and centred instead on Ireland and the secret *Path Finder* events scheduled for the next two weeks at Peace Castle on the west coast.

"We're in no position to do everything ourselves. In fact, we don't want to do anything. We'll leave it to the experts," said Mindy in a hushed voice that was far too loud. "We're gathering the great and the good to form policy boards; we're banging heads together." She frowned as she tried to remember the process, much like drunk people do when trying to remember how to get home, or where they've put their glasses when they're actually wearing them.

"The scientists arrive early on day one. We explain what we want. They spend the rest of the day discussing it, then we give them dinner and plenty of drinks. We're expecting lots of conversation during the meal and after it. Hopefully, those will continue the next day if they're not too hungover. With luck, they'll develop a bond as well as a science policy. Then we fly them home that evening and pick up the education group early on day three, and it starts again. After education, we have environment, followed by a two-day break, then manufacturing, culture and peace."

Pippa stopped scraping the barbecue grill for a moment. "These groups handle policy?"

"I'm sure there are better words. They're the experts. People, organisations, governments and political parties will work out how our policies translate in their own region or nation. The policy board will decide whether the local proposal is acceptable. If so, then that solution has our blessing." Mindy stopped and stared into the distance for a moment, then shuddered. "Andy and I don't want to deal with all that. It sounds really hard."

Simon couldn't help but nod in agreement. He would run a mile from that sort of responsibility and, from what he knew of Andy, he could understand him doing the same.

"What about the media?" he asked. "You won't be able to keep all of this secret."

Mindy shrugged. "Media interest wouldn't hurt. Some outlets may pick up on what we're doing, but we're recruiting the boards from credible individuals who joined *Path Finder* just like millions of others. We'll do our best to keep their involvement confidential until they say otherwise. All have signed non-disclosure agreements. We'll pick them up from one airport and drop them off at another with onward transportation organised for each individual." She stopped for a sip of wine while she collected her thoughts.

"All flights will be on Isaac Delemos's private jet and will use Peace Castle's own airfield. After two weeks, or even during that period, we'll be able to announce work has started on environmental, scientific, manufacturing, education, cultural and peace policies."

Even a tipsy Simon Pope knew how the media frenzy would build, how it could engulf them or just die out if there was nothing to fuel the fire.

"This needs to be a success," he announced with all the authority of a warehouseman hiding a secret past, who still dreaded a knock on his front door by a reporter and camera crew.

Mindy nodded and smiled.

"We have our best people on the case," she said.

The Best People

The 'best people' stood at the top of the steps to the entrance of the grand, castle-like mansion of Caisleán Síocháin, or 'Peace Castle', and watched as the jet belonging to Isaac Delemos completed its final approach to the property's own airfield.

"Not long now," smiled a tanned Mavis Barnwell, hugging her husband's arm. "Nervous?"

Martin Barnwell looked at the sky, even though the plane had disappeared from sight and, judging by the noise of the protesting engines, was just touching down. The former chief of staff to the UK's prime minister and recently voted the foremost political operator of his generation, frowned slightly.

"I'm never nervous."

"You were when I made you dance with me in that salsa class on the ship."

Barnwell thought back to their recent cruise in the Indian Ocean, and his realisation that the salsa was physical, passionate, sensual and not, in fact, the Cuban equivalent of line dancing. Agreeing over a liquid lunch to join a dance class believing it was the latter, when it was in fact the former had not been wise; a judgement confirmed by the confused, amused and horrified looks on the faces of the other dancers.

It hadn't been his best moment, he had to admit. Ridicule was not his favourite look, but it was a small price to pay for his wife agreeing he could take on a new role that might incur a lot more. *Time would tell*, thought the new chair of the *Path Finder* foundation. *And the success or otherwise of the next two days would be his first clue.*

Fifteen minutes later, a minibus crunched to a halt on the gravel at the foot of the steps. Five hooded figures emerged and headed into the lobby, while two hotel staff followed with their baggage. Like many visitors before them, the new guests removed their cloaks and took a moment to absorb their new surroundings.

The lobby reflected the timeless elegance and opulence of the entire building. An enormous crystal chandelier, suspended from the centre of the high ceiling, cast a warm glow that danced off the polished marble floor, even in broad daylight. A grand fireplace, with an ornately carved stone mantel, served as the focal point on one side, faced by a wall of dark wood paneling, onto which were mounted five large visual display units. An elaborately gilded digital wooden frame bordered each screen, within which was a portrait of one of the new guests, together with a quote from their illustrious career. If the newcomers didn't know why they were part of the *Path Finder* journey, the display and their own words left them in no doubt.

Martin and Mavis stood quietly in a corner of the lobby, watching five of the world's greatest living scientists, each representing a continent and their particular specialism, take it all in. As expected, the attention of each guest fixed on their own display first, before looking at the others. Smiles played on their faces as they caught each other's eye. Their hosts could sense any lingering nervous tension evaporate into the ether.

"Ladies and gentlemen, a warm welcome to Peace Castle."

The Barnwells approached their guests and introduced themselves to each before Martin continued.

"Each of you is here because you joined our organisation, are experts in your field and have a proven affinity with our own opinions on the world and its future."

He waited a moment as five members of the mansion's team walked across the lobby and picked up the visitors' luggage.

"Our team will show you to your rooms. You have half an hour to settle in and freshen up, then I will meet you back here. We'll take a short stroll down to the boathouse and, over brunch, will figure out what *Path Finder* is and how it will work."

"You mean you don't know?" The question came from French professor Camille Fournier, but the concerned look on the faces of the others suggested it could have come from any of them.

Barnwell shrugged. "We have an overall vision of where we want to be, but we are not qualified to set standards and guidelines. We will rely on a board of experts to design a practical, achievable policy in their particular field - in your case, science. Your specialisms complement each other. You hail from five different continents, each with its own strengths and its own challenges. We know you share our beliefs. You are better placed than we are to develop the pathways the world needs."

"And if we can't agree?"

"Then you vote. Majority wins. No abstentions." Barnwell held Mavis's hand and turned away, heading back towards the corridor that led to the dining room.

"That's why there are five of you. We'll provide support and general guidance. The rest is up to you. We hope to have the bones of a global science policy before you fly out tomorrow evening. See you in half an hour."

As the scientists identified their own bags and headed off with a porter to their rooms, the Barnwells walked down the corridor into the dining room. Sitting at the bare dining table were the pilots and cabin crew from the flight, plus the two staff who had driven the guests from the airfield to the mansion.

"Thank you all for waiting," said Mavis. "I'm sure you understand the importance of the next couple of days - indeed, the next couple of weeks - to *Path Finder*."

She waited a moment and received slight nods from the people in front of her. "We must begin well with our first guests. To do so, we need to understand them and their relationships."

Martin sat down at the table, opened a small notebook and removed a pen from his inside jacket pocket.

"Mister Widdock," he said, looking at the older, smartly dressed man who had chauffeured the guests from the airfield. "Perhaps we should start with you?"

Forty minutes later, a group of seven emerged from the woods and headed across a small clearing towards the old boathouse on the edge of the small, tranquil lough. The building retained its original charm; the moss and ivy clinging to the stone walls, blending the structure into the surrounding landscape.

As they approached, the large wooden door swung open silently, revealing an upgraded interior that blended tradition with high-tech comfort.

The arrivals wandered into the main room. Natural light flooded through huge, triple-glazed windows that provided stunning views of the surrounding hills and woodland, with the waters of the lough lapping onto the shore outside.

The grain of the long oak conference table matched the exposed, polished beams, while ergonomic chairs guaranteed comfort during meetings of any length.

"Who's up for some brunch?" Mavis led her guests to the buffet area at the far end of the room, while Martin tried to remember how to operate the room's control panel. Despite rehearsing what he planned to say, and knowing exactly what he wanted to achieve over the next day and a half, there was a pressure he had rarely, if ever, felt before.

Except for his own seat at the table, next to the laptop attached to the two electronic whiteboards he had lowered into place, anybody else could sit anywhere. Mavis would wait until they were all settled before taking her own seat, giving her the best possible view of each scientist. Martin watched his wife fuss around the people with brains the size of planets, making sure they had everything they needed and engaging them in friendly conversation.

Camille Fournier, a confident, passionate and outspoken woman who had the distinction of being France's youngest appointed professor, was piloting research into ecosystems augmented by AI and robotic species. She had achieved worldwide fame through a documentary about her work in the Amazon basin, where her so-called 'sentient drones' were helping to prevent deforestation. The smart money was on her winning a Nobel Prize within the next three years.

That she was talking to Mavis alongside Thiago Marques was no surprise.

The handsome native of São Paulo in Brazil became famous for copying how Amazon rainforest plants speed up chemical reactions to create powerful, eco-friendly chemicals for factories. Now running a thriving laboratory focusing on innovative green science at the University of São Paulo, the outgoing 35-year-old was adored by students and feared by the major chemical companies. Thanks to Widdock, the Barnwells had just learned Marques was launching a court bid to stop illegal deforestation, with Fournier's drones supplying important evidence.

Martin had met Isla Trenholm several years earlier, when the New Zealander had presented a paper at Davos on the evolution of physics education. He smiled to himself, remembering a heated discussion about outdated learning techniques, which resulted in the UK's education minister fleeing the room pursued by a plastic cup of water.

Words like 'charismatic' and 'blunt' often featured in articles about her, but 'diplomatic'? Never. That hadn't stopped thirty countries from adopting elements of her learning system since its launch at Davos, and it was certainly working in terms of student engagement, exam results and career choices.

Isla looked pale and tired, Martin thought, but that was hardly surprising given she had flown in from the other side of the world for this specific event.

Doctor Kenji Tan, CEO of NodGen Scientific, stood alone at the window. He gazed outside, perhaps using the reflection to observe the room. Barnwell moved his gaze elsewhere, just in case. The third generation of his family to lead the Swiss-based global manufacturer of advanced scientific equipment, Kenji studied molecular engineering at Oxford and joined the family business after a couple of years of volunteering as a teacher in India.

A quiet man, married to a professor of English and with four young children, Kenji had boosted the company's earnings by making science accessible to communities around the world. His vision, next to his portrait in the lobby, explained it all. Martin knew it by heart. "A world where every mind - no matter where it is born - has the support and the tools to discover, invent, and to change the future."

Fatima el-Hassan, the last member, was a Sudanese professor. She studied how diseases spread between animals and people, focusing on bats, mosquitoes, and related ecosystems.

Part biologist and part detective, she worked with international teams to predict where outbreaks of malaria and other diseases might happen before they actually did.

She didn't look happy to be there, thought Martin.

He caught Mavis's eye and glanced across at Fatima for a moment. Seconds later and his wife had extricated herself from one conversation, sat herself down next to Batgirl - as the media had named her - and had launched into another.

Martin was relieved to see Fatima's face light up as she smiled at a comment Mavis had made, even though he was sure he had lipread the word 'salsa'.

The Gambit

"People. Please..." Mavis threw her hands up in despair. Martin sat quietly, answering Andy Blackwell's text on his phone.

How's it going?

Disaster.

Have they decided anything yet?

That they hate each other. Or hate us for bringing them together. Or both.

The former prime minister had responded with several laughing emojis.

Within twenty minutes of convening the first meeting of the science policy board, both Barnwells felt less like facilitators and more like United Nations peacekeepers. The warm and tranquil vibe of the boathouse was intended to promote calm and thoughtful discussion between mature adults. The current meeting was now a multi-person, frenzied cage fight where the referees were receiving medical attention. Some fighters ignored the rules and battered each other with whatever lay to hand. The others tried to escape the cage, but there was nowhere to run.

The cabin crew had reported there was little need for air conditioning in the aircraft, given the frosty silence between Isla Trenholm and Camille Fournier.

The introductory remarks the guests made following brunch at the start of the meeting had provided the reason. The science community could be as bitchy as any other group in society. Camille resented a TED talk given by Isla, portraying her work as playing with toys that the children would swiftly discard. Isla blamed Thiago Marques for her recent failure to persuade South American governments to adopt her revolutionary educational methods, claiming he shared more with Camille than just an interest in deforestation.

Kenji Tan looked as if he would rather be in a war zone wearing only a pair of white briefs and requiring a surrender flag, while the smile on Fatima's face had been well and truly extinguished by her feeling that she didn't really belong here as she had nothing to shout about.

Martin stood and walked over to the bar, catching the attention of his surly policy board by doing so and quietening the row.

He poured himself a whiskey and ginger and made his wife a gin and tonic, then turned and looked at the group.

"Anybody else want anything?"

He took the silence as a no and returned to the table, handing Mavis her drink with an encouraging smile before settling in his seat and raising his glass to his audience.

"Congratulations," he said. "You'll go down in history as the people who killed *Path Finder* at birth." He took a sip of his drink, giving a chance for his words to sink in.

"Of course, you won't be the only ones. My good lady and I will be alongside you, together with everybody who believed you were the scientists to help put the world on a different path and inviting you to do so. We thought you were brilliant individuals with your hearts in the right place. We still do." Martin looked around the room, his gaze resting on each face for a couple of seconds.

Mavis gave him a quick wink. She had last heard this routine in discussions with train operators over pay and conditions. "But we didn't believe your vision, which is our vision, would vanish so quickly through petty arguments. It's very disappointing."

Then he shut up, took another sip of his drink and waited for someone else to talk, however long it took. He didn't have to wait long, although the source was unexpected. Fatima el-Hassan stood up.

"In our hearts, we are all disappointed, Martin. Disappointed… excited… nervous…and scared."

Isla Trenholm stood.

"We all have big egos. Yes, myself included." That drew slight smiles across the room, and Martin knew they were back on track. "We need them to survive in this business; we compete for funding, recognition, prizes and so on. But the prize here? Much bigger than all of that."

Camille stood.

"Clean sheet?" she asked, receiving a nod from Isla in reply.

Thiago Marques stood and looked at Fatima.

"That's the first thing you've said since we got here," he smiled. "You should speak more often."

All eyes turned to Kenji Tan, who stood slowly. "Mister Barnwell, I have always been an admirer of your work," he said. "You brought me here and surrounded me with geniuses. Brilliant people with incredible talent. Each on their own path to glory; willing to take on all-comers in their quest for victory. And you tame us all, using a gambit that last worked with train operators. You are the true genius." He smiled at Barnwell's raised eyebrows. "I told you. I'm a big fan."

Martin raised his glass and downed his drink, then collected his papers.

"Then you know what's coming next, Kenji," he said. "The tasks are on the whiteboard, and the bar is open. The doors will be locked for the next three hours. First passes at each of the tasks to be completed by our return."

Then he headed to the entrance door, accompanied by Mavis. As he walked through, he heard Fatima ask, "Going to practice your salsa?" and the group laughed. He stared at his wife, who grinned back at him.

As the door closed behind them, his phone pinged.

Mindy says have you thought about the train operators?

Martin laughed, partly at the timing, but mostly with relief.

The game was on.

The Unusual Dinner

Dinner at Peace Castle was a strange one. Normally, diners arrived relatively sober and departed drunk.

Not tonight.

Leaving five scientists locked in a room with an open bar for the afternoon had produced the desired - and some undesired - results. Conversation had flowed as well as the drink.

By the time Martin Barnwell returned to see how his guests were doing, the group had drafted, discussed and completed a *Path Finder* science policy and had then moved on to brainstorm suitable example projects for interested parties. Understandably, these concepts had become wilder as the meeting progressed, creating much amusement in the group that only died away after Kenji had fallen asleep and Camille had thrown up in the toilet.

"Impressive," was Barnwell's response to the group report. "It's thorough, easy to understand, and reflects the fundamentals of our philosophy. Some projects are genuinely exciting, and nobody's created problems for the cleaners. Well done."

The mansion's staff had ferried the group back to the main building in golf buggies. Mavis delayed dinner for ninety minutes to allow for a period of rest and recuperation.

Now, the group sat along with their hosts around the circular mahogany table while the staff flitted quietly between them, providing mostly soft drinks and taking food orders from the proffered menus. A hidden speaker system provided a gentle backdrop of classical music to fill the silence. The euphoria of the afternoon had waned somewhat, replaced by the quiet satisfaction of a job well done. It was a shared moment that none of the participants wanted to disturb by speaking, settling instead for eye contact, knowing smiles and fervently hoping the smell of the food didn't induce any projectile vomiting.

Mavis stood up, leaned across the white Irish linen tablecloth and flicked her wineglass with her fingernail. The *ping* was unnecessary to attract everyone's attention, but it stopped the background music.

"Fellow path finders," she started, pleased to see the response to the sobriquet. "Today is a monumental occasion for our organisation. We now have something to shout about in the vital area of science, and that is down to you. You have put aside your differences and your personal objectives to focus for a while on formulating something much bigger - a scientific movement that benefits the world. Before today, Martin and I were convinced of your individual bodies of work and your dedication to improving the lot of the planet. But we weren't sure you could work as a team. In the space of a few hours, you have removed any doubts."

She waited a moment as the guests looked at each other and beamed their affirmation, then she continued.

"You have done so much today that tomorrow we now have time to agree on the way forward; how we will announce our science offering, process the enquiries we receive, and so on. Martin?"

Her husband smiled his thanks as Mavis sat down to a smattering of applause, but he remained seated.

"Now. Housekeeping. As you know, we have all signed non-disclosure agreements, but we are coming to the moment the media will want to know who is involved in this pioneering work. In the *Path Finder* spirit of openness and honesty, we would like to tell them, but we won't do so without your permission. Releasing your names will put the spotlight on you, which will have its own pros and cons."

He looked carefully around the table, lingering slightly longer on Fatima, who glanced down at the table.

"Maybe agencies who are curious about us will see you as somebody who may be involved and could provide them with information. They might have tried to contact you already."

Mavis noticed that Camille and Thiago suddenly found the large silver candlesticks on the table very interesting.

"That would come as no surprise, and we understand why you would have kept that contact secret," Martin continued. "But if that is the case, we can help you provide them with just enough genuine detail to keep them happy and off your back, while still protecting the organisation's progress. We just need you to tell us who's involved. Have a quiet word with Mavis or me whenever you get the chance…"

"A lady from the General Intelligence Service talked to me. She had an American with her, but he said very little." All heads turned to Fatima, whose eyes remained firmly on the table. "She said the Americans would provide extra funds for my research if I helped them, but my government funding would disappear if I refused."

Mavis, sitting next to the Sudanese professor, put her hand on her arm and gave it a squeeze.

"Then we'll make sure you can cooperate," smiled Martin. "And if anything negative should happen to your funding, we will make sure it doesn't affect you or your research."

He looked around the table.

"The Brazilian authorities approached Thiago. I had a visit from my old university professor, who has government links. Similar message." Camille looked ready to burst into tears.

"I had lunch with the authorities on a visit to an exhibition in China, at their request," admitted Kenji. "It didn't go well."

"Well, nobody's hauled me in or threatened me." A red-faced Isla Trenholm looked incandescent. The room fell completely silent for a few moments. Then Fatima spoke.

"How rude," she grinned.

Isla stared at her, then she laughed. "Too right! I'm deeply offended."

Laughter, fuelled by the relief of sharing a major problem and discovering it wasn't so major after all, rippled around the table, feeding off itself and approaching hysteria, just as the staff returned with the starters and wondered what they'd missed.

Nose Up

Mavis and Martin finished their goodbyes and made their way down the steps leading from the jet, trying to ignore the rain. Airport staff stowed what little luggage the scientists had brought with them for their brief stay, while the plane's crew went through their pre-flight checks. Minutes later, safely back in the dry, warm minibus, the couple heard the plane's engines start with a low rumble and watched it taxi under its own power away from the terminal building towards the far end of the small airfield's only runway.

"I cannot believe how well the last couple of days have gone," murmured Mavis.

"I don't think anybody can."

Martin wasn't great on optimism, but today was different. This plane *had* to take off safely and return its 'science guides' - as its members had renamed the group - to Britain. Otherwise, the last two days had been a waste of time.

He thought back to the previous evening's dinner and the lively discussion during the meal and over coffee afterwards in the lounge.

It must have been the first time that guests at Peace Castle had finished their dinner more sober than they had started.

This morning, everybody had turned up for a convivial breakfast at the civilised time of nine o'clock.

They had stayed together all day as a group, making their way through the woods and down onto the beach for a stroll and lively conversation along the Atlantic coast, followed by lunch and a meeting to review and confirm their decisions.

An increase in the engines' roar disturbed his reflections, as the pilot pushed the throttle forward and released the jet down the runway. *Nose up. Nose up.* After what seemed an eternity, the plane rose into the air and the former chief of staff released the breath he hadn't realised he was holding. The plane climbed steadily and banked slightly to the west over the Atlantic before swinging east and heading across Ireland towards the Irish Sea and England.

The driver, Widdock, trotted out of the terminal, climbed in and drove back to Peace Castle without saying a word until he drew up to the front entrance.

"It starts again tomorrow then," he half-stated, half-asked.

"It certainly does, Widdock," smiled Mavis.

The driver grimaced, nodded, then drove off.

Mavis linked her husband's arm as they watched the minibus disappear around the corner.

"Highlight?" she asked.

"The change in group title. They're right. We're not a political party. We shouldn't stipulate policy. It's draconian, creates unnecessary pressure on our people and puts a target on our backs. We simply offer everyone a destination, where science should end up, based on what we think the world needs. How they get there is up to them. Our science guides will encourage and promote projects that represent a significant move in the right direction. What about you?"

"Watching a group of highly strung, very competitive geniuses, bearing grudges and harbouring fears, leave here as a motivated and united team, genuinely excited about the part they'll play in *Path Finder*." Mavis fell silent for a moment.

"I thought you were a fool for taking this on," she admitted.

"So did I."

"Now? I'm not so sure."

"Me neither."

They turned and headed into their home for the next couple of weeks to thank the staff and to send out the report on the last thirty-six hours. Martin would then call Mindy to discuss the addition to her role as CEO.

Keeping the intelligence services of the world happy while divulging nothing important would be right up her street.

The Call

The phone ringing in the early evening at the home of Matty and Jayne Hernandez wasn't unusual. The owner of the largest vehicle repair shop in the small Texan town of Van Gilbert was used to receiving calls at all times of the day and night.

Having just finished dinner with his wife in the large kitchen diner, he wiped his hands on a napkin, wandered into the hallway wondering when he would regret the third burrito and picked up the receiver, just before the call went to voicemail. Three minutes later, the burrito was the least of his worries.

"Mr Hernandez? Sir, my name is Omar Rahmani. I worked with your son, Daniel, in Afghanistan. Captain Hernandez gave me your contact details just before his unit moved out. Said I should call if I needed any help, sir. I hope you don't mind."

The accent was mid-Atlantic, but the caller wasn't from the US or the UK.

Rahmani sounded urgent. He explained he was Afghan. A doctor, he studied in London but returned to his country in 2012 to serve in the national army, initially as a medic and later as a medic/interpreter for allied special forces units including the Rangers.

He had worked closely with Danny Hernandez, who was training and advising Afghan security forces, as well as supporting special operations raids across the country. When the US withdrawal quickened in 2021, both had gone their separate ways but not before his friend gave him a scribbled name, address and telephone number on the back of an army food voucher.

"Danny said I could call if I ever needed help, sir. That time is now. My family evacuated from Kabul and are safe in America, but a bomb explosion near the airport caught me, and I missed the last flights out. I've been in hiding from the Taliban ever since."

Matty scribbled down vague details on the pad next to the phone.

"Son," he said, "I'll need to check with my boy, but I don't know how we can help with you being so far away."

"But I'm not, sir," came the reply. "I left my homeland six weeks ago. There are networks. I spent three weeks walking across the border into Tajikistan, then took flights to get here. It took me a month in total. I'm thirty miles from you."

"Then why do you need our help? Sounds like you've done pretty well by yourself."

"I'm in Mexico. In a migrant Mission. I have no special immigrant visa, and if I fail with an asylum claim, they could send me back to Afghanistan."

"Our government wouldn't do that."

"Let's just say I'd feel better if I were already in your country and had the support of the US military for my application."

Matty knew that reassurance on government policy from a car mechanic, who saw migrants picked up and deported or worse every day, was not very reassuring.

"I'll call Daniel, Mr Rahmani. Is there anything I can do in the meantime?"

"Call my wife, please, sir." Omar recited the cellphone number twice. "Tell her I'm safe. I'm in Santa Esperanza, helping the mission with translation, and they're looking after me. Tell her I hope we'll all be together again soon."

Matty hoped his sharp intake of breath hadn't made it down the phone line.

"I'll call them, Omar, but I can't make any promises about where we go from here. Santa Esperanza is a rough place, son. Full of bad people. And if you try to get over here… well, that's very dangerous. You take care of yourself."

"Thank you, sir. I'll call again tomorrow."

Matty hung up, stared at the notepad for a moment, then turned to see Jayne at the kitchen doorway.

"Was it him?"

"Seems to be."

"What are you going to do?"

"Call Daniel. After that, I don't know."

All Up In Smoke

Omar slipped the burner phone into his inside jacket pocket, emerged from the shadowed doorway and walked up the alley, back to the hot, neon-lit streets of Santa Esperanza. The road teemed with people, deafened by the cacophony of music blaring from the cantinas, accompanied by the angry horns of even angrier drivers and the loud curses of pedestrians.

The wide eyes and hesitant steps of new arrivals alerted the coyote guides to the prospect of fresh meat, while cartel lookouts monitored the chaos, on the alert for police raids or incursions by other gangs.

Despite only arriving in the city a few days earlier, Omar felt at home here, comfortable in his surroundings, and it showed in his demeanour. Despite the stifling heat of the evening, he flicked the collar up on his bomber jacket and strode confidently along the sidewalk towards the border crossing. The coyotes ignored him, and after a cursory glance, the lookouts did the same.

After three weeks and 260 miles dodging Taliban patrols and Tajikistan border guards; crossing the deep and fast-moving Amu Darya river over a ruined Russian transport bridge; and traversing desert and mountains on narrow trails in the dark, Santa Esperanza was a walk in the park.

Almost as stress-free, in fact, as the 48-hour plane journey via Istanbul, Madrid and Bogota to Mexico City, followed by the 21-hour trip in the back of the Mission's van.

For Omar, the real threat loomed ahead of him and, despite all he had seen in his time in Afghanistan's special services, it sent a shiver down his spine.

The border fence wasn't threatening as such. The huge steel wall topped by razor wire intimidated newcomers, but a cursory wander along its flanks revealed the behemoth's weakness - a mishmash of ancient barriers whose scars revealed how many times migrants had cut them open and authorities had welded them shut.

It was what it represented - the hope, the fear, the unknown; the obstacle to the fulfilment of dreams or the preventer of nightmares - not what it was.

Omar walked west, half a mile or so from the crossing point, away from the small groups gazing at the well-lit but closed gates, hoping against hope they would be on the other side of them tomorrow; the next stage in fulfilling their individual American dreams.

He bought his usual coffee from the usual small kiosk, smiling his thanks to the Asian man who owned the premises, then sat down on one of the four chairs at the establishment's only plastic table. For the past week, he had watched the frightened and the desperate gather here, their fears masked by curiosity or a frisson of excitement, depending on whether they were about to learn what they could do, or were just about to do it.

Omar wished them all well, but that was as far as his interest went. They were the fish, but he was more interested in the fishermen. Every evening, he would study the people who gathered them together and escorted them to safe houses, where they would find out what could be done and for how much.

Later on, he would walk to the edges of the town to watch the groups fade into the blackness of the desert. In the early morning, disguised in worker overalls and a cap, he would take another route to the same area to see which coyotes returned and who returned with them.

If any of the despondent headed for much-needed refreshment, he'd give them five minutes then follow them in, ordering a coffee and sitting nearby, using his language skills to pick up any useful nuggets of information in their conversation. Assailants had beaten and robbed some migrants. Others talked about those who had gone missing and speculated on their fate.

Now, he had a far better idea of what he would face on his own journey and a firm belief in whom he would trust. Himself.

As he watched, two men separated from the gathering crowd and walked across the road to the kiosk, where they bought coffees and sat at the same table; one facing him and one to the side. They were mid-twenties with gang tattoos on every visible skin surface. Probably cartel scouts; senior to the coyotes and with the group to identify prime targets.

The man facing him had a nasty scar on his cheek and a patch over his left eye. The right eye stared at him, and a cruel smile played on his lips.

"Are you planning to join us, *hermano*?" Patch asked Omar in Spanish. "You've been watching us for long enough."

"I don't have the money yet," Omar replied in the same language.

"Where are you from?"

"Afghanistan. Kabul."

"Your Spanish is good."

Omar nodded, never taking his eyes off his interrogator, who pulled out a packet of cigarettes and offered it across the table.

"I don't smoke."

Patch slid the packet across to his associate, who removed a cigarette and lit it.

"Same here," Patch said. "What other languages do you speak?"

"Pashto, Dari, English; other bits and pieces."

Patch sipped his coffee and looked at the border fence.

"You've come a long way, my friend," he said, "But the toughest part of your journey remains in front of you."

"I know."

"I could make it easier for you."

"I know."

A cloud of cigarette smoke wafted across Omar's face. He turned slightly to face the second man, his mind racing through a series of options depending on what happened next and whether these men were of value to him. *Time would tell.*

"Please don't do that," he said.

The smoker stared at him, his dead eyes betraying a glimmer of amusement, and blew again. Doing nothing wasn't an option. They were testing him, and in that moment, he knew their value to him could plummet to zero.

"Do that again, *hermano*," he said quietly, "I'll ram that cigarette so far down your throat, you'll blow smoke from your arse."

The smoker's eyes widened slightly, then he frowned and took another long drag on the cigarette. As he finished, Omar snapped the handle off the plastic coffee spoon and pressed the jagged edge into the skin on the man's throat.

"Hold that smoke there, my friend," he suggested.

Patch laughed, but it didn't sound friendly. He slid his coffee to the side and leaned forward.

"Like I said, I can make it easier for you, or I can make it much more difficult. Impossible, even."

Omar sighed and shook his head as the smoker's eyes watered.

"Thanks to your friend here, this situation does neither of us any favours," he said. "I'm losing your help. You're losing what little money I have, plus the chance to use my language skills for a while, to pull in more customers."

Omar stood, the spoon handle still at the second man's throat, and moved behind him, his eyes never leaving Patch while his hand searched for the pistol in the back of the smoker's waistband. Yanking the gun clear, he kneed the smoker in the back, and the man coughed a thick cloud across the table.

The momentary confusion delayed Patch's reaction. By the time he'd drawn his own gun, he was facing down the barrel of his friend's and carefully laid his own weapon on the table. Omar ushered him away, then shoved the smoker to the side and picked up the second gun, covering both men with the first.

"As you see," he said, "I could be useful to you if you treat me with respect. Maybe in a few days we can talk again, but seriously next time. Leave the donkey at home."

The smoker fumed, literally and figuratively, but Patch simply smiled.

"Oh, that bird has flown, *cabrón*. If I were you, I would pray to your god that we never meet again."

"Funny," said Omar, gesturing them both to rejoin the crowd, which had split into groups, "I was going to say the same to you."

The men turned and strolled calmly back to the migrants about to set off on their own journeys, almost reaching the nearest group when they heard footsteps trotting up behind them. It was the kiosk owner carrying their guns.

"He took the bullets," he panted. "Says if he ever sees you again, you'll get them back."

The Germ of an Idea

Major - formerly Captain - Daniel Hernandez looked at the handset he had returned to the receiver more than a minute previously, but didn't actually see it. His mind was working overtime to process what his father had relayed to him.

Fourteen months on, and Omar was still alive. And now he was out. The quiet, some might say shy, doctor had even negotiated the dangerous and difficult route from the centre of Taliban territory all the way to the Mexico-US border.

The relief he felt at hearing the news had come as a shock to him and would be the same for many of the Afghanistan veterans in the Regiment.

Thirty miles from his parents' home sounded trivial after all the former translator had been through. *Thirty miles*, he thought. Twelve hundred miles closer than he was, at Fort Blade in Georgia, and yet his journey would be much easier than the one his friend and former comrade had to make.

If the Special Operations Command recommended it, Omar would easily get a special immigrant visa. There was a position at Fort Blade waiting for him. Getting him away from the border area was the challenge, including avoiding cartels, immigration officials, and local vigilantes. The mission was to get him to a base, preferably Blade, with as little direct US Army involvement as possible.

He limped into the kitchen and made a coffee, then sat at the table to sketch out possibly the most important mission he had ever planned.

Omar had promised to call Matty again in 24 hours, and would probably need ten to twelve days more to reach his parents' home, given a fair wind. If the doctor succeeded, then the extraction had to be implemented soon after. The longer a migrant stayed in the US border zone, which could be 100 miles deep, the greater the risk of being found, held, and sent away, or something even worse.

Two weeks, Daniel thought. *For a regiment that deploys battalions anywhere in the world with less than 18 hours' notice, this should be a piece of cake.*

Even as he thought it, he knew he didn't believe it. He wrote four names on his notepad and considered each carefully while drinking his coffee and munching on a cookie. By the time the coffee had cooled, two of the names had gone, with one added.

He struggled back to the phone and dialled a number.

"Joey," he said. "It's Danny. I have great news."

The Situation Room

Aston Hail struggled to keep his volcanic temper in check – not something you want to lose when armed Secret Service agents surround your vehicle.

The seething, red-faced founder of Hail Electronics & Space Technologies was not used to inconveniences, and the last few weeks had been full of them. Security hacks and data breaches, legal subpoenas, unapproved access to his personal finances and a tidal wave of bad media coverage were more than enough for him to blow his top.

And now this. The public humiliation of queueing to access the Eisenhower Executive Office Building because his Level One High Security Government ID, the small card which entitled him to waltz onto any government property whenever he wanted, was no longer working.

Fortunately, the limousine had tinted windows and most of the checks were being conducted via the chauffeur, but the anonymity wouldn't last. Hail took matters into his own hands, wound down his passenger window and smiled at the agent nearest to him; a man who had been part of his own security detail before his recent 'issues'.

"How are you, Pete?"

The agent didn't look up from examining the identification card in his hand.

"I'm good, Mr Hail."

"How's the family?"

Pete ignored the question and compared the card details with the information on his electronic tablet. Hail tried again.

"How's your father doing?"

"Not good, sir." Pete handed the ID card back to the chauffeur and finally looked at the man in the back of the car. "Not since you made him redundant two weeks ago." Pete continued to stare at Aston Hail from behind his agency-issue sunglasses until the tinted car window completed its journey up again.

Ten minutes later, Hail sat in a waiting area close to the West Wing with several others, having had his fingerprints, his face and his body scanned, along with his briefcase and its contents.

He hadn't looked around, but he was sure security was recording the process, and the images would soon find their way into the media.

After what seemed an eternity, a junior staffer arrived to escort the billionaire to the Situation Room in the building's basement.

Hail was under no illusions. The Oval Office, virtually Hail's office just a few short weeks ago, would be out of bounds for the foreseeable future and possibly forever. The president, who had described himself as Hail's best friend during the election, didn't want to be seen with him in public and had only agreed to this meeting with considerable reluctance.

The looks thrown at him as he walked through the West Wing left him in no doubt that everyone in the building shared the same reluctance. It was a relief to reach the relative quiet of the dimly lit basement area. The escort used a coded access card to open the Situation Room door, but didn't follow Hail through it.

To his surprise, President David D. Clampett, a colossal figure, was already hunching at one side of the large, well-lit table in the middle of the large, windowless room alongside Jeanette Lusstey, his National Security Advisor. Two secret service agents stood motionless in the gloom behind the two executives. Nobody made a move to greet him.

Clampett - for some murky family reason, the middle D also stood for David - simply gestured to a seat across the table and looked down at the briefing papers in front of him before pushing them to the side.

"I am getting pissed with our allies hitting out, then hiding behind us when we're obliged to step in to discourage retribution," he said. "They're cowards, hiding behind the big guy. And when it spirals out of control, we're expected to clear up the mess. It's un-American."

"The Middle East?" Hail asked, as nobody else seemed willing to say anything and he hated awkward silences.

"The Final Breaths Nursing Home in Florida. You accept one lousy donation from these assholes, have a picture taken with them and they reckon they own you."

"At least it's not the Middle East."

"It's always the Middle East." The president looked rueful. "Anyway, what can I do for you, Aston?"

Hail ignored the fact Clampett didn't appear especially eager to do anything at all.

"Well, Mr President, you can start by explaining why my so-called best friend would suspend my security clearance without letting me know about it."

"Oh, that was my decision," smiled Jeanette Lusstey, her strong perfume wafting after her words across the table and engulfing the visitor. "We didn't want a compromised tech genius and potential criminal wandering around the White House. Not a good look for the Administration and a definite security risk."

Lusstey's smile broadened as she saw the effect of her words on her former husband's face.

"Surely even you understand that? It's hardly rocket science."

Clampett looked up and grinned.

"Ouch. She's sexy *and* sassy, your ex. *Sexassy.* If I weren't a married man…"

"I don't believe that's ever stopped you before, Mr. President."

Clampett ignored the challenging look from his NSA and cleared his throat, his eagerness to wrap up this meeting quickly taking precedence over the intriguing direction taken by the initial remarks.

"We've been through your email. I have our responses," he said. "The FBI can find no evidence of any cyberattack or intrusion other than the MisCox hack on your personal finance account. The Cybersecurity and Infrastructure Security Agency has reviewed the data and reassures me there is no threat to this government's cyber and physical critical infrastructure. We are *strucsecure.* If it's any consolation, we instructed the CIA's black ops hacker group to infiltrate your systems. Everything that the group tried failed. You're as secure as Fort Knox. *Secox.*"

Hail avoided rolling his eyes at the president's ongoing efforts to establish timesaving *Clampisms* to America's vocabulary and nodded.

The last thing he needed was to be the source of a national security issue, and the robustness of his systems was a relief.

But as welcome as the news was, it wasn't why Hail had requested the meeting or why Clampett had agreed to it.

"But that isn't why you're here, is it? Why are you here, Aston?"

Hail ignored his ex-wife and stared at the man he had helped to install in the White House the previous year.

"The hackers cost me $500 million, but that's okay. I'll recoup more than that from my legal action against Takahashi Technologies. What I'd like to see is this administration bringing forward the announcement on the satellites contract and using its influence to delay the Alcock investigation by the UK's Securities and Exchange Commission. That would give me some breathing space…"

Hail hesitated, disturbed as the president pushed himself gently away from the table and glanced quickly to his left, checking that the men sworn to protect him were nearby.

"Aston, I want you to drop the legal action against Tee Takahashi. In return, Tee will drop her claims against you. Neither of you needs the grief, the legal bills or the negative publicity. The *neglicity*."

Hail's fists clenched, and he felt his face flush.

"That wasn't what I expected to hear, Dave."

"First, it's Mister President. Never forget that. Ever. Especially in this building. In this room." Clampett's face flushed a dangerous shade of puce and, without even moving, his security detail loomed forward. Even Hail let the awkward silence drag on for as long as it needed. After what seemed an eternity but was, in fact, only an age, Clampett recovered his composure.

"Look. Almost every office in the government uses Takahashi systems and software. They're not something we want to rip out, but this publicity is raising awkward questions. You need to back off. You can use the information and the sources I've just given you to confirm Tee's non-involvement and to reassure the market about the integrity of your systems. Hell, you can even say you requested the investigation."

Both secret service agents stepped forward, their hands moving towards their shoulder holsters as Hail pushed back his chair and stood, then paced on his side of the room.

Jeanette Lusstey gently raised her hand off the table to stop the agents from shooting him. She knew her ex-husband needed to move when stressed, and this was certainly one of those times. Her role was to make sure he made the right decision. Her alimony depended on it.

"Everyone will understand why you took the legal action to protect your business, your clients and this government during the full investigation of the hack," she soothed. "The review of software use was equally valid, but now that the investigation is complete, there is no need to continue with either."

"I lost $500 million."

"You made significant charitable donations, which your tax advisers will no doubt recoup."

"And the satellite deal?"

"We're reviewing our options, which will take several weeks." Clampett helped himself to a can of cola from the ice bucket on the table. "That gives you time to calm things down. Make up with Tee. See if you can't come to some deal on the finance investigation. The *finanstigation*. Put the blame on a lower life form in your business. Get them to take the rap for some longer-term security."

Hail stopped pacing and stared at the dark wall in front of him, seeing a rapidly growing light at the end of the tunnel.

"That could work," he said.

"Good. Make it happen soon. You won't be welcome back here until it's done, so hurry. I miss you." Clampett took a gulp from the can and immediately launched a loud belch across the table. "Now, tell me what I need to know about this *Path Finder* stuff. Seems to have a lot of momentum… 48 million registered members… over $880 million in donations… You met Andy Blackwell in Ireland, right?"

"I did. A few of us did." Looking much calmer, Hail sat down again and smiled.

"It's a cute idea; a playground for those without power, where they can blow off some steam without actually having to do anything. Blackwell is still trying to work out what it is and how it will operate. He's genuinely surprised at its popularity and doesn't want to get into politics again. He was badly burned the first time. Our judgement? It's a safety valve for you; for every government. A harmless sideshow."

"Harmless?"

"Mostly. Yeah. Sure, they'll attract some names. They'll get media coverage. There'll be some ripples for a while, but when people tire of the *Path Finder* debate shop - all words and no action - that'll be it. Blackwell and his team may end up millionaires or in jail for fraud. Either way, it's over."

"Yeah. I'm hearing similar from some other folks. They reckon it's dead in the water. Nothing to worry about."

Jeanette smiled and nodded along with the president and her ex, although for different reasons. She had other thoughts about *Path Finder*, but nothing she would ever present to the president. Institutional complacency was exactly what the new movement needed to reach a critical mass.

The Last Recce

Early morning in Santa Esperanza was Omar's favourite time of the day.

Most migrants hoping to cross at the border point with real or fake paperwork were already in the queue. The coyotes and the cartel guides were still in bed after their nighttime activities, or somewhere over or under the border with the latest group of hopefuls. Most of the shops and bars were closed. The factory workers were just waking up. The city's cleaning department were clearing away the detritus from the night before, but only after the police department had picked up the murder victims after a cursory forensic inspection of the surrounding area.

The Mission where he was staying - a run-down former church now called La Casa del Peregrino, or The Pilgrim's House - was a mile from the border, in the centre of the city. The old church looked like a former champion boxer, now on his last legs and badly beaten, but determined to keep fighting. Its adobe walls were sun-bleached and cracked. The bell-less bell tower looked forlorn, deprived of its original purpose by metal thieves years ago. Most of the shattered stained-glass windows were covered with sheets of thick cardboard or wood. The remaining few cast coloured light onto the dusty pews inside.

Omar bought a coffee from across the road and looked back at his home of the last few days. It was no longer a place of worship, he mused. Now it was a far more spiritual place, really doing God's work.

Inside, rows of cots with blankets stretched across the nave and down one side, full of bodies huddled close together against the cold of the desert night. The other side used the remaining pews as storage for boxes of donated clothes, medical supplies and bottles of water.

Hopefully, today would be the last day he'd be helping, translating for travellers who had no way of making themselves understood or being able to understand. But first, he wanted to double-check his planned route, two miles east of the main crossing point and hopefully far enough away from the more popular routes to the west.

Dumping his empty cup on top of a nearby overflowing waste bin, he mounted the Mission's only means of mechanical transport since its van had broken down and cycled off, keeping one mile away from the border as far as the roads would allow. From the shelter of the church's main doorway, Sister Theresa watched him go. A battle-worn nun whose unusual habit of faded jeans and a Mexican Red Cross t-shirt was ideal for her position as Mission medic, her role was not to ask why the people were running, but to make sure they could continue to do so.

"Is he coming back?" she asked.

"*Si.*" The small, gaunt figure of the man she knew - they all knew - as Chucho, or the mongrel, stepped out of the doorway and watched the cyclist disappear around a corner. "But not for long."

He turned and walked past her into the church to debrief the three who had returned frightened and upset in the early hours after two days away, and to find out what happened to their friend.

Theresa watched Chucho go. *Such a valuable ally,* she thought. *But such a puzzle.* All they knew about him was that he had been a coyote, but something bad had happened and now he wanted to make amends; gain redemption. Certainly, he was a treasure trove of information on routes, safe houses and the cartels, but had made it very clear there were no guarantees.

The Mission team was aware of that. They knew they were helping people who would probably return, who might not make it, or who might disappear. But they also knew that without La Casa del Peregrino, many wouldn't even have that chance. Theresa looked through the inner door into the church, watching her flock waking and the volunteers setting up the coffee station.

My people help because no one else will, she thought. *Because a human being is not illegal. And the desert sun does not care who deserves mercy and who does not.*

Sometimes, the only thing standing between a person and the abyss was a warm meal, a soft bed, and a whispered prayer. La Casa del Peregrino.

***

Omar turned off the dusty track, which served as nothing more than the patrol route for the Mexican border guards, and onto the hardpan dirt that led between rocky outcrops and the occasional thicket of mesquite before breaking into the dry scrubland near the Rio Grande and, beyond that, the border.

Chucho had suggested this point because crossing the border here was the straightforward part; it was the river and the unforgiving, well-monitored chunk of America on the other side that made the cartels and the more experienced coyotes look elsewhere.

The gangs' record of relative success was key to maintaining their operations.

"Only a fool with a death wish would consider this route," he had warned. "It's littered with the bones of failure, picked clean by the animals or the cartels."

Omar checked his position using a compass and map - the Americans could easily detect GPS devices - and headed to an outcrop he had used three times already for monitoring border activity at different times of the day. Once in position, he turned his binoculars over the river and onto the access point, noting with satisfaction that the scrub he had placed across the small gap in the fence a couple of days ago was still in place.

He scanned along the fence, looking for recent installations of mobile camera posts, for repair activity, and for any telltale reflections off binoculars or rifle sights. After an hour, the heat of the day told him to get back to the city. Once on the main road, he stopped to make a phone call.

"Mr Hernandez? Omar. Did you call Daniel?"

"Yes. He's asked us to help you as much as we can."

"Thank you, sir. And my wife?"

"Daniel will call her when you're safe. He wants as few people as possible to know what's happening, for all our sakes."

"I'm leaving today, sir. Tonight. You won't hear from me again until I knock on your door."

"Then Godspeed, young man."

The phone went dead. Daniel's father was placing himself and his family at risk by getting involved. Omar removed the SIM card from the burner phone, then smashed both of them to pieces and kicked the remains into the scrubland just off the road.

Whatever happened to him, nothing would happen to them.

Time Stands Still

Omar had spent days in the mountains of his homeland during his escape, hiding in trees or sweltering under rocks, waiting for the sun to set so he could set off once again. Time had dragged its feet like a reluctant child on a trip to the dentist, but at least it had moved.

Today, he felt that time had stopped. No matter how busy he was with other migrants desperate for help, the clock never seemed to move. Eventually, Chucho laughed and put him out of his misery.

"The batteries are nearly dead, *compadre*," he explained. "I will find some more."

Omar held a chair as the former coyote stood on the seat to reach the clock and install the fresh power.

"I'm leaving tonight, Chucho."

"Tonight? I thought you needed to earn some more money."

"I had a little trouble last night with some cartel guys. I'd be safer on the move now."

Chucho stopped and looked down from his higher position.

"Did the man have an eyepatch?"

"You heard about it?"

"*Sí.*" Chucho replaced the clock and jumped to the ground.

"You picked the wrong man to mess with, my friend."

"Which is why I'm leaving today."

"You really took their guns?"

"I gave them back. Just kept the bullets."

Chucho shook his head.

"You should have shot them both. Dead. Taking their bullets… It's like taking their woman…"

He looked at his new friend as if trying to decide what to do next, then beckoned him to follow. They walked past the altar and up a small flight of stairs to where the organ used to be, then behind the pipes and up a ladder into a room in the steeple. Chucho's room.

The former gang member opened the doors of an old cupboard and pulled out a large plastic box with a lid, which he placed on a rickety table.

"Here," he said, lifting off the lid. "Take what you need. You can pay me back if you ever get the chance."

Omar stepped forward and looked inside at the Aladdin's Cave of head torches, matchboxes, knives, handguns, ammunition, rope, maps, compasses, and money. Wads of pesos and US dollars. Water purifying tablets, plastic bottles, water bladders and batteries. Camouflaged bivvy bags and protein bars. More wads of cash. Small gold bars.

"Chucho…" Omar couldn't take his eyes off the stash. "I can't take any of this."

"Sure, you can. Here…" Chucho pulled out a wad of pesos and two wads of dollars. "You know you need more money, so take these." He reached into the box again and pulled out protein bars, a water bladder and purifying tablets. "You're going nowhere without food and water, right? And you'll need to sleep without being spotted." Out came a bivvy bag. "Check the maps. They're better than yours - there are notes on mine. And check out the compasses too. You need a head torch?"

Omar shook his head, relieved that the night vision goggles he had brought with him meant he was going to leave this man with something in his box - although he may need some more batteries.

Chucho reached into the box again and brought out eight new batteries, a hunting knife and a handgun with a small box of ammunition. He weighed the gun in his hand, as if fondly remembering when it had last been used.

"The bullets you have already will work, but you can never have too many bullets!"

Omar shook his head again.

If he couldn't reach America without shooting someone, perhaps it was best he didn't reach it at all.

"Think, *muchacho*! What if you meet up with the cartel, or another migrant tries to rob you? How about if a pack of real coyotes or a jaguar stalks you? What if you fall down a ravine and need to attract help?"

They were all valid points, Omar had to accept, and time was of the essence.

There was just one question.

"Why me?"

Chucho sat on the chair and touched the pile on the table.

"All this was for my son and me, to start a new life in America," he said. "We had our own coyote operation. We were good. Many of our customers made it across; some got back in touch and paid for us to help other family members. And all the time, we stashed this wealth. Waiting for the day we thought we had enough to leave and never come back."

He picked up a map and opened it, stroking his finger over the marks he had made in anticipation of the big day - the best hiding places, the stashes of food, the safest water sources.

"What happened?" Omar felt he had no other choice but to ask.

"*El estúpido* went to say goodbye to his mother in Mexico City, fell in love with a waitress who now has *four* of his children *and* three restaurants and never came back. Not once. He called and asked me to stay - maybe live there - but that's not me; plus I'd have to see my wife. After a couple of years, I lost interest in guiding people over. It was getting more dangerous on this side of the border as it became more difficult on the other. So, I came here."

"Again, Chucho, why me?"

"Because you deserve a chance, my friend. You have proven your worth by getting here. And, unlike me, you are desperate to see your family again, so I will do my best to make it happen."

And So It Begins

Omar crouched behind a thicket of mesquite and watched - or rather heard - Chucho drive away carefully in the borrowed pickup truck, leaving the lights off and not touching the brakes in order to avoid attracting attention and arousing suspicion.

Using the night vision goggles he'd kept since his escape from his homeland, he scanned the narrow stretch of open desert ahead.

After weeks without rain, the Rio Grande was little more than a slow-moving ribbon here, its banks lined with reeds and scrub. The real challenge lay beyond - the fence, the cameras, the unseen eyes watching in the dark.

There were good reasons this was less popular than the well-traveled routes to the west, but an unfed river could easily change that perception. This place was quiet. Maybe forgotten. Maybe not.

He had packed his gear tight: a dark reversible poncho; water bladders strapped beneath his jacket to muffle their slosh; a compact backpack with a first aid kit, food enough for three days, and money that could last much longer. As in Tajikistan, he had wrapped his sturdy boots in strips of cloth to mute his steps. As much as he hated to think about them, a knife and a loaded handgun were within easy reach.

Ahead, the terrain was mixed - hardpan dirt breaking into dry scrubland, then a paddle through the river and a squeeze through the gap in the fence. If they had miraculously repaired that since this morning, he would climb quickly, then drop and move. Thirty seconds at most.

Beyond that, the night was his friend. Thirty miles - maybe more if he needed to avoid checkpoints - to sanctuary and a new life. *Inshallah*.

With Chucho's help and the 'new' old map, he had planned the first part of his route down to the hour.

He'd try to reach the old ranch road five miles away by dawn, then hunker down in the old coyote den a quarter mile into the scrub. If it were still there.

The trick was in pacing himself. Too slow, and the sun would pin him down. Too fast, and exhaustion would catch him before the end.

A gust of wind rattled the dry brush. He exhaled, adjusted his pack, and listened. No engines. No voices. Just the constant, rhythmic chirping of the cicadas and the occasional deep, resonant hoot of an owl to break the silence. *It was time.*

Omar stood, took one last look at the stars overhead, whispered a silent prayer and stepped into the night.

The First 24 Hours

To Omar's great surprise, he woke with a start in the United States of America, having settled down to rest never believing he would fall asleep. His adrenaline-fuelled overnight adventure ended once he found the shelter. It was a crude structure made of branches, discarded tarpaulins and a couple of old blankets, backing into a small thicket of thorny brush within sight of the old ranch road. That he had found it still under the cover of darkness had been a blessing. That it was unoccupied was a miracle.

After just two hours into the crossing, moving swiftly across the desert, selecting hard ground whenever he could, he had spotted fresh footprints. They hadn't been touched by the breeze and were heading in the same direction he planned, but had started from further west. The good news was he could now move faster, his footprints merging with those of his fellow travellers. The bad news was a group of seven, maybe eight, people ahead of him; some potentially armed. He would need to stop more often to avoid an encounter, using up the saved time.

Omar had checked ahead using his goggles. With no heat sources visible, he'd set off in the same tracks until they crossed a rocky patch, then started on a path of his own several yards away, but parallel to the group.

Two hours later, he'd spotted movement a quarter of a mile ahead of him; eight indistinct blobs in total. He'd crouched down close to a cluster of cacti, certain that the guides would check all around them, and concerned they had similar technology to his own. *Best to give them a bit more space.*

Taking a slug of water, he had checked his map, careful to avoid any light that could give away his presence. The old road was just over one mile away; the shelter not much further. But if those ahead were aiming for the same location, then he needed an alternative. *Fast.*

He didn't. The group had moved onto the old road, then headed towards the abandoned farm a mile further on, gambling on a fast dash to a larger refuge. Omar had watched them leave with a sense of euphoria. After ten minutes, he went to the other side of the road. To his relief, Chucho's shelter was in decent shape.

Once he stopped moving, the chill of the desert had ripped away what warmth he felt. He had put on another jumper and wrapped his poncho around him before settling down for some much-needed rest, making sure the gun was close at hand, just in case.

Now, after four hours of heavy sleep, he was awake, and the sun's rays were warming the air. Looking out of his temporary home, the desert terrain stretched for miles; dusty, stony ground broken up by rocky outcrops or sparse vegetation, with the suggestion of low hills in the distance. He listened hard for sounds; learning what to expect from his surroundings.

The cicadas of the previous night were quieter now, but he knew their loud buzz would increase in line with the heat of the day.

In the distance, he heard the grunts and snorts of the pig-like javelinas as they foraged for food. That sound would quieten as they sought refuge from the growing heat.

He could also pick out a humming sound, probably bees or flies, but very similar to the noise emitted by the high-power electricity cables at home. *Home.* Omar wondered if that was still the case and suddenly felt very alone.

A subtle drone noise disturbed his thoughts, and he edged slowly back into the shelter, not wanting any sudden movement to attract the attention of nearby border patrols. Safely inside, he repositioned the mosquito net he had placed across the entrance, using two branches as supports, and peered cautiously to the west.

A small helicopter - not much bigger than a dragonfly at this stage - kicked up a line of dust as it flew south over the desert towards the border, then turned in his direction, following the same road he had crossed just a few hours earlier. Omar eased back into the shadows, unsure if the beat he could feel through his body was his heart or the rotors of the approaching aircraft. He repacked his gun and other belongings in case he needed to hurry and to reduce the chances of being shot himself. There were no tracks from the road to his shelter, but there were plenty heading further east, towards the old ranch buildings. He wondered if the group were still in hiding there, or if they had moved on after an hour or two of rest.

The helicopter noise increased in volume and urgency. It seemed as if it was hovering over him, trying to blow away his cover, before it moved on down the road. Omar risked a peek westwards to see if any vehicles were travelling down the road towards him, then looked east to see what the pilot would do at the ranch. The helicopter kept going without any hint of hesitation. *A standard patrol flight.*

Omar removed his water and the map from his bag. Today would be all about observation, rest and planning. Then tonight he would move again, with a better idea of what he faced and how he would avoid it.

The Repair Shop

The heat of the desert baked the worn, long-suffering asphalt that stretched toward the horizon.

Matty Hernandez wiped the sweat from his brow, his eyes squinting against the sun filtering through the grime-coated windows of his small repair shop.

A couple of trucks sat idle in the yard, waiting patiently to be fixed.

The steady hum of his old and faithful ceiling fan had hidden the noise for a while, but there it was, the unmistakable sputtering of an engine in distress.

He wiped his hands on his faded, grease-stained overalls and watched a beat-up red pickup truck emerge through the shimmering heat.

As it drew closer, he could see something unusual in the cargo bed. Several figures huddled together, silhouetted against the bright sun.

The truck came to a jerking stop in front of the garage, disappearing for a moment in the dust cloud that finally caught up to it, the engine making a final sputter before dying altogether.

The driver, a man with a broad-brimmed hat pulled low over his face, climbed out and glanced around, just as two black SUVs crunched to a halt on the gravel beside him.

Local militia. Men wearing tactical gear emerged, mirroring their leader, with holstered guns and barely visible local "border protection" badges under their vests.

"Hey, Matty." The pickup driver stepped forward, held out his hand and shook the mechanic's, ignoring the grease and the dirt.

"Hey, Don. Sounds like you have a problem."

The back of the truck creaked as the tailgate dropped, revealing eight figures hunched together, weary and covered in dirt, with fear and desperation etched on their faces. Illegal migrants. It wasn't the first time Matty had seen this, though he never got used to it.

The men and women were mostly young, their clothes torn, their eyes wide with exhaustion and fear. Their presence was an all-too-common sight in this part of the world.

Matty had seen it all before, though he never got involved. He wasn't the type to pick sides - he was just a mechanic, after all - but Omar Rahmani was out there somewhere, or was here maybe. He scanned the shadowed faces quickly, searching for a standout among the South Americans.

"Got a problem, boss?" an identikit vigilante called out in a drawl, his eyes narrowing behind the standard-issue sunglasses.

"Hey, Maguire!" Don strode across to his underling, grabbed his shirt and slammed him against the nearby SUV. "You treat Mr Hernandez with respect. You understand me? The man is a true American. Lived here all his life. Works hard. Looks after his family. Has a son in the military. Don't you ever disrespect him." Don slammed Maguire again, then turned and looked apologetically at the mechanic.

Matty just nodded at Don and headed towards the truck. "I'll see what I can do."

The truck was a mess. The engine overheated, and the radiator broken.

Matty raised the hood slowly, the hinges creaking. The air was thick with the smell of burning oil and dust. With practiced hands, he leaned over the engine, scrutinizing it carefully. His eyes flicked to the cluster of vigilantes now gathered by the SUVs, each either eyeing him or their captives, watching for any sign of trouble.

"The water pump looks okay, but you're gonna need a new radiator. That's a bad leak; not much coolant left," Matty said, his voice calm. "I'll order a new one and see what I can do to keep you going in the meantime, but it won't be much. Maybe enough to drop off your… cargo… then get this back to me."

The vigilante leader nodded.

Matty could feel the weight of the moment. The tension was thick, but his hands were already working, checking the low level of coolant, inspecting the hoses and tightening the clamps. The migrants in the back shifted uneasily. Matty made sure not to look directly at them. If they thought he saw them as people, it might be harder to turn away later.

The heat beat down relentlessly, but he worked efficiently. The pickup truck was a wreck, but it had character. It served its purpose, even if that purpose was something no one in this town cared to admit.

He stopped a moment as one vigilante walked across to the group of migrants. A dark neckerchief covered the bottom half of his face, and a patch covered one eye.

"You're wasting your time, *amigo*," Don commented. "Your *hombre* is not here."

"Then it's time for me to go."

Don nodded and walked over to him, handing over a wad of dollars he took from his jacket.

"It's all there," he said as the stranger flicked through the notes. "You did well. Call me when you have others on the way. Jerry will take you back to the crossing."

The stranger nodded, then climbed into an SUV along with three others. The driver gunned the engine into life, and the vehicle disappeared in a cloud of dust. Matty watched it drive off.

The leader's eyes flicked back to him. "We don't have all day, my friend," he said.

Matty paused. "Just give me a few minutes," he replied. His voice was steady, but a small part of him wondered just how much longer he could keep pretending he wasn't involved in the bigger picture. He wasn't some hero; that was his son, and Don was well aware of that fact. Matty was just a man trying to keep his head down and make a living.

Half an hour later, he had added a bottle of sealant into the neck of the radiator, run the engine to allow it to circulate and then topped up the coolant level. It was a messy fix, but for now, the job was done. Matty wiped his hands clean on a rag and straightened up. "You're good to go," he said, not looking at the truck's passengers now the work was done.

Don nodded curtly and climbed back into the cab. "You're a good man, Matty Hernandez," he said. "I'll drop it back off later. Make sure you send me that bill."

Matty watched them drive off into the sun, the dust recommencing its chase in their wake. The truck's engine roared in the distance, but the mechanic felt the stillness settle around him. Another day and another set of choices he'd made without making a choice at all. The border town was full of them. But sometimes, you just had to fix what you could and let the world sort itself out.

Today had been pretty straightforward, he thought. *The next few days could be very different.*

Nighttime Adventures

The sun dipped below the horizon, casting long, creeping shadows across the desert. Omar could feel the temperature drop rapidly, the searing heat of the day giving way to a chill that seeped into his bones. He took a last sip from his water bottle, listening intently. The desert hummed with life - the breeze through the brush and the constant chirping of insects, interrupted by the occasional distant coyote howl - but there were no voices, no footsteps, and no hints of a human presence.

Time to move.

He emerged from his thorny shelter, careful not to snap any dry branches, and slung his backpack over his shoulders. The sky was clear; the stars beginning to reveal themselves as the evening darkened, but there was no moon tonight; good for concealment, but bad for navigation. He double-checked his bearings and headed east towards the smuggler's hideout.

The first half-mile was slow going; the uneven desert floor was littered with loose rocks and cactus spines. Omar kept low, moving in short bursts and pausing often to look and listen. He skirted a dry wash, using its shallow dips for cover.

The wind picked up slightly, rustling the brittle desert brush and good for covering any inadvertent sounds he made, but also masking any approaching danger.

As he closed in on the ranch, tension coiled in his gut. The feeling brought back brief memories of the special forces raids back in his own country and, more recently, his escape over the mountains to safety. He forced himself to focus on the ranch. Last night, it was full of migrants, but tonight, it was eerily silent.

He crouched behind a cluster of mesquite trees, scanning the silhouette of the building. A faint movement - maybe a flutter of fabric, maybe a tarp - caught his eye near the entrance. *Someone could still be there.* Or it could just be the wind.

Deciding the risk was too great, he veered north and then east, giving the ranch a wide berth and running parallel to the track. The detour cost him time and energy and forced him across an exposed stretch of terrain. His pulse hammered in his ears as he walked steadily across, trying to avoid attention, but half-expecting a shout or a sudden flashlight beam to pin him in place. Nothing happened.

An hour later, fatigue had set in. The terrain became rougher; the land dipping into dry arroyos and climbing back up to rocky ridges. His legs burned with every step, and his concentration faded as his mind tired. He almost missed a rattlesnake coiled near a clump of yucca, catching the telltale hiss just in time to freeze and sidestep around it. He had expected the delay in progress, but not the effect on his nerves, which made every shadow look like a lurking danger. Forcing himself to stop in the shelter of a rocky outcrop, he grabbed a protein bar, put on another jumper to ward off the cold and used his night goggles to establish his location on the map and to look for heat signals in the area. Satisfied with his progress and feeling calmer, he set off once more, keeping the road to his right in sight, but far enough away to give him the chance of concealment or escape if anything came along.

Two miles later, something did.

Omar heard the truck engine first, then the low growl of tyres on dirt. He threw himself flat behind a cluster of prickly pear, barely breathing. The truck wasn't using headlights. He could make out just a faint glow from its dashboard, visible through the windshield.

The vehicle slowed and then stopped. A door creaked open; then another. Flashlights clicked on, sweeping the ground on both sides of the track. Omar pressed into the earth, his body trembling as he tried to keep still and resist the urge to run. Boot steps crunched nearby, then mercifully moved away.

The minutes crawled by before the searchers finally gave up. The flashlight beams headed back toward the truck; the doors slammed shut, and the vehicle rumbled off into the night. Omar didn't move until the sounds faded completely.

The last few miles were gruelling. Hunger gnawed at his stomach, thirst parched his throat, and exhaustion made his feet clumsy. He stumbled several times, catching himself just before falling. But as the eastern horizon glowed faintly with the first hints of dawn, he finally spotted the smuggler's hideout - a low, crumbling adobe structure nestled in the desert scrub.

Omar staggered towards it, his muscles screaming for rest. Keeping his eyes firmly fixed on the doorway, he removed the handgun from his waistband before advancing and gently pushing the battered door inwards. The door cracked open, restrained by a forest of cobwebs as it did so. Omar dropped to the ground. Sliding his rucksack in front of him and keeping as low as possible to avoid disturbing the cobwebs, he crawled into the gloom and closed the door behind him. *Safe. For now.*

The Wake Up Call

The rattling of the shutters covering the broken window woke Omar from his disturbed sleep. For one terrible moment, he feared he was about to be discovered.

Instinctively, he felt for the gun, then came to his senses and shoved it under a pile of rags just to his right, in a corner of the small building. If there were vigilantes about to force their way in, they would carry more than handguns and wouldn't be afraid to use them. Just in case, he sat up cross-legged, with his hands high in the air.

The shutters rattled again, their movement coinciding perfectly with the sounds of the wind battering against the adobe walls.

It wasn't just stronger than anything he'd experienced since arriving in Mexico, Omar thought; it was wrong. It blew in every direction at once, as if it were arguing with itself.

Despite his protection from the outside, even the air inside the building felt thick, as if it had weight. His ears popped, like he had experienced on the flights away from Afghanistan.

The wind almost tore the door out of his grasp as he stepped outside the shelter, pressed himself close to the wall and looked upwards to see the sky boiling. He couldn't think of a better word for it. *Boiling*.

It wasn't clouds. It was something alive, a malevolent airborne maelstrom, turning in on itself, churning black and green and... growling... a low, threatening growl that hit him deep in his chest.

The ground around him came to life, as if every grain of sand, every stone, every bush and tree was trying to flee from the behemoth's path.

Omar ducked back inside, shouldered the door shut and wedged an old and broken chair against it. Grabbing his rucksack, he buried himself under the pile of mouldy tarps and rags in the far corner. Everything shook. The walls flexed, the roof groaned, and Omar flinched as he felt something heavy slam into the building. The wind was howling, screaming, full of pain and rage.

Omar burrowed deeper into the corner, pushing himself into the wall and raising his rucksack in front of his head and chest, feeble protection against whatever this monster could throw at him. His head throbbed, and his ears ached. And still the onslaught continued.

He did not know the time. It could have been two minutes, five minutes, maybe twenty. Just him and the elements determined to kill him, frustrated in their mission by walls of sun-dried earth and straw, constructed decades ago. Surely, the end had come. So close to reaching safety and salvation, only to have it ripped from his grasp as he was torn from the earth.

And then it was gone.

Just like that. No more wind. Just the sound of heavy rain, soaking the loose impediments that had failed in their escape bid and dropped onto the ground. Omar struggled to his feet and moved the old chair, miraculously still holding the door shut. Debris smothered the ground outside. Wood, metal, branches. A truck tire. Three barely recognisable oil drums. What looked like part of a smashed barn.

He slipped on his poncho, walked to the road and saw the blockade of fallen power poles, snapped like matchsticks. Repair and rescue teams would focus on the more populated areas. Border patrols and the local vigilantes would have their own issues, as would anybody caught crossing the border in the storm.

Looking southwest, back towards Mexico, a fresh, wide brown scar had torn across the land towards and then beyond his shelter.

Flanked by all kinds of debris, it looked as if some god had dragged a giant knife through the earth, ripping out everything in its path. The scar had passed within 100 yards of him. He had been lucky, but there was always the chance his luck could change.

He checked his watch. Late afternoon, although the darkness suggested it was much later. He didn't care that it was early. There were too many unknowns to risk staying in the area and so close to the road.

It was time to go.

The Dilemma

Omar closed the door of the hideout firmly behind him and used a nearby branch from a long-gone tree to cover his tracks back to the road. Such was the flatness of the earth around here, he could still see the tornado twisting across the land like a drunk through a crowded bar, gouging its path of chaos through the baked dirt, scrub and cattle wire flung high into the air.

He followed way behind it until he was half a mile or so north of the farm road, then bade the twister a fond farewell and headed eastwards, keeping a watchful eye out for any traffic to his right.

Now that the wind had gone, and the rain was following, the smell of uprooted everything - soil, gasoline and cows - hung in the air. Omar crouched beside what he imagined had been a chicken coop, now a pile of lumber wearing a patio umbrella like a hat. He checked Chucho's laminated smuggler's route map, hoping it continued to be accurate. The next waypoint was an abandoned gas station, about six miles east, near where the farm track met asphalt. Reaching it hadn't been an issue until the tornado had complicated things - *just like America*, he thought. There was also the chance of a mobile checkpoint to negotiate, but he was hopeful - maybe even pretty sure - that recent events had put paid to that.

He skirted along the route, moving through low ditches and tangled mesquite whenever he could, his rag-wrapped boots squelching in storm-sodden earth.

The filthy American university hoodie and worn baseball cap he had found tangled in a barbed-wire fence gave him more of a local look, even if it was a look that Americans may well studiously ignore.

Half a mile on, walking across open land between two sets of useful cover, he stopped.

About two hundred yards away, closer to the road, was an overturned pickup, wheels still spinning slowly, as if it was refusing to accept its fate.

It was too far away from the carnage for the tornado to be responsible for its predicament. A man, shirtless and bleeding, stumbled around it, waving a flannel shirt in all directions like a surrender flag, desperate to attract attention.

Omar dropped flat. Reflex. It could be a trap. He'd seen this before; decoys set up on Afghan roads to target helpful types. You bend over a fake injury, and someone plants an IED in your shadow.

But then again, Texas didn't work like Afghanistan. Or maybe it did. He was still figuring that out.

He pulled out an old Mexican peso coin - a gift from Chucho to help when he needed a quick decision. Like now. *Heads: help. Tails: move.* He flipped it.

Heads.

Of course.

Omar approached slowly, hands visible. "You okay?" he called, adding the slight American accent he hadn't used for over twelve months. The man staggered toward him, his face a grimace smeared with blood and disbelief. "Jesus. You - are you Border Patrol?"

Omar gave a bitter half-smile and shook his head.

"My wife's in the cab. I'm not sure..."

The man clutched his ribs and pointed at the truck, which lay like a dead animal, a web of glass across the crumpled windshield. Omar peered in. The woman was pinned upside-down, seatbelt jammed, one leg bent awkwardly. Eyes wide open. Breathing, but in shock.

"Ma'am," Omar said gently, sliding into medic mode. "Can you hear me?"

She blinked. "My legs," she whispered.

Omar yanked open the bent door and crawled in. He used his knife to slice the seatbelt, then took her weight as she dropped like a stone. *Too shocked to scream.* With the driver's help, he pulled her free and laid her as gently as possible on a coat her husband had placed on the ground.

"Are you a doctor?" the man asked.

"Medic. Yeah," Omar nodded.

He worked fast while the man - Burt - dialled 911 along with hundreds of others and bitterly regretted gazing at the tornado rather than focusing on the road.

Omar made a leg splint from two pieces of broken fence post. Strips of an old t-shirt made basic bandages.

Pain relief. The one thing he had forgotten about in his preparations.

And him a medic. Idiot. But he'd learned long ago that eye contact and calm instructions could postpone pain.

"Keep talking to her," he told the man, who still had his phone to his ear. "Touch her face. Say her name."

The man did as he was told.

"Beverly. Beverly, sweetheart, you're gonna be okay. This guy, he's - he's some kind of… Hello? Yeah. We've been in a crash. Eighteen miles southwest of Van Gilbert on the border track. Truck's upside down. Wife badly injured."

Omar waved for the phone to be handed to him and relayed the patient's status to the operator, directing Burt's attention back to his wife.

"They've made you a priority case," he said when he finally handed the phone back. "I exaggerated Beverly's condition to get you there. They should be here in thirty minutes. Maybe sooner."

"You'll stay, right?"

Omar shook his head.

"I need to go. Beverly will be fine. Just don't leave her, give her water if she wants it and keep talking to her."

"But I can get you where you need to go. The paramedics…"

"I appreciate it. But others will still be on the lookout for people like me."

He turned to go, but Burt held his arm. "You're not American? What's your name, son?"

He hesitated for a moment. "Omar."

"We appreciate your help, Omar. If there's ever anything I can do…"

Omar nodded and pointed back the way he had come.

"If anybody asks, tell them I went that way. Tell them I'm going back. Say I said the tornado did for me. America's too dangerous."

Then he winked and headed off away from the road and back towards the brush. The landscape looked cruel. Trees splintered, livestock carcasses bloated in the waning heat of the day, and all kinds of detritus flung all over the place.

But he moved fast now, lighter somehow. Partly because he had done the right thing; partly because doing so had put him in greater danger.

He followed an old oil pipeline trench, half-buried under storm debris, leading east. As the sun dipped lower, just before it slipped away, he found an American flag, flapping weakly and caught in a barbed wire fence. Out of some instinct, Omar freed it carefully, folded it and slipped it into his pack. It felt stupid, but it felt necessary.

In the early hours, he reached the gas station; abandoned, just like the empty checkpoint he had almost fallen over at the end of the track. The roof had partially collapsed; soda machines listed sideways. But there was shelter. And stillness. For the moment, everyone focused their attention further west, on Beverly, Burt, and the many others affected by the day's weather.

He dropped his backpack and wandered over to a half-submerged sedan, its hood under the water in a flooded ditch, its bumper sticker - faded but legible - pointing to the night sky: 'REAL AMERICANS DON'T RUN.'

Omar crouched beside it, put his hand on it and laughed. Then he picked up his backpack and headed into the remains of the building to search for a place to sleep.

He didn't know whether he was running or surviving. But he was still here. For now, that was enough.

The Reluctant Hitchhiker

Omar woke to the sounds of a clanking chain and rubber tyres on asphalt - the first unnatural noises he had heard since bedding down in the gas station. He bolted upright, hitting his head on what used to be a price sign for unleaded premium, now lying flat across two rusting barrels. The station, once a landmark monument to fossil-fuelled freedom, now served as a desert drop-in for anyone who was extremely broke, wanted or unlucky.

He held his breath and waited. The vehicle sound faded, replaced by the desert's usual playlist: wind, sand, the bark of a coyote and the occasional existential groan of an unhappy tree. He scrambled over to a shattered window, peered through a louvred slat, and spotted the culprit - a smart black and red tow truck, turning onto the farm road and disappearing in a cloud of dust.

He waited a couple of minutes, just long enough to convince himself that the universe was unaware he existed in this place and at this time, then grabbed a protein bar and a few swigs of water for breakfast. Supplies were getting short. He spread out Chucho's map and looked for any nearby location that offered a faint prospect of supplies. The closest in the right direction was eight miles away.

Sweat dripped off the end of his nose and onto the map.

The heat had arrived early. The sensible option was to wait for the relative cool of the night, but the border patrols may be operational again by then, progress could be slow and he would be weaker. There was only one thing to do. The peso coin came down tails. He debated trying for the best of three tosses, but decided against it. *Time to move.*

Two hours and just a mile and a half later, he was sweating like a politician wired to a lie detector. The need for speed dictated that he kept near the road, ducking behind the occasional rock or bush, or lying flat or sitting still anytime he heard a noise, which was uncomfortably often.

The tow truck had been the least of his worries; an early indicator of a rush-hour that had started almost as soon as he had set off and showed no sign of stopping. Every few minutes something would pass by - ambulances, construction vehicles, FEMA vans, cars carrying rescue workers or worried relatives passed by - all heading west and, judging by the dust cloud behind him, off the asphalt and onto the farm road.

Omar had been quick to adopt a stop, scout and move strategy, making short dashes from cover to cover, or moving low and slow if there was nothing to shelter in or behind. As soon as he saw or heard something, he would stop, wait until the vehicle passed, then move on.

The key was to make the most of the gaps in the traffic. He put the tiredness to the back of his mind, imagining instead what was waiting for him at the next stop; commending himself on the progress he was making and the success of his strategy. The soporific heat continued to beat down, making concentration hard to maintain. Then the black and red recovery truck appeared from nowhere, its smart paint job covered in dust. It overtook him from behind, towing a battered pickup with a crumpled windshield and - Omar would have bet his life - a sliced passenger seatbelt.

The vehicle slowed to a crawl, like an animal would when deciding if you were something to run from or eat.

Omar kept walking, hoping the truck driver would keep moving. Hope faded fast. Brake lights lit up under a film of dust and the truck manoeuvred to the side of the road, the pickup following dutifully behind like an obedient puppy. Nobody got out, and the engine continued to tick over.

Omar considered his options. Run like a paranoid jackrabbit or walk like he had every right in the world to be here, in the middle of a desert, close to where a tornado had cut a swathe through the landscape just hours earlier.

He adjusted his baseball cap and opted for a swagger. Not too much; just enough to say, "I'm local, but emotionally distant. There's nothing to see here. Be on your way."

As Omar walked past, the driver leaned over and rolled down the passenger window.

"Need a lift, son?"

"I'm good, sir. Thank you. My friend is waiting for me just up the road a way."

"Kinda hot for a stroll in the desert. Jump in. I'm heading to town. I'll take you to him."

Omar hesitated. This was a miracle or a trap. But at the moment, he'd risk arrest for air-conditioning.

He opened the door and climbed in. "Do you… need papers or anything? I'm afraid I don't have any and…"

The driver snorted and shook his head. "After yesterday, half the area's fallen down and the other half's helping to pick it up again. The only papers I care about are the labels that say 'cold beer'."

He checked the road and pulled out, slowly picking up speed as the damaged truck behind them groaned its objections. "I'm guessing this isn't the first time you've seen this mess I'm towing."

"You'd be right, sir."

"Burt reckons you saved Beverly's life. Said if I saw a guy heading this way and looking like he'd give anything to be anywhere else, that'd be you. Told him I'd help if I could. A favour deserves a favour."

Omar turned and looked out of the passenger window, watching the miles it would have taken him days to travel pass by in minutes.

Two empty checkpoints were each dealt with by driving through them in a split second rather than spending hours keeping a healthy distance and traversing through the surrounding desert.

He flinched as a police car overtook them with lights flashing, but soon relaxed as it continued on its way.

Eventually, as they headed into the town's suburbs and skirted around the centre, the driver spoke again. "What are your plans, son? Got anywhere you can stay? Any friends?"

"I have some money. I'll buy a bus ticket and head north."

"There's no bus north until the day after tomorrow at the earliest. Tornado damaged a road bridge, and the army corps of engineers is repairing it."

"I'll find somewhere to stay. I think there's a Mission…"

The driver glanced across at him incredulously.

"You've come all this way from God knows where, and now that you're here you've nowhere to go?"

Omar didn't reply. He just looked straight ahead, worried that any gawping at the town's streets might raise suspicions and create problems.

"Look. My wife and I… we have a spare room if you need it. Bed. Shower. Probably got some clothes that'll fit you if I look long enough."

"That's very kind, but I don't want to put you to any trouble. If someone saw me…"

"Son, what's your name?"

"Omar. Omar Rahmani."

The driver turned a corner towards the edge of town, heaved the steering wheel to the left and pulled into a workshop parking lot. He reversed the damaged pickup next to a row of vehicles awaiting attention, switched off the engine and turned to face his hitchhiker.

"Hello, Omar. I'm Matty Hernandez."

The Final Report

Widdock waited until the jet had taxied to the far side of the airfield before heading over in the passenger van. He arrived just as the steps were being lowered to the ground and walked round and opened the passenger door just as two cloak-clad figures exited the plane.

"Widdock! As I live and breathe!" boomed the familiar voice in the first hood.

"Mr Blackwell. Welcome back, sir." The tone exuded as much warmth and friendliness as a single ice cube, trapped in the dark by itself in a refrigerator's freezer compartment.

Mindy didn't bother with anything more than a "Hello Mr Widdock" and stepped into the van with no expectation of a reply, which was just as well. The driver walked around to his open door, climbed inside and started the engine.

"The three of us again!" laughed Andrew. "It's just like old times!"

"Indeed, sir." Widdock flashed a wan smile, which disappeared a split second after its arrival. "We're heading straight to the boathouse. Everyone else has arrived."

Six minutes later, the van descended a newly laid track through the hilly woodland and came to a halt outside the building by the lough.

"Oh," sighed Blackwell. "My favourite boathouse."

The couple exited the van and watched as it was driven off without so much as a vague wave of farewell.

"You are such a wind-up merchant," Mindy said without looking at her fiancé.

"It's just banter between good mates," Andy protested.

"Banter is a friendly exchange of teasing remarks, not a one-sided, vaguely embarrassing barrage of comments at someone who plainly is not your friend and has no desire to be so."

Blackwell watched as the only love in his life sauntered towards the large wooden door, which swung open as she approached.

"Ah," he pointed at her triumphantly. "That was banter!"

"Nope. Fact," she said, leaving him pointing at mid-air.

They walked into the main room, briefly took in the stunning views of the surrounding hills and woodland through the large windows opposite, then focused on the figures approaching them.

As the hosts of the event, Martin and Mavis Barnwell reached them first and greeted them with hugs. Martin looked pale and tired. *But who wouldn't after engaging intensely with the best and brightest minds the world could offer over a lengthy time period?* reasoned Andrew. Mavis looked nervous, glancing anxiously across to her husband even when she was trying to give someone else her undivided attention.

Former gangland boss and proven master of deception Declan Kelly wandered over munching a Danish pastry, closely followed by brother and technical genius Connor and the third key element of Kelly Industries, their close friend Brendan Dunne.

"Andy. Mindy. A warm welcome to your third home. Try the pastries. They could be the highlight of the day." He turned away, then turned back again and winked. "Although I seriously doubt it."

Greek billionaire Isaac Delemos had been in deep conversation on his phone, facing out of the room towards the waters outside, when he caught sight of the new arrivals' reflections in the glass. Hurriedly finishing his conversation, he pocketed his phone and strode over, hugging Mindy and offering Andrew a firm handshake.

"It's good to see you again, Isaac," said Mindy.

"And looking much happier than the last time we met," beamed Blackwell.

"I don't deny it," Delemos smiled. "It's an exciting time to be alive. I have never been so popular - even amongst my workforce."

"Let's see if you feel the same in a few hours." Mavis had sidled up beside them all. "Sit yourselves down, or we'll never get you home tonight."

Everybody settled around the long oak conference table, and the front door closed silently, while Martin took his place alongside the screen and cleared his throat.

"Welcome everyone. Here is an overview of our achievements during the last couple of weeks. You'll know I'm not one for overstatement, so you'll understand what it means when I say I am quite excited to have played a part in a historic… historic… series of events."

"That's enough for me," said Andrew, pretending to stand up. "Just give me the full report to read and I'll be on my way."

"Andy!" Mindy slapped his arm, and the former prime minister settled back down with a broad smile on his face. If Martin felt so strongly about this, then the next few hours promised to be very special.

They were.

Martin reiterated what they already knew; that *Path Finder* would not be a political party or have a range of policies apart from one, which would be never to have any.

It had taken a while for some of the invited groups to come to that conclusion, but they had arrived there eventually. He fell silent, feeling strangely overwhelmed for a moment, and stared at the table, considering how to convey the enormity of what they had accomplished.

"As you all know, I worked in politics for decades," he started. "I spent longer than I care to remember patiently and not-so-patiently persuading, cajoling or threatening egotistical, resentful individuals and groups into working together for the benefit of either the party, the people, the country or themselves. I was pretty good at it."

He looked up from the table and gazed at the others.

"Never, in all that time, did I meet one person who matched most of the delegates we've entertained here in terms of sheer genius, infuriating smugness, unbelievable self-confidence and bitter competitiveness."

"Present company excepted?" Andy asked hopefully.

"No. You don't even come close."

"And that's a good thing," assured Mindy, patting her fiancé's arm. "Try not to be too disappointed."

"My point is," interrupted Martin before losing the moment completely, "This bunch of self-centred individuals set aside their differences, vendettas and fears to work together and provide *Path Finder* with a mission and a structure. Not only that, they left here recognising they are now an important part of a mission that is bigger than themselves. Each group left here as a motivated team of guides, ready to help others to find the right path for themselves and united in their ambition for the movement and, ultimately, the world."

"Tell them the best bit," urged Mavis.

"That we're done here and can finally leave?"

"Martin Barnwell! Tell them the best bit or I'll tell them what I call you at home!"

The group stifled the gasps around the room, but that didn't stop the stifled gasps from being heard. Threatened by the nuclear option and knowing damn well that it would be at the forefront of everyone's mind, Barnwell moved on.

Each team of *Path Finder* guides was to create a general 'destination' or 'goal' for their specialist area, he told them. This could be, for example, as broad as environmental improvement or universal access to quality healthcare. Individuals and organisations could then submit a proposed path towards that destination on a local, national or international scale, taking into consideration the capabilities and resources available in their geographic area.

The guides would review and select proposals with real potential, advise on their development to the approval stage and work alongside the implementers of approved projects, which *Path Finder* would help to promote and potentially fund.

"Promotion is key," he said, looking at Mindy. "If this is to work, we need to capture the imagination of the people, so they look to organisations, political parties and governments in their own area to support and build the paths. Questions so far?"

Six hands went up. Martin pointed at Connor.

"Is your nickname Grumpy?"

Martin counted slowly to ten, aware he was the sole focus of attention in the room. Mavis put her hand over her mouth to cover her laughter.

"No, Connor," he replied evenly, aware of the Kellys' artificially manufactured reputation for violence, but unwilling to test how artificial it actually was. "And I won't be responding to any further guesses."

The remaining five hands dropped like stones, and Martin used the moment to press on as quickly as he could from the topic of nicknames.

"So, we have a structure and a strategy. But the guides didn't stop there. We have a start. They've provided some intriguing ideas in our five key areas of education, environment, industry, culture and peace. Some are credible and genuinely cutting edge; others were created as the night went on and the alcohol intake increased, so make of those what you will. Each one is a signpost, showing the kinds of ideas we're hoping to see, and not to see. View them as sparks to ignite excitement and interest... Andy?"

The former PM put his hand down as quickly as it had gone up.

"Sorry, but it's just occurred to me... politics and all that... Is your nickname the Honourable Member for Mavis?"

As promised, Martin ignored the question and the sniggers that followed, but took some satisfaction from the severity of the thump his former boss received in the chest from his girlfriend.

"Let's start with science and the environment. Genetic research is already under way into merging chloroplasts with human skin cells, enabling people to generate up to 20% of their calorific intake through basic photosynthesis..."

"Like plants do?"

"Exactly. If it works, it would reduce food consumption and agricultural demand and would give everyone in tropical countries a better chance of survival."

Before anybody could think of a smart-arse comment, Martin moved swiftly on to other examples. He talked about virtual cows, created by artificial intelligence and existing in a 'meadowverse', where they would produce a lab-grown dairy product that tasted exactly the same as milk. Each cow would come with a heartfelt, emotional backstory to make consumers feel invested in the product, plus there would be massive reductions in methane emissions and related land use.

Scientists in Japan were developing toilet turbines, which generated power every time a toilet was flushed and fed it into a battery storage facility for local use or into the national grid. *Poo and pee equals power* was the current branding proposition, explained Martin, looking at the frown on Mindy's face and the smirk on Andy's, but the product was still in development and was nowhere near ready for marketing yet.

Forestry experts in Canada were in the early stages of genetically engineering emotionally needy trees that would absorb up to ten times the usual amount of carbon if talked to daily and told they were special.

Moving on quickly again to avoid any comments, Martin talked about flat-pack factories, shipped in container-sized kits to communities in developing regions, then constructed and used to manufacture local necessities cost-effectively with no global supply chains or middlemen, or middlewomen.

Two tech giants were talking about free or low-cost internet access for all, creating massive potential benefits in terms of access to education, economic development opportunities and cultural exchanges. Finally, a conference of peace campaigners had concluded with a list of proposals for resolving current global conflicts and reforming global attitudes to new ones, which they planned to drop off at the United Nations.

Martin halted and took a drink, concealing his anxiety about how the ideas were going down with his audience. He needn't have worried. Connor was busy scribbling notes; his elder brother was grinning at Brendan; Mindy stared at the key points staring back at her from the screen; and Mavis looked at her husband with genuine pride and affection. Isaac Delemos studied the notes he had made during the presentation, tapping his finger on the table at the same time.

Andy Blackwell stared at the ceiling.

"It's happening, isn't it?" he asked nobody in particular. "We'll have ups and downs, no doubt, but we're offering another way. We're giving people a chance wherever they are."

Isaac stopped the finger tapping, which was a relief to everyone else, as it was becoming annoying.

"It's happening," he confirmed. "And credit to Martin and Mavis for making it happen. I'm not sure it would have done without their persuasive skills."

The group burst into spontaneous applause.

"I'm delighted with the progress and the direction of *Path Finder*," the billionaire continued, "But I am concerned about the reaction of certain organisations to its development. How do we defend ourselves against what may come? What stands in their way?"

He looked at Martin, who turned to Andrew, who looked at Declan, who turned to Connor, who pointed at Mindy, who smiled brightly at the group.

"Oh, I wouldn't concern yourselves with that," she said. "Just focus on turning the success of the last fortnight into a lasting triumph."

"By not getting involved?" asked her fiancé hopefully.

"By doing what we said we'd do."

"Nothing?"

Mindy stifled a sigh and looked at the man in her life, her face a picture of controlled contempt, barely hidden behind a winning smile.

"You promote, you encourage, you support. Everything is positive," she said. "Leave the defence to Connor and me."

"Then we have nothing to fear," Andy beamed. "Unlike our enemies."

The Late Gift

Pippa parked the car on the drive by the garage, picked up the shopping bags and walked through the back garden into the kitchen. Three weeks had passed since the barbecue, and she had just about recovered from the lack of sleep and the excess alcohol.

The dogs heard the door closing and raced from the lounge into the kitchen to inspect the groceries. Pippa lifted the bags out of harm's way onto a work surface, threw a biscuit onto each dog bed and walked into the hallway.

Simon sat on the third stair, staring at his mobile phone.

"Everything okay?" she asked.

"I'm trying to decide. That was the RSM, with an offer."

Pippa bridled. "Did you tell him what he could do with it? Ireland was bad enough."

Simon couldn't argue. The mission had been stressful, but worth it. Nobody had died. Stuart Morris and Dave Westlake now had serious love interests. Morris had found a new purpose in life. The Clonbrinny community and its priest were no longer under threat, and Ireland's most powerful gangster had morphed into a powerful ally.

However, there had also been threats, guns, death and a significant amount of fishing, none of which were Pope's cup of tea.

Plus, if anything *had* gone badly wrong, there would have been no cavalry to come to the rescue. Simon would have been on his own, but he hadn't known it. And now the former regimental sergeant major, who had instigated all that in the name of the Garden Club, was back with another proposal.

"He's offering a holiday as an apology."

"Strings?"

"None, apparently. Someone offered him a last-minute chance to chase storms in the States, but he doesn't want to go and thought I would want it."

"Because lightning, which killed your current wife twice, also hit you?"

Pope didn't get the sarcasm. His mind was thousands of miles away in Tornado Alley.

"No," he said. "He knows I'm interested in that stuff. The problem is that the flight out is in two days, with the tour starting a day later. The organisers had a cancellation."

Pippa stroked her husband's hair.

"We haven't sorted a honeymoon yet," she said. "I can get out of work, but we'll need to make sure the kennels can take the dogs."

Pope cleared his throat, wary of the reaction his response could trigger.

"The offer was for me, Pip. Not both of us."

She waited until he finally found the courage to lift his eyes to hers before she replied, using the soft and even tone he recognised as signalling murderous intent.

"Then you have a decision to make, don't you?"

She smiled a smile that didn't reach the eyes, patted his head and walked back into the kitchen to put away the shopping.

Pope sighed and looked down at his mobile phone.

Decisions, decisions.

Apologies and Thanks

A couple of days later, Simon Pope stepped out of the car at Heathrow Airport's Terminal Three departures and waited for the driver to remove his case from the boot. The driver simply pressed a button and the boot lid opened. Pope heaved the case out and onto its wheels before returning to the open passenger door.

"Whatever happened to good old customer service?" he asked.

"The same thing that's happened to tipping, apparently," came the reply.

Pope closed the door with slightly more force than was actually required, ignored the glare thrown his way and headed towards the terminal entrance, swinging his rucksack onto his back with one hand while pushing the case with the other.

Once inside, he checked the time and walked away from the check-in desks to a nearby coffee shop, where he bought a cappuccino and a muffin before struggling towards an occupied table in a busy area of the store.

"Making friends with the locals?" asked the former regimental sergeant major, who had observed the mild altercation with the vehicle driver through the vast windows nearby.

"A slight misunderstanding over the definition of service and reward," grunted Pope, settling into a seat. "How can I help you?"

"And it's good to see you too," beamed the RSM, looking as uncomfortable as ever out of uniform, despite having officially returned to civilian life some eighteen months earlier. "I'm here to apologise once again for providing you and your friends with a memorable break in Ireland four months ago, and to give you the opportunity to fulfil a lifetime ambition."

"Why me?"

"Because you're the only fool I know who wants to go storm chasing despite being hit by lightning not too long ago, and I don't want to drive around Texas for a week, looking for death in a van full of people I may not like."

"And why just a couple of days' notice?"

The RSM sighed. "So much suspicion," he observed. "You must be a nervous wreck."

"Only when you're involved, Pete."

The RSM reached inside his jacket pocket, removed a promotional flyer and slid it across the table.

"The guy who owns this business used to work in air traffic control in Iraq for the US military many moons ago. He was good. Very good. Helped us get around the country, even when the weather was terrible. We got to know him well. Once, we were extracting at night in a couple of Chinooks. A huge thunderstorm hit us; appeared from nowhere. We were getting battered by the wind and the lightning... well... you know how terrifying that can be."

The RSM poured himself more tea, recollecting the night he thought he was going to die and giving Pope time to reflect on his own near miss with nature.

"He took over the controller comms. I'll always remember how calm he was. Very cool. Within a minute we noticed a drop in the weather's impact. Don't get me wrong, it was all around us, but not where we were. He was using the same military-grade weather radar as the other controllers, but he saw things they didn't or couldn't see. Navigated a path out of there for us and saved our lives. And probably his."

"Oh?"

"He was a real weather buff. It wasn't just the fury of the storm that fascinated him. It was how nature could turn so quickly and unpredictably. That night he experienced the adrenaline rush of navigating that chaos in real time, and he loved it. His tour of duty was ending. He had planned to extend it, but with his curiosity about storms piqued, he left the service two months later. Took a job as a driver with a storm chasing group, then set up on his own."

"So how did that night save his life?"

"One week after he left, they attacked the air base he worked at. Two shells hit the controllers' quarters." The RSM took another sip of his tea. "He got lucky."

Pope looked at the photograph on the front of the leaflet. Excited, happy customers by a well-equipped van with a huge tornado a mile or so in the background, hurling debris into the air. The back cover featured some testimonials from all over the world, plus the Storm Stalkers' contact details and a photograph of the owner.

"I stayed in touch," the RSM continued, anticipating the line of questioning. "Liked his photos online, that sort of thing. I made the mistake of commenting one time that it sounded great, but I couldn't afford it. Four days ago, he got in touch, told me there'd been a cancellation on his next tour and there was space for me. I gave my excuses but suggested you might be interested. The Garden Club bought your flights."

He reached into his inside pocket again and withdrew two envelopes.

"Here are your tickets," he said, pushing one envelope across.

"What's in the other?"

"I'd like you to give that to him. It's a gift. I never had time to thank him properly for what he did for us that night. This is my chance."

"What is it?"

"A replacement passport."

"But he's American."

"Dual nationality. We found his UK passport after the attack. Damaged and burnt beyond repair. He must have dropped it before he left. I've been meaning to do something with it for years. Just give it to him and say Pete says thank you."

Pope eyed the envelope. "It's a forgery, isn't it?"

"It's a favour. For an old friend."

The RSM pushed the second envelope across the table and stood up.

"Don't worry. It won't set off any alarms." He patted Pope on the shoulder. "Good to see you again, Simmo. Enjoy yourself, send some pictures and come back alive."

Pope watched as the man he'd first met soon after joining the regiment as a chaplain all those years ago limped across the concourse and out to the roadway. Thirty seconds later, a car with tinted windows pulled up, the RSM climbed into the front passenger seat and the vehicle was gone.

Pope put the second envelope in his inside jacket pocket and examined the contents of the first. The flight to Denver was definitely today and - he checked a nearby departures board - on time. The boarding passes were in order and the tickets… premium economy. *Excellent.* The other three pages were the accommodation voucher for the hotel, an itinerary for the start of the tour and a letter of introduction to the chief tour guide and business owner, 'Twister' Mitchell.

"Well, fancy meeting you here."

Pope didn't even look up from the correspondence.

"We're flying premium economy," he smiled. "A nice touch."

Pippa plopped herself down in the recently vacated chair, having dropped their car off at valet parking. "Did he ask how I was?"

Pope considered lying but wisely decided against it.

"He didn't even ask how I was," he shrugged.

The Ambush

Briefing Room A in the Cabinet Office building had not changed since Martin and Mindy's meeting with Damien Crockett many months before, following Andy Blackwell's vanishing trick. It was still full of piled furniture, decorator's ladders, sheets and pots of paint.

The repainting of the usual venue for the Cobra cross-departmental committee, which meets in times of national emergency, had yet to be completed. Fortunately, there had been no national emergencies in the meantime; not major ones at any rate. Until the requested two pots of the specific pink paint arrived, policy dictated the room remained out of use, which is why prime minister Damien Crockett was sitting at a large boardroom table in a nearby room, alongside chancellor Emily Helms and junior minister Henry McInnes, staring at a laptop.

"We said eleven, didn't we?" asked McInnes, desperate to thaw the icy silence.

Crockett seemed deep in thought, but Emily Helms wasn't.

"You organised the call," she patronised. "You tell us."

McInnes looked as if he was about to say something, then withered under the chancellor's glare and thought better of it. He walked over to the refreshments and made himself a cup of coffee.

Having embarrassed his prime minister and chancellor, his political party, the government and the entire media corps by concocting the 'Blackwell is back in the fold' story at Chequers, this call was his chance to rectify the situation and his career. Blackwell's positive response to his request for an online chat had saved his bacon, for now. The former prime minister had appointed him in the first place and was keen to support him in his hour of need. McInnes was grateful for that, but was wishing he had told Blackwell that the PM and chancellor would also be on the call.

Fourteen minutes later than scheduled, the laptop ping announced the former prime minister, and he appeared on screen immediately, red-faced and in a sweat-stained t-shirt. The three people crowded around the laptop in the Cabinet Office had a few moments to recover from their shock at his appearance, as he was facing away from the camera, talking to someone out of shot.

"We talked about this, didn't we? We decided it was better to have a crap in the woods rather than in the house. But it appears *somebody* wasn't listening, were you, Fred?"

The three eavesdroppers quickly ran through all the Freds they knew in politics and what little they knew of their toilet habits, then relaxed when the head of a black greyhound moved into view and licked Andy Blackwell's face.

"Alright. Apology accepted. Here..." Blackwell took something off the desk and gave it to the dog. "Have a sleep with your sister. Go on..."

Fred grabbed the biscuit and shot off without so much as a by your leave.

"You daft dog!" Blackwell laughed, then turned towards the camera. His expression changed to mild shock as he realised he was facing two people more than expected, a slight frown as he recognised them and then a tight grin as he addressed them. "Quite the welcoming committee," he said.

"No doubt this chat will be in the media within a minute of its conclusion?"

"And good morning to you too, Andy," said the current prime minister, deciding to ignore the question, as thousands of politicians had done before him. "How's retirement? Up to anything interesting?"

"Damien. Emily. Henry. How good to see you all looking so well. It's been quite a while. If I'd known you were all going to be involved, I'd not have bothered to call. You could have just made up our discussion. Like you did last time."

"Point taken, Andy." Crockett flashed a murderous glance at McInnes, who was studying a blank sheet in his notebook. "My sincere apologies for that error of judgement. But we want to move on from that… water under the bridge and so on…"

"Although we would love you back in the fold, Andrew," Emily Helms was eager to move the conversation onto firmer, more positive ground.

"Your *Path Finder* thing is galvanising the public and is ticking quite a few boxes within our pre-election campaign committee. We just want you back and our party to be the home of *Path Finder*."

Not all of her words landed initially.

Blackwell was about to decide her description of *Path Finder* as a 'thing' insulted him, then realised it was as good a description as any, given he didn't know what it was either. Eventually, all her words landed.

He looked surprised for a moment, then leaned back in his seat and put both hands behind his head, exposing sweat stains under his arms.

He kept his face straight when he saw the prime minister gulp and the chancellor suppress an involuntary heave, then spared them further discomfort by leaning forward and resting his elbows on the desk.

"*Path Finder*'s home will be everywhere, Emily. It isn't a political movement with a set of policies. It is a set of destinations designed to improve the planet and everything on it. How individuals, governments and nations move towards those destinations is up to them. We have teams of world experts in different fields ready to consider and evaluate proposals, provide guidance and to recommend which ideas we promote, but no group can claim the adoption of *Path Finder* as their own. *Every* political party should read the room and recognise it has no future unless it moves in the direction the people want to be led. We're all in this together."

Unusually for a meeting of four politicians, no-one spoke for a minute. Three of them absorbed the ramifications of Blackwell's statement, and Blackwell tried to remember what he'd made up on the spur of the moment, as it sounded as if it could be quite useful.

"And what are these destinations?" asked Henry McInnes.

Blackwell smiled what he hoped looked like a confident, knowing smile.

"Monitor the website," he said. "Although I'm pretty sure the media will let you know as soon as anything goes up."

"Will you come to the party conference this year, Andy? It's at Brighton again. My idea." Henry McInnes looked hopeful, like a poker player revealing his last hand with the swagger of someone pretending they didn't just bet the rent on a pair of threes.

Brighton, where Blackwell's political career took off after he upset almost every delegate in half an hour. Where he'd met Mindy for the first time. What a global media fest that would be if he spoke at Brighton.

"Great idea, H. No."

"Many people - including royalty - have urged me to recommend you for the New Year's honours list, Andy."

Crockett was desperate to get his man onside. "A peerage and the House of Lords would be a great platform for you. It won't take up much of your time either. Money for old rope. And the food and drink are cheap."

"Me? In the Lords? But I'm *an embarrassment. A grubby footnote in the unsavoury pages of our nation's history.*" Andy waited while Crockett remembered the insults he had thrown at Blackwell just after his return. Once he saw the event dawn on the PM's face, he graciously let the issue slide. Point made. "I would probably fit right in."

He gave the idea serious consideration for three seconds. "I appreciate the thought, Damien, but leave me off the list. I don't want to upset anyone by refusing."

"Come back and be prime minister, Andy. The country needs you!" Even as she almost shouted the words, Emily's brain was telling her to stop, because the country's prime minister was watching her with his mouth wide open. The chancellor turned to look at him. "Oh, for heaven's sake, Damien," she said, as her brain slammed itself against the inside of her skull in a vain attempt to shut her up, "Do you realise how far up the creek you are without a paddle? Dear God, man, you don't even have a boat."

Crockett looked crestfallen.

"Look." Andy felt embarrassed for the three of them. "If you agree with our destinations, work out paths you can sell to the party and the people. If we like them, we'll endorse them. Good to see you all. Speak soon."

He closed the call, keen to commit what he could remember to paper or keyboard. Other parties in the UK and from around the world had requested meetings of one form or another. He needed to give them all the same story. Andy smiled as he wrote. The call had been a bit of an ambush, but thinking on his feet had focused his mind. *Path Finder* was on the move.

The Cabinet Office room was deathly still. The three occupants could hear footsteps, conversation and occasional laughter on the other side of the door, but that was all a world away.

Crockett was still trying to process the call and its ramifications.

McInnes was worrying about the size of the Brighton venue and hoping that the booking was provisional.

And Emily Helms prayed the others would forget her outburst, at least until she included it in her memoir once she was out of office.

The Denver International Experience

Denver International Airport had a well-deserved reputation for creating chaos and confusion in the head of any unsuspecting and weary first-time visitor.

Sadly, neither Simmo nor Pippa had been there before, and the ten-hour flight had done nothing to sharpen their senses.

The man in the suit on the other side of the cabin aisle had had the best idea. As soon as he sat down, he had asked for a plastic glass and three small bottles of the airline's red wine, and the cabin staff had smiled knowingly and obliged.

By the time the plane pushed back from the gate, all three bottles were empty and the rubbish had gone. Twenty minutes later, he was fast asleep, his body leaning forward with a blanket over his back and his head resting on his flight bag, shoes and a pillow, all piled carefully onto his tray table.

"No need to look concerned," smiled the air hostess. "He's fine. He'll wake up fresh as a daisy just as we hit Colorado. Does this all the time - usually twice a week, each way."

"Twice a week?" asked Pippa. "What's his job?"

"In-flight security," the hostess maintained the smile she had hoisted thirty minutes earlier. "Dave's one of the best."

She handed them their refreshments and moved on, leaving Pippa to wonder exactly how good Dave would be in an emergency.

Simmo didn't care. He was too busy wishing the airline put more thought into the terminology used by its cabin crew. He, for one, had absolutely no desire to hit Colorado.

Now, safely on the ground in Denver, and just about awake after 20 hours of travel and waiting around, they had other issues to concern them. Where, for example, was their baggage and where, for another example, were the exits from the terminal building?

"This feels surreal, and the art and the cowboy announcer are not helping," observed Pippa. She wondered if the giant murals depicting bewildering creatures from another world were by one artist, or were simply additions by passengers who had given up on getting out and needed something to do to pass the time.

"I have a feeling we'll end up staying here the week, then flying back home and not saying anything to anybody," worried Pope.

Fortunately, it was a spritely, wide-awake Dave who came to their rescue.

"You're not in the terminal building," he explained, as if talking to an old couple struggling to cope with this newfangled flying thing. "It looks like a terminal building, but it's Concourse A. There are a B and a C as well. These are the gate areas, where you get off and on your plane. You could walk to the Jeppesen Terminal, but you'd be better off getting the train."

"The train? How far is it? And we need to get our bags first."

Dave shook his head and smiled kindly. "Your bags are already there, waiting for you. Here, I'm heading for the train. Come with me."

Five minutes after saying goodbye to Dave and retrieving their bags from the pleasant, always-happy-to-help representatives of the US Customs and Border Protection

Force, the Popes caught their breath with the help of a coffee at one of the many eateries in the building, then headed out to the taxi rank.

"At least we know we're in the right place for storm chasing," observed Pippa, pointing to the *Tornado Shelter* sign on the wall. Simmo nodded absently, having noticed the time displayed on an enormous clock.

"How come it's only two in the afternoon?" he asked nobody in particular.

A Warm Welcome

The Welcome Home Hotel, Denver, had a cute name but looked very similar to every other hotel on the road five miles from the airport. Five stories high with a welcoming entrance, an impressive reception area and surrounded by a substantial car park, the Welcome Home offered all the amenities expected by the modern-day traveller apart from one. Excellent customer service.

"You're not on the system and we're full," explained the receptionist, looking at his watch and fretting he'd be late for his rodeo clown class as Carlos was late for his shift, yet again. "There's a ballroom dancing convention in the main conference hall."

"Sounds wonderful," smiled Pippa, before her husband could say anything, "But we have a reservation and the paperwork to prove it."

The receptionist, Michael, grabbed the offered documentation and examined it carefully for two seconds before tossing it back.

"There is nobody called Pope booked in for tonight," he sighed, failing miserably to hide the exasperation he felt at his present circumstances and Carlos. "There are Popes booked in for tomorrow night as part of the storm chasing group, but not tonight."

"But that's us," interrupted Simmo. "We're with that group. We have the booking for it."

"That's such good news!" declared Michael. "Then I'll see you tomorrow."

"Please." Pippa got in quickly before Simmo exploded. "There's a reference number. There's a room booked under it for us, for tonight. Could you search for that rather than our name?"

Michael held his hand out for the sheet, feeling a great sense of unease under the intensity of Pope's glare. He tapped the booking reference into the system and stared at the screen.

"I see the problem," he announced. "You've given me the wrong name."

"Excuse me?"

"The name. You gave me Pope, but the booking reference brings up the name Hope."

"So our name has been input incorrectly into your system."

"Or you gave me the wrong name."

"We gave you the right name."

Michael swallowed hard. "Well, let's agree to disagree, and I'll get you a key."

Half an hour later, after quick showers and a change of clothes, the Popes sat in comfortable chairs in the hotel bar.

The drinks menu featured local craft beers, overpriced airport-style cocktails, and a house speciality called The Turbulence - a whiskey-based concoction that started smooth but ended with a kick that made you question your life decisions.

For the adventurous, there was also the half-price Standby Surprise.

This included a random mystery ingredient which, like a standby air ticket, meant you might not know where you were when you woke up.

In the afternoon, the place was fairly quiet. A handful of regulars sat at the bar, including three hotel cleaning staff who had just finished their shift and were chugging espresso martinis before moving onto their next job at a hotel down the road.

A businessman in a crumpled suit mumbled today's orders into his Bluetooth headset between mouthfuls of complimentary peanuts, and a confused-looking guy named Larry told anybody who would listen that he'd been stuck here for five days and didn't know what to do about it.

Simon and Pippa passed the time people-watching and fighting the tiredness through the traditional methods of drinking and eating. At least, they would have been eating if there'd been anything to eat.

"I'm so sorry, folks." The waitress returned empty-handed for the third time. "We don't have the Philly cheese flatbread or the shrimp scampi flatbread either."

Simon laughed. "So, you don't have that, or the oven-dried tomato flatbread, or the cheesy spinach pesto flatbread?"

"I'm afraid not." The waitress, Naomi, shifted uncomfortably. "We're out of flatbreads."

"Of course, of course." The surreal day obviously hadn't finished with them yet. "What do you have?"

"Burgers or pizza."

"Burger, fries and salad will be fine," Pippa said, before Simon could even form the word "Pizza?"

The couple sitting at the bar had been watching with interest.

The woman laughed out loud at the end of the conversation and then, realising her laugh had drawn the attention of the Popes and the waitress, pushed playfully at her partner, as if he'd said something funny.

Unfortunately, the man hadn't realised that the laugh or the subsequent shove were coming.

He staggered awkwardly off his stool, his legs preventing him from falling to the floor, and caught most of his beer, but only thanks to his sweater getting in the way.

"Goddamn it, Amy!"

The bartender rolled his eyes and then flung a clean beer towel at the guy to help with the mopping up, while the flustered lady tried to make amends by getting in the way. Naomi finished writing the new order and headed for the kitchen, praying burgers were still on the menu.

Pippa caught sight of the tornado on the front of the woman's t-shirt and called across to her.

"Are you here for the storm-chasing trip?"

"We are!" Amy Johnson stopped making amends and walked over, hand outstretched. "I'm Amy. That's Rob. He's a storm chaser. I'm just here for the fun!"

She sat down and plonked her glass onto the table. Once he'd handed back the beer towel, her 'good friend' Rob joined them.

Amy's experience of storm chasing was slightly more than the Popes'. Having watched a tornado movie or two and a couple of weather documentaries, the slim, thirty-three-year-old blonde from Boston had had storm chasing on her secret bucket list since she was a child. When her friend Rob showed her images from his chases over the years, he fell into the bucket himself.

"And so here I am, second year running," she smiled, "Killing two birds with one stone."

"And Rob let you come again?" Simon asked.

Rob nodded. "Amy's a wide-eyed, jittery ignoramus," he began charitably. Amy nodded enthusiastically. "Once we're chasing, she thinks that every cloud could be a tornado. Every gust of wind is the end of the world."

"We were driving through big hail last year, and I asked if we were going to be sucked into the sky," admitted Amy.

"And I genuinely wondered if the tornado knew we were chasing it. In fact, I still do."

Rob shook his head. He had studied meteorology from the age of eight and liked nothing more than watching clouds swirl while calculating the likelihood of a tornado forming based on the dew point and wind shear. He showed them the weather apps on his phone and explained briefly what each of them did.

"I guarantee you'll know far more about Convective Available Potential Energy at the end of this trip than you do now," Amy assured them. "But don't worry, you'll have forgotten it all by the time you reach home."

"CAPE is basically the amount of fuel available to a developing thunderstorm, based on the instability in the atmosphere and an estimate of the updraft strength within the storm," explained Rob, while Amy decided on a fake yawn. He smiled.

"As well as being beautiful, Amy's super enthusiastic and funny. She'll photograph every cloud she sees, just in case, and that can drive you mad. But her energy's infectious, and you need that when you're standing in a field or on a dirt road, waiting for Mother Nature to unleash chaos and being regularly disappointed when she doesn't."

"And we'll see tons of other cool stuff," said Amy, eager not to disillusion her new friends too quickly about the downsides of storm chasing; the weather could do that on its own. "There are the dust storms, the lightning shows…" She stopped, catching the glance exchanged between the Popes.

"We know quite a lot about lightning," Simon explained. "We were hit a few years ago. Pippa's heart stopped twice…"

"Girl!" exclaimed Amy, rushing to her new best friend and hugging her tightly. "It killed you twice, but you're out here wanting to stare that mother in the eye. That is so badass. I love you!"

New Friends

Despite being exhausted by early evening and getting to bed only after trying to enter the wrong room, the Popes were wide awake at five the following morning. While Pippa nursed her gentle hangover with a book and a coffee from the machine in the hallway, Simon tried out the hotel gym - a decision his wife found hilarious.

He eventually located the gym tucked away on the second floor, past a vending machine that offered a range of expired granola bars and dusty bottles of unchilled water. The entrance featured a motivational sign that read *Sweat Now, Board Later* - a nod to the air travellers who formed most of the hotel's residents.

Bathed in the unforgiving neon light that makes every ounce of unnecessary flesh very obvious, the gym looked and smelt as if it could do with a good clean. It boasted three treadmills: one that worked fine, one that made a disturbing grinding noise, and one that appeared to have been out of order for the last decade.

One of the three stationary bikes seemed to have been used for delivering bread in the 1940s.

The dumbbell rack had a good selection, assuming that meant a 5-pound weight or a 50-pound one, because the middle range didn't exist.

A single sad yoga mat draped over the stretching area, looking like it had seen one too many downward dogs. Next to it, a whiteboard offered a 'class schedule' that comprised a single entry reading *Zumba - Cancelled*.

The air conditioning was intermittent, meaning some areas of the gym felt like the inside of a blast freezer while others were noticeably humid in ways best not investigated. From a temperature perspective, jumping onto any piece of equipment was akin to playing Russian roulette.

Still, the showers looked fairly clean, and there were at least two towels that weren't soaking wet; just damp.

Pope jumped on a bike, sweating out the alcohol from the night before and stretching legs that had been confined to an airplane seat space for too much of the previous day.

Much to his surprise, yesterday afternoon had flown by, thanks to an enjoyable few hours with Rob and Amy. Like themselves, the couple had met when serving in the armed forces.

Rob Davidson was a logistics specialist whose pre-army experience involved providing students with an impressive range of party supplies, most of which had vanished mysteriously from other university frat houses.

Fortunately, acquisition was a talent appreciated by the military, although delivery was where he'd made his reputation.

During a mission 'abroad', Rob was part of a supply convoy heading for a forward operating base when it ran into an insurgent ambush.

Displaying the cool-headedness needed to remove cases of spirits from a faculty bar one bottle at a time, Rob grabbed a map and coordinated an alternative route while under fire. Not only did the water, food, medical equipment and ammunition get through, Rob also produced an unexpected bonus supply of chocolate bars and candy.

"They called him the supply king after that," Amy announced with pride. "He wanted me to call him Your Majesty, but that idea didn't last very long."

"Two seconds," reported Rob.

Amy's army career had come as a surprise to the Popes, but both hid their amazement incredibly well. Appearances can indeed be deceiving. In fact, her army career had come as a surprise to everybody except Amy.

Despite excelling at high school, she turned down college, enlisted in the army and became an intelligence analyst, where her first role involved analysing satellite images and intercepted communications. However, what made her stand out from the crowd was her ability to read people as well as she read data. Unashamedly taking advantage of her looks and personality, she could get almost anybody to feel better about themselves and to open up a little more than they would normally. But it was her ability to detect a speaker's inadvertent verbal and non-verbal cues that made her special.

Promoted to the role of military intelligence officer after four years, she ended up seconded to a special forces team planning a series of raids. Reviewing the data being used to identify potential targets, she read the transcriptions of radio intercepts, then asked to hear the original sound recordings, alongside a translator.

"The transcriptions are correct," she'd reported, "But I don't focus on *what* is being said. I focus on the *how*, and there's something not quite right."

Eighteen hours later, having analysed a wider range of intercepted communications, she presented the raid team with an alternative list. One waste dump, a recruitment office and a training facility - all justified by a range of speech indicators, which suggested these locations were more important than they seemed.

"Check them out, then hit them hard," she said.

The raid team had done as they were told and were not disappointed.

Amy had left the army and now worked as a forensic linguist consultant for businesses and government organisations who wanted to know when people were being economical with the truth.

"I enjoy shopping," she revealed. "My job pays for a lot of shopping."

The conversation moved seamlessly from that statement onto plans for the next day, with the tour group meeting around six in the evening for a briefing and a getting-to-know-you dinner. Pippa's eyes had widened at the word 'shopping', so the girls were heading into downtown Denver on an expedition.

After fifteen minutes of cycling, Pope stepped off the bike and onto the working treadmill, intending to run, then opting to walk after remembering why he hated running. The machines had views over the parking lot and across a square mile or two of waste ground, with snow-capped mountains in the distance. *Not an unpleasant scene to keep you occupied*, he thought.

A movement on the far side of the wasteland caught his eye. He watched as two runners ran towards the hotel, pounding out the hard yards over dusty mounds and clumps of brush. Despite the difficulty of the terrain, they maintained a good pace and only paused for breath at the edge of the hotel premises. Both laughed and chatted as they made their way into the building, their sweat-stained t-shirts a testament to the effort they had spent in the rarefied air.

Pope's eyes wandered back over the wasteland, wondering how far the paramedics would have needed to venture before coming across his exhausted body. And how anyone as drunk as Rob and Amy had appeared a few hours ago could be awake at this time, never mind completing a serious run.

Storm Chasing 101

Storm chasing was Rob Davidson's favourite pastime, but talking about storm chasing wasn't far behind. The couples met after breakfast, and the women departed soon after for the delights of Denver, promising to be back well in time for the group gathering and not to spend too much money.

The men settled in the lobby area, just off reception, so Rob could look out for fellow chasers who were checking out after the previous week's tour, or checking in for the next one.

"I love this day, and that's why I got here early," he confided. "It's like a school reunion, but with more alcohol and the chance to meet new people."

The briefing he had prepared for Simon wasn't what Pope was expecting. Rob would not talk about the science; that would happen later in the day at the meeting. Rob wanted to explain what the week was going to be like; what to expect; how to cope; who to avoid and how to make the most of your time in Tornado Alley. Pope couldn't decide if he was disappointed or intrigued.

If they were really lucky, said Rob, they could see several tornadoes this week. If they weren't that fortunate, they could still land on some highly impressive storms that might choose to hurl baseball-sized hailstones or spear bolts of lightning at them.

Failing that, they could witness cloud-to-cloud lightning to rival the light show of any rock concert and last just as long. Or they could run for cover as a downdraft kicked up a curtain of red Texan dirt that would make the getaway drive hellish in more ways than one.

"And if you're really unlucky, the biggest thrill of your trip could be a hotel that makes breakfast waffles in the shape of Texas."

Rob spotted the dismay flit across Pope's face.

"Look," he continued. "Storm chasing involves failure, tiredness, frustration and luck, but every time I've been here, I've had adrenaline-pumping, heart-stopping moments that result in memories for life. They put a grin on your face and keep you coming back. Plus, there's a lot more to this week than sitting in a van for hours, travelling hundreds of miles a day hoping to track down a monster."

"Is there?"

Rob hesitated a moment.

"There are bits and pieces," he replied, "If the weather's a bust, expect local tourist attractions to be on the agenda. Use the opportunity to relax before things get hectic again. One thing's for sure. Every day involves a lot of travel in a confined space with a bunch of people who have just one thing in common - storm chasing. You do not know at the start of the journey whether you'll be on speaking terms with them by the end. That interaction has a major impact on the success of your trip. And here's how you get that right."

The role of everyone in each vehicle, he explained, is to help reduce the boredom and the stress levels; to make the experience of hours and hours in a van each day as pleasurable as possible.

"That doesn't mean incessant chat, deciding everyone should listen to your music or your life story, mandatory singalongs, interminable games or snoring," he said.

"And it certainly doesn't mean lively discussions about politics, or religion, or the environment. Everyone wants a happy camp, and nobody is going to change the mind of anybody who can't escape, has an aching butt, is hungry or desperately needs a restroom. The chemistry between a van's occupants is extremely important."

The restroom issue fascinated Pope.

"Good bladder control is key," Rob offered. "Drink little and often. Toilet breaks will not be as regular as you had hoped! Everyone takes turns behind a mound of sand or gravel by the side of a road. Just leave your dignity on the van and pick it up again when you get back in."

The lecture halted as Pope realised he needed to work on his own bladder control. On his return from the restrooms, he saw Rob walking over to the reception desk and making some comment to a couple focused on checking out. The man, whose size made Pope wonder if he'd had a van to himself, spun round to attention and saluted smartly, before cracking a smile and extending his hand. Rob shook it, then hugged the woman, who gently pushed him away so she could spin around, showing off her weight loss since they had all last been together.

Unwilling to break up the reunion, Pope sidled into the bar, waited for the bartender to realise he had a customer, then took a couple of beers back to the lounge. Rob was sitting down once more, and Pope could see the couple through the enormous glass doors, lifting their bags into the back of a cab.

"Friends of yours?" he asked, nodding in their direction.

"Pete and Jean," Rob replied. "Just off to the airport. They've had a decent week, but not a great one storm-wise."

Both men sipped their drinks. Rob was quiet, his mind working through whatever he had just been told. Eventually, he spoke.

"They were at a steakhouse three nights ago. Pete took up the 72-ounce challenge. Finish the steak and trimmings in less than one hour and get it for free. Otherwise, you pay 72 bucks for the meal. He finished in 38 minutes 20 seconds."

"Impressive." Pope felt indigestion rising in his gut just at the thought.

Rob shook his head.

"That's his worst time ever. Every year, the manager offers him a bonus for finishing under 30. Pete makes it look so easy that everyone thinks they can do it, especially after a few beers. The restaurant makes a lot of money. Pete usually gets a free pudding, but not this year. Jean had to buy him two just to cheer him up. Then someone fell onto a glass cabinet and the rattler got out." Rob smiled. "Those times make the week memorable."

The Storm Killers

Rob put Storm Chasing 101 on hold for a while as more of the storm chasers on their way home recognised him and wanted to catch up as they checked out of the hotel. Pope marvelled at the variety of characters from across the world who had been willing to pay thousands of dollars for the chance to risk death with a bunch of strangers. Rob introduced him as a friend from England; a lightning strike survivor who still wanted to chase storms. The response was overwhelming. Everybody wanted to shake his hand. Some wanted their photograph taken with him. Their faces revealed respect, delight, admiration, and more than a little envy.

"You'll get the same response from people on our tour," promised Rob. "Being hit by lightning is a badge of honour."

An elderly couple appeared and checked out, each wearing an old t-shirt bearing an image of a tornado breaking in half and the words *Storm Killers* underneath.

"Three couples had them made towards the end of a miserable week on a different tour a few years ago," revealed Rob. "Gallows humour. Everything they chased vanished, so they concluded they could kill storms before they wreaked havoc. Locals bought them drinks in appreciation. Everyone thought it was funny. There are bars in New Mexico and Texas where they're still remembered."

"And they still come back?"

"Every year," Rob nodded. "Fred and Jackie are the only two left from that group of six, but they still turn up as regular as clockwork. Storm chasers are a community. It gets in the blood."

At that moment, a shuttle bus drew up at the entrance and off-loaded half a dozen people, who spent a long time ensuring they had all their gear before checking in. One man stopped and surveyed the reception area, nodded at Rob - who responded in kind - then returned to the reception desk. A couple of seconds later, the rest of his party turned around, stared at the two men, then turned back again.

"Friends of yours?"

"More like acquaintances. They have a name. We call them photographers."

Pope laughed. "Aren't we all?" he asked.

Rob considered the notion, then explained that photographers spend the entire trip focused - pun intended - on capturing the perfect shot.

"They're a law unto themselves on the chase," he said. "And they'll want all the space in the van to prepare their kit or to edit shots they've just taken."

Pope watched two of the group glance over yet again, then resume their discussion.

"And how do we deal with that?"

Rob grimaced. "The last time I was with them? Badly. But things have changed."

Tristram, Rob explained, had devised a specialist photography trip and, to date, it had gone down very well with the target market.

The photographers had a dedicated van with an experienced storm chaser driver/photographer as their guide. They shadowed the main group, but parked up sometimes as far as a mile or two away to get their shots.

In the evenings, they had lectures while the rest drank the night away. They felt special, and they paid more for the privilege.

Pope listened politely, then asked a one-word question. "Tristram?"

Rob almost coughed up his beer.

"I misspoke. I meant Twister," he clarified. "Joseph Tristram Mitchell owns Storm Stalkers. Never call him Tristram. If you do, he'll leave you stranded in the middle of New Mexico in the heat of the midday sun. He hates that name with a passion. Stick with Twister and you'll be fine."

The Girls Return

Simon Pope was approaching the outskirts of an Afghan village, squeezed into the hot and sweaty bowels of an armoured troop carrier. He watched the young soldiers around him laugh at the banter, but they couldn't see or hear him, so he couldn't warn them of what was about to happen.

A loud bang woke him suddenly. Pippa stumbled through the guest room door, dropped the three shopping bags and collapsed onto the bed.

"I am knackered," she announced in a voice that suggested she was also slightly drunk. "What a busy day! So much shopping! So much to see! You should have…" She stopped when she saw the sweat on his flushed and confused face, and grabbed his hand.

"You're okay, sweetheart. We're in a hotel in Denver. Remember? Going storm chasing?"

She smiled, still holding his hand. "You must have fallen asleep. Did I disturb you? Sorry about that. You're safe though. We're both safe. I think you were having a bad dream."

She waited until his eyes focused again, and he nodded.

"Let me get you a coffee," she smiled. "God knows I could do with one."

He found his voice. "Me too."

"Was it the usual?"

Pope nodded and headed unsteadily to the bathroom to wash his face and collect his thoughts.

Half an hour later, both were sitting at the table near the suite's window, overlooking the front parking lot. Pippa revealed her purchases, which essentially comprised a couple of cheap t-shirts each, plus food and drink supplies for the first couple of days and some medication. Then she listened carefully while her husband tried to forget the nightmare and remember everything Rob had told him.

"All we do later is network to prepare for the dance tomorrow morning," he concluded.

Before Pippa's face could contort into a frown, he continued. "The dance makes or breaks our week. Vans turn up tomorrow and everybody piles in. The van groups stay the same throughout the tour. We have to stay close to the people we think we'll bond with and get in their van."

"No pressure then."

"And even that effort comes with risk. Van atmospheres can be warm and friendly, or quieter and colder."

"And probably both, given it's a seven-day trip. It all sounds very stressful."

"I thought so too," said Simon. "That's why I said we'll jump in the van Rob and Amy pick."

"Interesting," Pippa smiled and took another sip of her coffee. "I accepted Amy's invitation to do the same thing."

"Makes sense. They're a pleasant couple."

"I don't think they are." Pippa said. "A couple, I mean. Maybe they're having an affair. They're certainly likeable enough, and they get on well together. It's just that when we were chatting today and I was telling her bits and bobs about you, she had nothing to tell me about Rob. She was very vague about the two of them and changed the subject as soon as she could."

"What bits and bobs exactly?"

Pippa smiled to herself. *Hook, line and sinker, every time.*

"Oh, you know, this and that. Right, I'm off for a shower."

She walked over to him and kissed his furrowed brow before heading to the bathroom.

"Try not to fall asleep again."

Sandy Irvine

After an interesting evening and a late night, meeting and making new friends, Simon was up in the early hours. This was mostly due to jet lag and partly because the dream of the previous afternoon made him reluctant to go back to sleep once he was awake.

Twister Mitchell had been delighted to meet them both, asked after his old friend the RSM, but declined the package because he tended to lose stuff when he was so busy. He'd take it off Simon at the end of the tour. He then gave a warm, friendly and amusing welcome speech before explaining that tomorrow's departure would be at ten, as an interesting weather front was on its way to see them. They could end up being the chased rather than the chasers.

After the late night, a late breakfast was the order of the day, because there was no guarantee when they would eat once on the road, so the group of seventeen guests plus drivers and guides had agreed to meet in the restaurant, packed and ready to go, at nine.

The time was just after six, and Pope had quietly filmed Pippa snoring off the effects of the previous day - you never knew when such footage might come in useful - before heading to the gym on the fourth floor. By the looks of it, nobody had been in there since his last visit.

Today's visit had a different purpose, but all the equipment silently pressured him into making some kind of effort, and he headed for the treadmill. Being military or ex-military types, Rob and Amy were probably creatures of habit, and Pope wanted another look at them together, when they didn't suspect they were being observed. Pippa's comments about the relationship between their new best buddies had piqued his curiosity.

Sure enough, after fifteen minutes working up a sweat on a machine that had probably last been used to grind wheat using manual labour, he saw two familiar figures lope into view over the rough waste ground. As before, they came to a halt at the edge of the car park and walked between the rows of vehicles into the rear entrance of the hotel. Body language and facial expressions suggested they were a little more serious today, he thought. There was none of the affection displayed last night. Maybe it was their game face. Tornado hunting was a serious business, and Rob and Amy's careers had them pinned as serious people.

"Mind if I join you?"

Pope almost fell off the machine. He hadn't heard a sound until the soft Scots accent almost caused a major bowel incident. He stopped the treadmill and turned to face an old, thin man standing next to the free weights in a loose grey t-shirt and track pants that looked as if they were about to fall down. Alexander 'Sandy' Irvine, the oldest member of the group and, like the Popes, a first-time storm chaser.

"Morning, Simmo," he said, his voice gravelly, as if he'd just woken up. "Thought I'd get here early and beat the rush."

The former sheep drover, Royal Marine and pub landlord didn't look like a gym bunny. In fact, he didn't look like he should be up at all. He looked like death warmed up. Simmo waved his arms around the room.

"I think we *are* the rush, mate," he said, a little breathlessly. "Take your pick."

The old man gave a half-grin and walked over to an exercise bike, settling on with a creak of old joints and a faint grunt, then pedalling at a slow but rhythmic pace.

"Couldn't sleep," he said. "The room's too quiet. Morag used to snore like a chainsaw. Now I can hear my own thoughts." He stopped pedalling for a moment. "I wish I didn't."

Simmo had those thoughts himself, and he knew what it was like to love someone and to lose them. He couldn't decide what to say, so said nothing. Instead, he just nodded at his new friend, hit the treadmill button once more and walked a little faster.

Standby For Take Off

By midmorning, the sun had pushed the haze off the Denver skyline, casting sharp shadows across the hotel's front car park. At ten o'clock sharp, three white passenger vans rumbled in from the bigger car park at the rear, each bearing magnetic decals that read Storm Stalkers in a cracked, weathered font. Their pockmarked bodywork suggested they'd seen more than their fair share of hail.

Simon stood at the curb alongside Pippa, Rob and Amy, his rucksack balanced on the small suitcase at his feet. His hiking boots felt too new, and the branded cap that Twister had handed out the night before was too stiff, as if it didn't belong on his head and wanted him to know it.

The other guests milled around him - mostly Americans, a mix of science hobbyists, adrenaline junkies, and what looked like a coastguard in neon rain gear who had missed his own group and had joined this one instead. The photographers stood at a distance, making sure their kit was well away from the nearby excitement and smugly certain that their special van would stop exactly where they were. There would be no dancing for them.

And then Sandy appeared, emerging from the lobby with a canvas rucksack slung over one shoulder and a windbreaker zipped halfway.

He moved with the same careful gait, but there was a subtle shift - a straightness to his back and an alertness in his eyes. Simon waved him over, having agreed with the group that the old man should join their party. Sandy stopped beside him, squinting up at the sky. "I do not know what I'm looking for, but I doubt it's what I can see up there."

"Oh, honey." Amy walked over and linked the Scotsman's arm. "You are going to learn so much these next few days. I got really excited at a gas station one day last year when I saw some strange formations in the sky. Turned out they were soap bubbles some kid was blowing."

"Dammit, Amy," Rob said in mock annoyance. "That's a half-hour of entertainment gone."

The group laughed, knowing there would be plenty more where that came from, then Sandy looked to the vans, appraising them with the same cautious respect Simon imagined he once gave to a Chinook on an airfield.

"Is it silly?" Sandy asked quietly, "To be nervous about chasing weather?"

Amy shrugged and squeezed his arm. "Only if it's silly to want to feel something real."

That got a low chuckle from Sandy. "Good. Because I'm seventy-five, Scottish and I've no time left to be sensible."

The first van in the convoy stopped close to them, and a tall, wiry man in mirrored sunglasses, combat shorts and a hoodie that read *I BRAKE FOR FUNNELS* across its back stepped out and walked around the front of the vehicle. A shout went up from the crowd. "DEEEEEE-KE!"

"Hell yeah! Deke's back!" he grinned, finishing the breakfast burrito. "Let's get loaded up, folks. Storms are already getting ready to rumble later today near Amarillo. Twister will update you on the road. Remember. Usual rules. No biting, kicking or pulling hair. And no sex, politics or religion on board, unless the sex involves me!"

The group fired a few catcalls at the laughing driver, then shuffled towards the vans. *Not so much a dance; more a pilgrimage or a zombie apocalypse,* thought Simmo.

As agreed, Amy and Pippa headed towards the guest seats in the front van with Sandy, while Simon and Rob stowed their cases in the back.

Rob turned and grinned at Simon. "This is it, my friend. No going back now!"

And with that, they climbed aboard. Twister Mitchell completed a final count and jumped into the front seat next to the driver. He flipped open the laptop, double-checked his settings and picked up the CB radio, broadcasting to the rest of the fleet.

"What a fine day, people! What a great day for heading south through Colorado, into New Mexico and then east into Texas to pick up some baby storms that could turn into monsters. Let's go see the sky come alive!"

The van's speaker blasted the cheers and whoops from the other vans as Deke gunned the engine into life, lurched away from the sidewalk and onto the main road. Twister put down the CB mic and turned to the group behind him.

"Get comfortable, folks," he smiled. "Now's the time to chill, because things are going to get hot over the next few days."

Safe At Last

After a fitful night's sleep in Danny's room, Omar stared at the bedroom ceiling, listening carefully to the noises outside. The sounds of the town had replaced the sounds of the desert.

The house and vehicle workshop were on the edge of town, on a tight bend of a main road that led north. Every vehicle had to slow to take the bend, and Omar found he was holding his breath until he heard each engine pick up speed again and not turn into Matty's forecourt. At the moment, every vehicle could be an ICE patrol or local vigilantes. He had been careful getting into the house from the truck, but you could never be sure.

Exhausted after the efforts of the last three days, he felt a range of emotions. Relief - maybe exhilaration - at making it this far and feeling relatively safe. Excitement about what may happen next. Fear for himself and his hosts. Nervousness at reconnecting with a family that may have forgotten him over the last year. Optimism that he was nearing the end of one journey and approaching the start of another.

His appearance the evening before alongside her husband had surprised Jayne Hernandez, but she was quick to organise his room, towels and a fresh set of clothes.

Once Omar had showered and changed, he had come downstairs for welcome food and drink. Conversation had been stilted, and focused mostly on details of his journey over the Mexican border. Matty had called Daniel to give him the news and to confirm the vehicle parts being ordered. His son had promised to call back the following day once he had completed the extraction timings.

"We'll need you to stay out of sight," Matty explained at the end of the meal. "Many folks in this town have sympathy with people who want to make a better life for themselves in this country. Many others feel they're fighting on the front line, defending our nation from potential terrorists and gangsters who can't enter the USA through official channels. The problem is, it's difficult to know who's who."

Omar had nodded. After the last few days, relaxing in a comfortable and safe environment for a few more sounded very appealing.

Now, still lying on his bed and looking at the ceiling, he gave silent thanks once more for the blessings he'd received by helping at the crash site. Truly a miracle. If he could just have a couple more over the next couple of weeks, they wouldn't go amiss either.

Driving Through Paprika

By early afternoon, the scenery had shifted from Colorado's suburban sprawl to the Texas flatness where you soon hankered for a hill of any size and could see tumbleweed coming at you from 30 miles away.

Twister picked up the CB handset, his eyes not shifting from his laptop screen. "Attention all. We're tracking a conveyor belt of storms that could develop into a juicy supercell somewhere northeast of Amarillo. That means towering cumulonimbus clouds, possible rotation, and maybe, maybe… no, not gonna say it… let's not jinx it!"

Amy leaned forward and asked, "So, when do the margaritas come out?"

Deke cackled. "Amy, if we see a tornado, you can drink the wind."

The cackle faded as he saw his boss's shocked face.

"You jinxed it," Twister stated, then returned to the laptop.

By late afternoon, as dusk was preparing its appearance, they had reached a dusty rise near Panhandle, just in time to watch a supercell grow like an angry deity, woken from a peaceful slumber in the sky.

The clouds bulged and churned in slow motion. Sunlight pierced through in golden shafts, creating an eerie scene that lost some of its impact in Van One thanks to Sandy's snoring.

Warm winds kicked up from the south, wrapping around the convoy like invisible snakes. Twister muttered into the radio, "Even in the van, you can feel the inflow… this thing's got classic supercell structure… I think the meso's starting to spin…"

Deke couldn't resist adding his own moment of profound truth.

"It's sucking up air like a vacuum cleaner in heat," he beamed, one eye on the road, the other on the growing storm and blissfully unaware of the impact his poetic turn of phrase was having in the rest of the convoy.

Keeping south of the storm, three of the vans raced ahead of it and parked in a roadside lay-by. The chasers piled out and crossed the road, lining up on the far side with cameras at the ready. The photography van carried on another mile where the view was supposedly more photogenic, but actually kept them out of the way of the rest of the group.

Sandy didn't bother to take his camera. He simply stood by the Popes with his hands in his jacket pockets and stared at the seething mass in front of him with a look of gobsmacked wonder on his face. "Amazing," he whispered, the inflow behind almost blowing him across the prairie in front. "Majestic." Indeed, it was. To the west, the storm flexed its muscles - anvil cloud, rolling thunder, the sort of sky that seemed less a meteorological event and more of a divine tantrum.

Twister marched up and down the roadside and announced in the solemn tones of a man unveiling nuclear codes that there could be lightning and to be prepared. Prepared for what, he didn't say, although probably not cremation by static electricity.

Simon and Pippa were chatting politely with another couple about weather apps when the sky lit up like a malfunctioning disco ball.

Dozens of cloud-to-cloud flashes stitched patterns across the heavens, each one accompanied by the *oohs* and *ahhs* usually reserved for firework shows. "Two minutes, then we go!" Twister shouted, pointing at his watch like it conferred immortality.

Almost immediately, Pippa's hair levitated in a halo of impending doom, and Simon looked as though he'd licked an electric socket. Before they could compare notes with others sharing the hair-raising experience, Twister yelled, "Scratch that! Back to the vans!"

The crowd bolted; a stampede of hobbyists galloping toward safety, while other storm chasers in their SUVs nearly flattened them in the race to avoid, but document, Armageddon.

Simon made it across, chest heaving, and turned just in time to see Sandy stumbling away from the road and into the field, as if searching for a bus stop. Pippa was chasing behind him, screaming at him as she tried to keep her balance over the rough ground.

Simon pushed himself off the van and risked death as he ran back across the road, bellowing their names in tones that suggested both marital concern and the imminent need for a new larynx.

Pippa finally caught up with the old man and grabbed his arm, but Sandy - eyes wet and jaw trembling - was going nowhere. Not on Earth, at any rate. Apparently, the express lane to heaven was a lightning strike in Texas; an option the travel agencies rarely advertise.

"You go!" he shouted above the storm. "This is my chance to be with Morag once again."

"This isn't noble, it's stupid!" Pippa snapped, invoking her own brush with death-by-lightning, which had left her in pain and shock for weeks, when she wasn't being resuscitated.

Simon grabbed them both, tugging with the grim determination of a man refusing to try out his holiday insurance. Behind them, the van's horn blared, and the storm cracked. Sandy's defiance sagged into embarrassment, his planned grand exit downgraded from Greek tragedy to farce, and almost dragging two fellow tourists into his obituary. The three of them stumbled back across the road as the thunder ironically applauded the drama.

Rob hauled them into the van like damp sheep, slamming the door behind them. The convoy took off, engines whining to stay ahead of the storm. Behind them, the sky raged on in magnificent indifference, too busy ripping itself apart to notice three fragile humans silently coming to terms with their own mortality.

Twenty minutes down the road, the tease that is Mother Nature left them all disappointed. The updraft weakened, a downdraft crashed into the ground, and a wall of cold air spread quickly in all directions, carrying with it an apocalyptic wave of red Texas dirt.

"You have one minute for pictures, then the vans leave sixty seconds later," shouted Twister. "If you start feeling cold, then you've missed your ride and you'll have to shelter as best you can."

The threat hit home, and just ninety seconds later, the vans were on their way with full payloads. Deke floored the accelerator, the van battling against the winds now battering into its flank. The other two vans scrambled to keep up as the dirt wave surged over the plains and across the road. A thick, red dust filled the air.

"It's like driving through paprika," Pippa half shrieked.

Deke settled the van down to a steadier speed, now he could barely see the road.

"It's like driving through hell, man," he observed, a strange, ethereal smile playing around his lips.

A tremendous bolt of lightning cracked overhead, as if confirming the opinion. The Popes and Sandy weren't sure what to think. Simon held Pippa's hand tightly and gave her what he hoped was a reassuring smile. Sandy smiled uncertainly, but his eyes sparkled.

Twister gave Deke a couple of directional instructions, and the convoy's diversion helped it outrun the red tidal wave and shelter from the wind by parking behind an abandoned grain silo, where they waited until the photography van caught up. The chasers milled about outside the vans and watched as the storm wandered off, throwing the occasional lightning bolt in a random direction as if warning off any pursuers. "Don't expect the camera guys to come out," Deke told the Popes. "They'll be cleaning off their gear and downloading their shots."

Simon realised how quiet - almost serene - everything had become.

"Those supercells sound like mega jet engines," Amy laughed. "That's down to the turbulence created by the warm air smashing into the cold air and the movement of hailstones within the storm."

Rob looked on with pride. "My girl remembered something," he stated, grateful to have anything to take their minds off the recent drama, before catching the disparaging look on her face and adding, "Just one of the many, many things she remembers."

Pippa smiled and filed away the exchange for future reference.

The Hap Win Motel

After a stop for dinner at Tornado Terry's Vehicle Lube Supplies & Steakhouse, where the smell and taste of half the business had found its way onto the plates of the other, the convoy finally rolled into Lubbock. The birthplace of rock 'n' roll legend Buddy Holly, the city let nobody forget it and - according to Deke - it was a place where everyone had attitude. Even the planetarium was called Moody.

The group had narrowly outrun a dirt tsunami, avoided electrification by Zeus himself, risked a fair chance of food poisoning and now faced one of every chaser's biggest gambles: lodging options. They pulled up to the Happy Winds Motel, a squat concrete slab painted beige in a way that deeply offended the concept of colour.

"We rarely stay here," Twister apologised in advance, surveying a building that would not have looked out of place at Kandahar. "Our usual hotel cancelled our booking this afternoon when they realised we had the photographers with us again. Let's just say those guys get very annoyed if you question why they need all that kit when smartphone cameras are so good nowadays."

A flickering neon sign blinked *Hap Win* over and over, like it really couldn't bother with the full name any more. Next to it stood the reception desk and a harshly lit office.

The clerk looked like she would prefer another couple of divorces, a direct tornado hit, and a third year living with two growing kids in the home of her disapproving, former mother-in-law, rather than one more night in her current role.

"Rooms are out back," she grunted, throwing a bunch of keycards onto the top of the desk without looking up from her mobile phone. Deke doled them out while Twister checked his own phone.

"There's a food plaza just across the road, folks, so I suggest breakfast at eight and we'll head out around nine."

Deke stopped and looked inquiringly at his boss. "There's nothing coming through here tomorrow?"

"There is, but I reckon we'll have a lot more on our plate for the rest of the week if we head towards the border. The tornado that hit down there a couple of days ago wasn't a one-off. We'll intercept storms with potential on our way south."

There was a murmur of excitement throughout the group, despite their tiredness after a long day.

A lot more on our plate. Deke nodded and continued to distribute the keycards, his heart beating significantly faster in his chest. Ever since Afghanistan, he had felt he was in the presence of meteorological genius when he was with Twister, and events since then had continued to justify that belief. His boss was a reasonably quiet, understated man, but there were some tells if he was genuinely excited. The plate phrase was one of them. *This wasn't a promise that the week was going to be special,* he thought. *It was a guarantee.*

Gesture Politics

The Oval Office smelled faintly of lemon polish, beef burgers and political cynicism. Sunlight blagged its way through the bulletproof south-facing windows and slumped across the Resolute Desk, which bore nothing but an intercom, a framed photo of the president with a dolphin, taken during a badly misconceived ocean summit, and a silver laptop that David D. Clampett was reluctant to use.

The president stared suspiciously at the screen, which currently displayed a heat map of nationwide Path Finder activity. It looked to his eyes like America had contracted measles or - worst case scenario - had been hit by multiple nuclear warheads.

"What in the holy hell is this?" he asked, one hand hovering over the keyboard like it might bite. "Is this TokTok?"

"No, sir," said Jared Pfist, twitchy and tired, as usual. The baldheaded, thirty-year-old deputy chief-of-staff searched for words his boss would understand. "It's from their public data dashboard. They're mapping community involvement. It's... impressive."

Clampett frowned. Aston Hail had declared the movement nothing but a global talking shop, and now - just two weeks later - this. The growth of activity certainly was impressive.

A thought suddenly occurred to him. "Are they communists?"

"They're volunteers, sir."

"Is there a difference?" The President leaned back in the historic chair - which creaked like it wanted to resign and spend the rest of its days in a museum or a Boston bookshop - and reached for a can of cola, now rebranded as 'performance hydration' in internal memos. His eyes flicked to Grace Hampton, the self-titled head of optics, who wore a blazer like it was armour and carried herself with the urgency of someone constantly five minutes ahead of the apocalypse.

"They want equality. And peace. And..." Pfist paused, "... sustainable governance."

"That's not even a thing," Hampton snapped, her speed-blinking revealing the stress she was feeling. "Governance is like cholesterol. You don't even know it's there until it's killing you."

"Sir," Pfist interjected gently. "They're building real momentum. Even suburban moms in Ohio are saying words like solidarity. I think it's time we... we made a gesture."

"What kind of gesture?"

"A compassionate one," he said, like it physically hurt him. "Something human. Real. The tornado in south Texas..."

"Oh, God. Don't say FEMA." Clampett felt himself getting sweaty. "Every time I say FEMA, somebody somewhere files a class action, claiming nothing works since we halved its budget."

"It's an opportunity." Hampton's blinking was almost back to normal. "You stand in front of a church in Texas - hopefully a damaged one. You hug a weeping family. Maybe... brace yourself... a bilingual family. We pivot to unity. Immigration. Climate resilience. You say things like, 'We're all Americans, whether we live in a mansion or a mobile home.' Then we fly back before anyone asks why the shelters are full of mould."

Clampett scratched the side of his face, staring malevolently at the laptop, as if it were personally responsible for the coming insurrection.

"You think I should hug a weeping bilingual?"

"If it tests well," Hampton replied. "Yes. Hopefully, someone who's lost their home."

Pfist cleared his throat. "Also, you could say something nice about trees."

Clampett looked at him as if he'd grown antlers. "Are we running for re-election already, or can we do some governing first?"

"We're running." Grace Hampton sounded surprised, so much so that her eyes forgot to blink and simply stared at the president. "We're always running."

The room fell silent. Outside the Oval Office, somewhere just beyond the double doors, a staffer sneezed, sounding like a gunshot. Hampton opened her notebook.

"I'll get comms started. Bomber jacket or windbreaker?"

"Which one makes me look slimmer?" the president asked.

The Waiting Game

The Storm Stalkers' vans sat in a row alongside a gas station on the outskirts of the catchily-named Somewhere, in Texas. The group's breakfast and the morning journey south had been unusually quiet for the early days of a week-long tour.

Staying at the Happy Winds motel had been neither a happy nor a windy experience. Air conditioning in the rooms was sporadic at best, with the sealed windows ensuring a hot, uncomfortable and unhappy night's sleep for everyone.

A man more at home in the cold, Sandy had opted for a cooling shower around three in the morning, turning the water on just as a fire alarm sounded throughout the complex, forcing the other guests outside and into the parking lot. It had taken seven minutes to switch off the alarm and allow guests back into their rooms to continue their overnight hell.

The next morning, across the road in the local restaurant, the Scot looked on confused as his fellow diners discussed the night's events.

"But you must have heard the alarms going off," insisted Amy. "That loud, mournful wail…"

Sandy burst out laughing. A real belly laugh - something he hadn't thought possible ever again after Morag; a laugh that caught the others by surprise, which amused him further.

Eventually he calmed down enough to explain.

"I thought that noise was my shower," he said. "It started as I turned the water on and stopped when I turned it off again. I was half expecting someone to bang on a wall, but figured you were all asleep."

"We were outside and wide awake," grumbled Pippa, while Simon grabbed a third coffee to prevent himself from falling asleep face first in his ham and eggs.

"And alive," Sandy nodded, "But not awake enough to check if I was okay. Just an observation…"

Suddenly, everyone's breakfast became incredibly interesting, as they looked down to avoid catching the old man's gaze. Everyone except Simon, who stared straight at him and was the only witness to the wink and a smile.

And so, the air-conditioned journey south had been unusually quiet. Up front in Van One, Deke had focused on his driving.

Twister had spent much of his time sending and receiving messages on his phone, his face a study of intense concentration. Occasionally, his eyes had flicked across to his laptop, but the satellite images gave him no cause for concern or self-doubt.

Behind them, the guests had made themselves as comfortable as possible and dozed fitfully. Alone on the last passenger seat, Sandy had made the most of the extra space available. Having slept well after his motel shower, he spent the morning resting with his cap pulled down over his eyes, ears alert to every sound.

Inside the gas station's café area, the guests sat in their van groups at different tables, fuelling up with coffee and burgers and stowing snacks and cold drinks into their bags for the hoped-for chase later that afternoon. Twister sat with the guides and drivers, staring at laptops and with brows furrowed.

"Is that a worrying sign?" Pope asked Rob, nodding across at their leader and his crew.

Rob washed down his burger with a gulp of coffee and turned his head to follow Simon's gaze.

"I'd say it's normal for this time of day," he said. "So much has to fall into place to develop a storm - more to create a supercell and even more for that supercell to drop one or more tornadoes. At some stage, Twister will narrow down the options based on data, predictions and geographic location, then we'll be on our way."

"Things will get quiet in the van," Amy warned, having just returned from the restroom. "It can feel quite stressful, even though it's exciting."

Pippa glanced across at the photographers, who sat by themselves a few tables away, sharing their best photos from the day before on their laptops. "Are they competing?" she asked.

"Yes and no," Rob said, taking another sip of coffee. "They used to when they were looking to sell their pictures to the news channels and so on. The problem now is anyone with a decent smartphone camera and an internet connection can beat them to it. And with so many chasers now, people are basically giving their shots away just to get their name on TV or the web."

"Now, they see themselves as the masters of the art," sniffed Amy. "They resent the rest of us. We're just getting in the way, which is why Twister makes sure their van stops at locations that give them a different view of the storms."

"To give them a unique perspective of the drama?"

"Yes. But mostly to reduce the risk of arguments or fights with the rest of the tour." Rob caught the doubt flicker across Pippa's face and shook his head. "Honestly. It happens. War was almost declared between the USA and South Africa in Nebraska last July."

The sound of a metal knife tapping against a glass brought the conversations in the café to a halt, and all attention turned to Deke.

"Time to mount up, folks," he announced. "We're heading east."

As chairs moved and the groups stood up, Amy used the noise cover to mutter to Pippa.

"We might start east, but we won't end up heading that way. Watch how many others move out of here when we're gone."

Sure enough, as the Storm Stalkers clambered into their vans and drove off, people trotted out of the gas station and towards their own vehicles. Some held up their phones and reported live where they were heading to their dozen followers online. Others raced to the pumps to fuel up.

Deke led the Stalkers at speed towards the nearest junction and then took a swift right, heading south until swinging into a parking lot and pulling to a halt behind a large, modern church. The other three vans swung in beside him. Twister climbed out and jogged to the corner of the building, then walked across the empty lot and stood behind a lamppost, peering back towards the junction. Ten minutes later, he was back and on the radio.

"You folks have paid good money for this adventure of a lifetime, and some of that investment goes to buy our technology and our expertise," he explained. "I don't like freeloaders taking advantage of the same for nothing. Oh, and praise the Lord for allowing us to use His house as a hiding place."

"Praise the Lord!" intoned Deke, heading out once more, this time in the general direction of southwest Texas.

Aaron's Dirt

The Popes had quickly discovered one irrefutable fact very quickly. Texas is vast.

It takes an age to get anywhere over a flat, featureless landscape accompanied by telegraph poles and power lines.

Only the occasional small town, dilapidated and deserted homes, battered cars and the pervading smell of cattle shit literally miles from the actual herd provided a distraction outside the confines of the vans.

Inside Van One, Amy and Rob were doing their best to keep everybody entertained with stories from their time in the military and from previous storm chasing escapades.

Even Twister closed his laptop for a while and joined in the conversation, reminiscing about his time in the air force and comparing notes on US military life with the couple.

Sandy joined in and talked in the respectful silence about his service from another era in the Royal Marines, firing up new topics for discussion and helping to pass the time. Pippa slipped her hand onto Simon's leg and gave it a reassuring squeeze.

Neither had any inclination to talk about their experiences in the army, and managed to avoid doing so by asking questions of the others, suggesting they knew nothing of military life.

Two hours down the road, with cloud formations gathering like members of different gangs in a city park who had arrived too early for something to kick off, Twister called a halt at a crossroads somewhere in the middle of nowhere in south Texas.

Deke turned the van off the tarmac onto the edge of a dirt track, which disappeared on both sides of the road towards the horizon between huge, recently ploughed fields. A genuine tumbleweed - the first of the week - blew gently across the road, stopping politely now and then to pose for photographs.

The storm cell they were tracking meandered along with brooding intent but with little inclination to do anything else in the sweltering heat of the day. Until it turned into something more dramatic, or until a cell with more potential revealed itself on the radar, the plan for the Stalkers was to stay where they were.

Those who had had their fill of photographing clouds, the photogenic tumbleweed and the Stop sign with three bullet holes in it settled in what shade they could find and raided their food and drink supplies. The photographers searched for more creative compositions by venturing along the main road or into the surrounding fields. In the distance, farm machinery churned away at the earth.

A small dot on one track gradually transformed into an old, dirty pickup, which crunched to a slow halt at the junction and disappeared for a couple of seconds into the dust cloud it had created. The driver looked out of the open passenger window.

"Howdy. What are you folks up to?"

Pippa walked across and placed her hand on the roof of the truck.

"Hi. We're storm chasing. Just stopped to see if that cell up there's going to turn into something interesting."

The driver turned around to look out of his own window at the looming cloud formation.

"That's doing nothing for a while. Leastways, ah sure hope it don't. We just finished these fields yesterday."

If anyone knew what the weather was going to do on that patch of ground, it was this man. Aaron was the owner of 4,000 acres of Texas dirt, and he'd farmed cotton on them for over forty years.

Every single day of that time span - the trials and tribulations, the scorching heat and the furnace-like winds - had etched into his face.

This wasn't a simple life. It was damn hard work, but it was his. He was proud of it and was happy to talk; the conversation with strangers providing a welcome interlude in his arduous routine.

Simon and Rob joined the conversation, chatting for a few minutes about the weather, where they had all come from and what they'd seen to date, omitting Sandy's walk towards sweet oblivion. Aaron's roaming eyes took it all in and sparkled with a mixture of amusement and bemusement. They narrowed ever so slightly when he spotted the photographers on the edge of the recently sown field.

"I hope you don't mind," Pippa said. "They're keeping to the edge."

"As long as they stay there, my dear, that's fine," he replied, before adding reasonably, "But if they're in the field when I get back, I'll shoot 'em."

And on that note, with his face creased even more, but this time into a grin, he bade them all good day and drove off down the road. The loyal dust trail followed in his wake for a short while, then gave up.

"I like Aaron," Pippa announced. "It would've been good to share a beer with him one evening and listen to his stories."

"You'll see Aarons every day on this trip," Rob said. "Friendly locals, curious to know why we're there; bemused and amused at our reasoning when they see storms regularly; and occasionally concerned that our arrival may mean impending catastrophe."

Sandy watched the truck disappear.

"They live with the dangers," he said. "We take our photographs and get out of there, but they stay and take their chances."

A beep from Van One gathered the group together, and Twister stood on the step before making his announcement.

"We've picked what could be a small, isolated supercell following behind a multi-cell storm to our south," he said. "It's a gamble, but there's limited shear and moisture everywhere else, and I reckon it's our best shot. We're heading for the mountains in southwest Texas, and I'll keep you updated as we go. Stay safe and listen to what your drivers and guides tell you. Mount up."

With whoops and hollers from the two youngest guests, everyone returned to their vans. Twister ran across to the photographers and talked briefly to a couple of them and their driver before jumping into his seat and opening his laptop. The clouds above them seemed to churn a little more, concerned they were losing their audience, then slowed down and carried on their merry way as the convoy departed.

Amy could barely contain herself. "I love this time on the trip!" she exclaimed. "It's so exciting!"

"She's not talking about the storms," warned Rob, before anyone could comment. "She's on about Twister working out where we're going to stay tonight."

"No, I'm not!"

Rob cocked his head to one side. "Really? Having waffles the shape of Texas for breakfast is not a big deal for you?"

"A girl can dream, Rob." All eyes turned to Pippa, who had a spirited gleam in her own.

The US army's best logistics specialist held up both hands in submission.

"If they're there, I'll make them for her myself," he smiled.

"Pippa Pope. You are my new best friend!" exclaimed Pippa's new best friend, squeezing her arm.

The Drum Solo

By the time the convoy reached the expected interception point, a brooding stillness had settled across the West Texas desert. The vans drove east through Marathon and pulled up in a lay-by; the groups stepping out a little wearily into the sultry warmth to stretch their legs and to witness the meteorological drama unfolding on the far side of town. Late afternoon light filtered through towering cumulonimbus and, from the jagged silhouette of the Davis Mountains, two majestic supercells writhed upwards, each sculpted in shifting greys and purples, illuminated by internal flashes of lightning.

The air was thick, thought Simon. *The atmosphere felt charged - almost alive.*

The updraft of one storm grew broader, sharper, more organised than its twin. It inhaled humid thermals and exhaled a deep rumble.

Slowly, it turned eastward, churning threateningly towards Marathon. By the time it neared Highway 90, the mesocyclone had tightened, and the vault of the storm glowed pale green.

"There's a lot of hail in that beast," Twister shouted over the growing rumble and the excited chatter. "We want to keep it at arm's length if we can, so be prepared to move out."

Almost as soon as he had spoken, a dense hail shaft emerged from the supercell's churning base and slanted towards the earth like a curtain of shattered glass. Locals pulled their vehicles into whatever shelter they could find as Deke pumped on the van's horn and started the engine. The guests needed no second bidding. In Marathon, hail the size of golf balls was already bouncing off tin roofs and skidding across caliche roads.

But it was right on the tail of the convoy, close to Sanderson, where the storm reached its crescendo. With a roar like a freight train overhead, it unloaded its heaviest payload. Tennis-ball-sized hail, measuring over two inches in diameter, smashed into the roof of each van with the violence of a rock concert drum solo.

"Bags and coats against windows," came the abrupt instructions over the radio. "We're stopping here. Drivers park up behind Deke. Windscreens facing the storm,"

The drivers did as they were told while the guests peeked from behind their window defences at the mayhem outside. Amy screamed part in fear and part excitement. Lightning forks zipped horizontally through the vault, and a near-instantaneous thunderclap caused the hail to pause for a moment, wondering *What the hell was that?*, before recommencing its assault on everything below.

"Windscreen's gone," Deke reported, as if it was the most normal thing in the world.

After what seemed an age, the storm pushed past them and east towards Sanderson, its anvil spreading across the fading twilight, trailing virga - or 'jellyfish clouds' as Amy called them - and casting long shadows across the desert floor. Behind it, the ground glittered in the dim light, as scattered hailstones melted away. The guests fell out of the vehicles, took photos and talked excitedly while the drivers and guides took stock of the vehicle damage.

"Pretty intense, huh?" Rob beamed, watching Amy dance a giddy jig as she waved at the supercell.

"I've been through worse," Sandy grinned, "But that was definitely memorable."

Simon sat in the relative quiet of the van, holding Pippa's hand as she watched the occasional lightning bolt through the rear window, the smile on her face frozen in place.

"How are you doing, Pip?" he asked quietly.

Pippa said nothing, because she felt... nothing. She searched inside for some fear or anger; maybe a feeling of victory or elation at having survived a strike by something so powerful and deadly. Instead, nothing. From the relative safety of the van, she had watched the overhead drama unfold with something approaching professional interest, but without feeling emotion of any description.

"I'm okay," she said eventually, squeezing his hand, her mask finally slipping into a puzzled frown. "I feel... numb... disconnected... I don't know how to describe it..."

"It did not freak you out though? Not frightened? Upset?"

Pippa shook her head. "I remember nothing about that day, so I associate nothing that happened to us then with what we've just seen. I didn't feel thrilled or excited either. Just... curious. And now it's gone, I'm thinking *Is that it?*"

Pope tightened his grip on her hand and nodded slowly.

"Since that day I've looked for answers to what happened and why. I've found nothing that... makes it real, I guess. I thought this trip would give me what I'm looking for, but now I'm not so sure."

The side door of the van slid open, breaking the moment, and Twister climbed in, closing the door behind him.

"Folks," he said, "I think it's time I had the package. And here's the reason..."

The Great Conundrum

Most of the Van One Gang, as they called themselves, sat on the veranda of the Pesos Motel and Bar, each nursing a cold bottle of the local beer and watching the nighttime light show way out across the desert towards the Mexican border. Their storm had gusted out; the outflow kicking up a cluster of new cells that were producing the evening's entertainment. The heat of the day had long gone, and so had the range of food supplies by the time the convoy reached its destination. The group made the best selection they could from the snacks still available at the bar, using alcohol to dull any hunger pangs.

From a weather perspective, Twister had warned them, the following day could be a damp squib not just in southern Texas but throughout Tornado Alley.

"I'm not seeing much potential right now, and there's no sense in trying to chase something that's not there," he explained at the group meeting. "Tomorrow you'll have a lazy start to the day. Van One needs to get a new windscreen, so we'll head into town first thing, then we'll catch up with the rest of you at Big Bend National Park. If you haven't been before, it's one of the most dramatic and remote landscapes in the whole of America. By the time you've taken your shots of the Boquillas Canyon, the hot springs and the desert scenery, you'll need a new SIM card for the rest of the trip."

A tremor of excitement rippled through the crowd until it hit the granite cliff that was the distinctly unimpressed group of photographers.

"There is a slight chance of some activity heading over the border," continued Twister, throwing the awkward squad some hope. "You'll remember the tornado they had around here not that long ago. That came out of nowhere. We'll review the data in the morning. Who knows? We may get storms forming early afternoon. If we do, then we'll be chasing before the clouds know they're storming."

"Quicker than a chicken after a June bug," grinned Deke.

"Just try to avoid them big hailstones tomorrow!" yelled a voice well-hidden in the crowd.

"I'll be in front of the van with my baseball bat," the driver promised. "There'll be ice dust all around, but the windscreen will be spotless."

The drivers and Twister had gone now, followed shortly afterwards by Sandy, who was feeling the effects of a long and tiring day.

"Did you see his face after he realised the air conditioning works perfectly in his room?" laughed Amy. "I didn't think we were going to see him again tonight."

Pippa nodded.

"He looked so shattered today," she said, "But, for a moment, I didn't think he was going to get back in the van when the hail came. He loved every minute."

"And the company," said Rob. "Even when he wasn't directly involved, he was listening intently to everything that was going on. I think he appreciates the company."

The group fell silent, watching the last of the lightning fade away and stars appear in the rapidly clearing sky. The noise in the bar behind them diminished as others turned in for the night. Pippa linked her arm with Simon's and laid her head against his shoulder.

"A morning wandering around Van Gilbert might be fun," she yawned. "We've not really seen much of the real America on this trip."

"What *is* the real America?" Simon asked nobody in particular. He caught his new friend's glance at each other, then Amy laughed.

"That, my friend, is the $64,000 question. And if I dropped you into a different location in this country for every day over a year..."

"I'd have 365 different answers?"

"366 if it was a leap year." Rob raised his beer bottle. "To America, the great conundrum."

The others joined in the toast, clinked their bottles, then finished the dregs.

"Time for bed," said Pippa. "I've a feeling we're in for another big day tomorrow."

"Over here, every day is a big day, but tomorrow promises to be bigger than most," smiled Amy, and gave her a hug. "Welcome to America!"

The walk down the long corridor to their room took the Popes past Sandy's room, where Simon slowed.

"Has he got someone in there with him?" he whispered.

Both of them listened carefully to the recognisable soft Scottish burr, coming to the end of recounting the day's events. Pippa grabbed his arm.

"Oh, bless him. We have to go. Now," she said in a hushed, urgent voice. "He's talking to Morag."

Simon hesitated a moment as he processed what his wife had said.

"I promised you I wouldn't be long, my dear," the muffled voice said through the door. "But I think I've got more life to live first. People to help. More things to achieve. Please, understand. I want you to be proud of me; not sad for me. I miss you. Love you."

The faint glow at the bottom of the door disappeared as Sandy switched off his bedside light, leaving the Popes staring at each other for a moment, then sharing a long hug of relief, before sneaking off to their own room.

The talk in the van with Twister had been on their minds all evening, but both now felt that sleep would be slightly easier than either of them had dared to hope.

The Haunted Raccoon

The settlement of Van Gilbert started life in the early 1850s as a station on an overland mail route. They named it several years later after Lieutenant Donald Van Gilbert, the first commander of the town's army garrison. His appointment lasted just 18 months and ended once the Confederate forces finally realised the post was there, seized it and took the lieutenant prisoner.

The Texas and Pacific Railway further boosted the town's importance in the 1880s, and its population increased to a peak of 3,000 in the mid-20th century, before dropping to its current figure of 1,500, excluding the occasional, usually lost, tourists and the exhibits in the local taxidermy museum. The townsfolk had little, but they had a self-deprecating humour, cultivated over generations.

"Welcome to Historic Van Gilbert," said the sign at the edge of town. "Named after a Loser and Your Gateway to Far More Interesting Places."

Van One halted in the middle of the high street and was on its way again almost before the Popes and Sandy were on the sidewalk. Deke seemed concerned that the locals might use the opportunity to dive through the open doorway to escape their current lives, much like the thousands on the other side of the nearby border.

The three newest arrivals in town stood blinking in the early morning heat as their storm-chasing van pulled away in a cloud of dust.

"He is going to come back, isn't he?" Pippa asked nobody in particular.

"Oh God, I hope so," Simon muttered, looking around and wondering how they were going to fill the next few hours.

Sandy examined a dilapidated mural of a rattlesnake apparently wrestling a cactus. "I camped in the Falklands with more amenities," he observed. "At least there we had morale."

"And here, we have coffee," Pippa said, having turned around to find Jenny's Diner & General Store waiting patiently just behind her for its first customers of the day. "Let's start with that."

Just as expected, the bell jingled as the diner door opened. The diners sat on chairs fixed to the Formica table and checked out the menu.

"Well, y'all sure don't look like you're from around here." The customers turned to see a woman the wrong side of sixty appear behind the kitchen counter, dressed in a figure-hugging, leopard-print tracksuit, sporting a wig that appeared to be made from candy floss and holding an empty cigarette holder that suggested classy dementia.

"Is it our accent, or our general air of discomfort?" Simon asked, warming slightly to the quirkiness of their host.

"None of those," Jenny replied, blowing and bursting a gum bubble for dramatic effect before continuing. "You're reading the ketchup bottle like it's a wine list."

Pippa asked what coffees were available and was offered four options - black or white and mug or cup. The trio ordered coffee and doughnuts, resisted requesting the doughnuts with the fewest flies on them and selected a box of doughnut bites instead.

Sandy sipped his cup of black coffee and grimaced. "The gas in Iraq tasted better than this."

Conscious their reactions were being monitored, Pippa attempted to maintain a smile on her face as she sipped from her mug.

"No, no, it's... complex. I'm getting a combination of... some type of nut and... I want to say burnt rubber..."

"Oh bless you, hun," Jenny beamed. "That's my husband Larry's blend. He brews it in the same vat he uses for hog dewormer - once he's given it a good clean, of course. Reckons it 'adds kick' to the aftertaste."

"Ah. It certainly adds kick," nodded Simon, ignoring the flies and cramming two doughnut bites into his mouth to mask the flavour.

After an unpleasant half hour trying to avoid eating or drinking anything whilst listening politely to Jenny as she provided her new audience with an update on all things Van Gilbert, the three made their excuses and left, promising to visit Dwight's Taxidermy and Historical Curiosities. This turned out to be an error, as Dwight's museum of nightmares was straight across the street, and Jenny stood at the diner window, sucking on her empty cigarette holder, until she was happy the three of them had entered the building.

Inside, an unnervingly cheerful man showed them his "Famous Possums of Texas" exhibition and an albino raccoon he insisted was haunted.

"Tell me something stranger," Dwight asked Sandy. "Have you ever shot anything that wasn't trying to shoot you first?"

Sandy thought carefully before replying.

"Yes," he said, and received a hearty guffaw and a clap on his back.

"That's the spirit!" Dwight exclaimed before adding seriously, "Do you want to hold a petrified squirrel?"

"No, but thank you."

"That's a smart accent, my friend. Are y'all from the BBC?"

Sandy shook his head. "I'm from a part of Britain that still carries a knife in the sock and distrusts vegetables."

Dwight nodded sagely at the revelation from someone who was obviously a kindred spirit.

"You can never be too careful with vegetables," he announced enigmatically. "Especially them from under the ground."

Renewing Aquaintances

Having installed and connected the new radiator in the old red pickup the day before, Matty Hernandez had been working on the vehicle in his repair shop since dawn. He filled the radiator with a mix of coolant and distilled water, checked for leaks and then ran the engine with the cap off and the heater on full blast to purge any air from the system. These weren't jobs for the heat of the day.

Once the air bubbles stopped and the thermostat opened, he topped up the coolant, checked all the connections and took the beat-up vehicle for a test drive.

The desert towards the north already shimmered, the heat reflecting the sky and creating a lake-like mirage that made the view towards the mountains much more appealing than the reality.

Matty loved this drive. It was an opportunity to be away from the day-to-day stresses of keeping his business afloat; to be alone with his thoughts.

The events of the last few days had done little to lower his blood pressure.

Omar's unexpectedly early arrival, coinciding as it did with Don's vehicle issues, was as unhelpful as it was welcome. The Afghan had been the model guest; polite, patient and helpful.

Mindful of the problems his presence created, he had kept himself hidden away in his - or rather Danny's - room, spending most of the time committing to memory the two pages of fake biography forwarded by his friend from contacts in the UK. Matty had printed the document for him, then removed any proof of the email's existence. The pages themselves were to be destroyed before Omar's departure. And if all went according to plan, that would be today. Everything was set.

Matty had one last, long look at the view in front of him, let out an enormous sigh, then turned the vehicle around and headed back to the workshop. Once there, he just had time to check the job was a good one and to wash and dry his hands before the crunch of tyres and the sight of Deke's huge grin through a badly cracked windscreen announced the arrival of Omar's rescuers.

The side door opened as soon as the van stopped, and Amy flew out and into the arms of the old man. "Matthew Hernandez," she scolded. "Where has my invitation been these last couple of years? And where is the loveliest lady in the whole of Texas?"

Rob followed her out, but scanned his surroundings carefully before walking over and shaking Matty's hand. "It's good to see you again, sir."

"And you, Captain. My son's leaving nothing to chance."

"If you mean he's sent in the A-team, Mister H," smiled Deke, "You're damn right."

Twister emerged from the back of the van, carrying a holdall.

"Where is he, Matty?"

"Joey Mitchell," called a female voice from the house, "What kind of heartfelt greeting is that?" Jayne appeared on the front verandah, obviously delighted and definitely relieved to see her son's friends.

"Jayne!" shrieked Amy, pushing away from Matty and running to the house where she almost knocked over the older lady.

"Let's all go in before Amy destroys the house," suggested Matty. "I'll get to work on your van once we've introduced you to our guest."

Omar sat at the kitchen table, nervously fiddling with his watch; reluctant to show himself at such a crucial stage in the proceedings but eager to discover the identity of his rescuers. The extraction plan was deliberately vague, Danny had explained, depending as it did on the vagaries of the weather, the tour group's location and the need to build a plausible-enough back story to get past the border patrols they could run into at any time. Omar understood. *Caution was the name of the game*, as his professor at med school reminded his students regularly.

He stood as he heard movement at the front door and turned to face the silhouetted figures heading down the hallway. Jayne walked in first.

"Omar," she smiled, "We have some visitors." She walked over to the kettle and filled it with water as Rob and Twister stood in the doorway and grinned.

Rob rushed over to his Afghan friend and shook his hand, realising too late that he hadn't thought of what to say once this moment arrived. Twister had no such issues.

"Where the hell have you been, Doc?" he asked, hugging his old comrade. "I reckon you're at least twelve months late."

"Make that fourteen."

Omar's eyes widened as he recognised the female voice and peered over Twister's shoulder to make sure his ears weren't deceiving him. There she stood. The same bright smile, but with eyes shining from the tears he could see rolling down her cheeks.

Twister instinctively stepped out of the way of the mini-tornado that swept past him. Amy threw herself at the illegal immigrant, knocking him backwards into the wall behind him, as she wrapped her arms around his neck and held on as if she never planned to let go.

"I have missed you *so* much," she sobbed. "I have worried about you every day."

"And now I'm here," he replied, conscious he was simply stating the obvious, but uncertain what else to say, given the current circumstances.

Amy suddenly realised she was the centre of attention and that nothing could move on until she did. She stepped back and patted his cheeks.

"Indeed, you are," she smiled, "But not for much longer."

Deke stepped forward, removing his sunglasses as he did so, and offered his hand. "Deke Scanlon, Doctor Rahmani. We've never met, but I was a grunt for eight years and did two tours in your country. I've heard a lot about you."

Omar looked into the taller man's kind eyes and felt reassured - even optimistic. "I hope it was all good, Deke. If it weren't, then I could be on my way back to Mexico."

It was a weak joke, but it raised smiles across the group.

"Omar, did you leave your sense of humour on the other side of the border?" Rob asked with a smirk.

"I did Rob. I had to travel light and was told I wouldn't need it over here."

"And so it begins!" Amy clapped her hands delightedly.

Twister pulled the package the Popes had given to him from his pocket and handed it over.

Omar opened it and pulled out a British passport complete with visa stamps, proof of his ESTA visa confirmation and a return flight ticket to London. There was also cash and various credit and membership cards in a worn, leather wallet, together with a couple of receipts.

Two small photographs showed Omar and a fictitious wife by the seaside, and a picture of the couple in a park, laughing with an older man.

"Your 'father-in-law' is on the tour," Twister continued. "You'll meet him once we've sorted out the windscreen. In the meantime, we'll go over your backstory to make sure everything's covered."

Matty nudged Deke.

"C'mon, son. Let's get you guys back on the road. Did you use a hammer?"

Deke looked affronted. "How dare you, sir! I'm a storm chaser. You'll find every crack is genuine and formed by large hail. I would never stoop to such artifice."

Matty frowned and looked at Twister.

"He's discovered some old BBC series on cable," Twister shrugged. "I doubt he knows what it means. Just a lucky guess."

"Yessssss!" A thrilled Deke fist-bumped Rob, put on his sunglasses and followed Matty out of the door.

The Orange Vest

The presidential C-32A was a modified Boeing 757, used for VIP transport and able to land on shorter runways than those required by Air Force One. It touched down on a makeshift tarmac just outside South Texas Falls, a name nobody in the White House had heard until recently, when the media had made the most of the town's location and its relative proximity to the recent devastation. A motorcade of twelve cars and vans, escorted by several police vehicles, rolled quietly into place while the media exited the plane from a rear door and gathered expectantly behind a hastily constructed rope.

Eventually, President Clampett descended the forward stairs in a navy windbreaker bearing the stitched words: 'President David D. Clampett - Committed to Recovery: *Comcovery*'. The words had been debated for three hours in the Situation Room and only agreed once someone switched off the air conditioning for 90 minutes.

At least half of the sweating, exhausted members of the group left the room wishing they had never reached these political heights, and believing that the president should indeed be committed. Crowded behind a rope now held at waist height by two police officers, many of the media felt the same.

The moment Clampett's shoes hit dirt, a staffer from advance sidled up and whispered, "We have a refrigerator for you to stand by."

"A fridge? Here?"

"At the site. About twelve miles away. Symbol of domestic resilience. The house behind it is part gone, part upside down so... you know... optics."

Clampett nodded grimly. "Just don't let it fall over."

The staffer nodded. "The press are waiting," she said. "Don't smile."

A crowd - mostly media, local officials, and two dozen pre-screened victims cleared by FEMA's PR people - had gathered along with a few curious clouds at the disaster site. The victims were deemed photogenic but not too angry, as was the rest of the crowd. The people wore clean shirts and looked emotionally, mentally and physically shattered. One held a small dog.

The presidential element of the convoy halted eighty yards away, while the media vans rushed their occupants ahead, so the photographers and TV crews had plenty of time to take shots and footage of the inspection of the ruins. Clampett, his team and security, walked past twisted trees and insulation caught in fences like cotton candy from hell. A child ran towards him, or rather was pushed from the crowd of locals, and handed over a drawing of a rainbow with the words *Thank You, President Person*.

Clampett crouched down, hugged the child, admired the picture and posed for photos. "Tell comms this one's going in the campaign video," he muttered.

Nearby, a volunteer in a bright orange vest was directing debris clearing with the calm competence of someone not paid by the hour.

She had dreadlocks, gloves, and *Path Finder: Local Coordinator* stencilled on the back of the vest.

Pfist noticed before the president did. "Sir, we have a Path Finder in the shot."

Clampett turned. "A what now?"

"The orange vest."

The president squinted. "Is she going to shout at me?"

"Unlikely, sir. But she might offer you a reusable water bottle."

Pierce turned to Hampton, whose eyes suggested her stress levels were increasing. "Grace. Do I hug her?"

Grace paused. "Yes. But just a hug, okay? No tongues."

Clampett approached the woman, a member of his security detail close by, but out of shot.

"Hey there," he said, voice loaded with presidential warmth, which mostly sounded like someone trying to remember your name at a funeral.

She looked him over calmly. "Hello, Mr. President."

"What are you folks doing here?"

She gestured behind her. "Feeding people. Tarping roofs. We've got solar chargers, med supplies, translators, childcare…"

"Wow," he said, impressed despite himself. "Are you with FEMA?"

She shook her head. "Just neighbours helping neighbours. You know. Radical stuff."

Pierce chuckled a little too loudly. "You one of those Pathmakers?"

"Path Finders."

"Right. Right. Trees and feelings."

She smiled politely. "Also logistics, education, outreach, and resource equity. Check the website. The list grows every day."

He blinked. "You got any press?"

"No. Just massive impact."

The cameras clicked.

The President turned slightly, creating a perfect three-quarters profile, and threw a casual arm around her shoulder.

Grace gave a discreet thumbs-up from the media line.

Someone handed him a bullhorn.

"Ladies and gentlemen," he said, "We stand here today and witness the heart of American resilience. Here in South Texas, amid wind and ruin, we see not despair, but a steadfast and steely determination. We see families helping families. Organisations, stepping up to the plate and doing a fantastic job. And we see..." He leaned back and looked at the volunteer's vest, squinted, and improvised, "...path... finding."

Pfist winced. Grace didn't blink. The media would love it, and the public would lap it up.

The Garrison

Back in Van Gilbert, the cultural exchange continued. What claimed to be America's first-ever sporting goods store was essentially a catalogue of methods to kill things. Apart from three baseball bats (which could still be in the catalogue), and two mitts and two footballs (which couldn't), the rest of the store was a weapons arsenal and ammunition dump.

When Simon asked with tongue firmly in cheek where he could find the rocket-propelled grenade launchers, he wasn't laughed at or kicked out of the store. The 'weapons advisor' apologised profusely and explained they had run out after the Pentagon bought the manufacturer's entire production run for an ally currently fighting a war in Central Europe.

Sandy tried out a US-built model of the AK47 on the range at the back of the shop and pronounced it the lightest version of the Russian classic he had ever used. Despite firing a lot of rounds in what was essentially the town centre, nobody batted an eyelid. Pippa tried on a lady's ghillie suit, which made her look like a swamp creature. "It's hot in there," she reported. "The next time I need to lose weight, I'm getting one of these."

The unisex hair salon nearby had two hairstyle photographs in its window - a crew cut displayed by a male model and a bob haircut modelled by a woman.

"This must be the busiest shop in the town," murmured Sandy. "Look around."

Sure enough, every passer-by had one hairstyle or the other. And the selection of hairstyle wasn't determined by gender.

"Depends on the season," explained the six feet, eight inches farmhand Herman when Sandy engaged him in conversation on the matter. "Crew when it's hot; bob when it's cold."

The meeting point was to be The Garrison; not so much a saloon and more of a glorified shack with a pool table, a stage at one end protected by chicken wire, and a jukebox that played only Johnny Cash, southern rock and, inexplicably, Eurovision hits.

After a friendly chat with the clearly inebriated bar tender, who explained he drank to keep the chef company, the trio settled with beer and surprisingly good burgers at a table that gave them a good view of the bar while also being close to the only working air conditioning unit.

Simon peered at a stuffed iguana on a shelf, wearing a cowboy hat. "This town is a batshit-crazy nightmare after one too many of the wrong mushrooms," he declared quietly. A couple of locals, dressed in matching black logoed shirts and combat trousers, wandered in and settled onto stools by the bar, talking to the barman but throwing the occasional glance towards the trio via the large mirror behind the bar.

Pippa finished her mouthful of burger and took a sip of her beer.

"Would it be inappropriate to say I've found this entire experience oddly... charming?"

"I've seen this before," Sandy grunted. "Textbook Stockholm Syndrome. Give it another hour, and you'll be writing five-star reviews online for Dwight's haunted raccoon."

"We were talking about the real America with Bob and Amy last night," Simon grinned. "They didn't think it could be defined easily, and I'm believing them."

"Excuse me, folks." The trio looked across to see one of the men at the bar had stood up and turned to face them. "Mind if I ask what brings you to these parts?"

"We're on a storm chasing tour," smiled Pippa. "Just killing some time here while our van's windshield gets replaced."

The man rubbed his stubbled chin with one hand, placing the other on his hip, close to his holstered handgun. "Can you prove it? Got any ID?"

"Do you? I'll show you mine if you show me yours." Pippa's smile didn't leave her face, but the affability in her voice had definitely disappeared. The man frowned and shifted his hand onto the butt of the gun, while his friend stood to reveal he too was armed.

"We have proof and ID," interrupted Sandy. "Check my camera if you like. I took some braw pictures of the storm. The weather was awfy dreich, but the major problem was the van. Those seats are not designed for my bahookie."

"What the hell did he say?" asked the first man, looking at Simon Pope for help.

Simon shook his head. "I wish I could tell you," he shrugged. "He's from Scotland."

"Wheesht, you loon." Sandy was growing into his role. "Dinnae be so gallus. Away and grab me another beer. Yon's heid's mince and we should keep it there awhile."

"He called you a loon…" Pippa looked stunned and turned to the two men for help. "He called my husband a loon. Is that allowed in Texas nowadays? Surely not?"

"And gallus! Who says that anymore? Gallus!" All eyes turned to the bartender, who felt he was missing out and wanted to be involved.

The two black shirts looked at each other for what seemed an age, before the stubbly one shrugged and offered, "The First Amendment protects the right to free speech. But I don't know if that extends to the words 'loon' and 'gallus'. That's all I got."

"Then that's settled!" said Sandy. "Now, where's my beer?"

Simon stood up, walked to the bar and ordered three bottles.

"That was embarrassing. I'm sorry you had to hear that. Can I get you both a drink?"

Before either could reply, two black SUVs with tinted windows pulled up outside and the first beeped its horn. "Duty calls. Good luck with the old guy."

Both men finished their drinks, nodded and walked out.

"Are they police?" Simon asked the bartender. The man shook his head.

"Worse, if you're a migrant. Local border patrol. Bit of advice? Don't get on their wrong side."

Sandy called across. "Did you really understand what I was saying?"

"*Dinnae be so gallus*? Don't be so… cheeky?" The bartender blushed as Sandy applauded. "I worked for a season at a hotel in Scotland about fifteen years ago - The Spittal of Glen Shee," he continued, keen to impress even more. "The place was fantastic, and the people were really kind, but I never met Glen."

"Glen who?"

"Mister Shee. The owner. The others did, but I just kept missing him."

Simon looked up at the mirror behind the bartender and saw Sandy nod, then look down at the table with his shoulders shaking. Pippa suddenly found her phone very interesting.

Feeling embarrassed, he bought the bartender a large drink *and* left a generous tip, then returned to the table with the bottles. The trio clinked glasses and sat in silence for a while.

"I'm not sure what to make of all this," confessed Sandy eventually.

"I feel I'm looking face-to-face at the real America, but I'm not sure what to make of it," shivered Pippa. "That was going south quickly."

"You did well there, Sandy. The distraction worked a treat." Simon leaned forward so he could clink bottles once again with his new old friend. "That was some quick thinking."

The old Scot nodded his thanks and smiled. Inside, he was buzzing, feeling alive for the first time in a long time.

"We make a good team," he said. "A good team."

The three of them sank back into silence, reflecting on how the situation had started and was finally resolved. Eventually the tour van drew up outside, complete with a new windscreen. The three returned their bottles and plates to Earl, the happy and still inebriated bartender, and walked outside.

"Y'all come back any time you like," Earl called after them. "We've got a meteorite museum opening next week. Turns out they're just rusty manhole covers, but no one's gonna tell Dwight. Keeps him busy."

Surprises

The rain started falling from a bland, overcast sky just as they left the bar, spattering the dust on the ground and providing welcome relief from the early afternoon heat. All three of them dawdled slightly to relish the change, then climbed into the van through the open side door. It took the three of them a couple of seconds to realise the van was fuller than usual.

The first to cotton on was Sandy, who no longer had a row to himself. Omar sat by the window, dressed in slightly worn clothes and a golf cap brought over by his 'father-in-law' from Britain and handed over to Twister on the night preceding the tour. The old man flashed a reassuring smile and sat down beside him as if he'd known him all his life.

"Good to meet you, Omar," he said, not looking in the newcomer's direction. "We can talk in a while once we're out of town. I counted at least three people with eyes on us as we got on board."

Both Simon and Pippa overcame their ingrained English politeness and ignored Omar completely as they walked past him and settled onto the seats just behind. Eventually, Pippa could stand it no longer. She leaned forward just as the van moved.

"Hello Omar. It's nice to meet you. I'm Pippa," she murmured, receiving a slight nod in return.

Nobody else spoke during the ten-minute trip out of town. Even Deke kept quiet. Most of the passengers scanned outside, looking for anything or anyone that looked suspicious whilst trying not to look suspicious themselves. The daylight disappeared quickly as the cloud cover intensified, along with the rain, which made its presence felt on the roof of the van.

"This is going to mess up our day, I'm afraid," muttered Twister, checking his radar data. "But we'll be out of it in a couple of hours. Time will tell."

Simon stared at the back of Sandy's head, his mind spinning. Twister had mentioned no one else's involvement in the rescue. Rob and Amy were no surprise, given their military background and the fact they had stayed on the van rather than visiting the town; but the old fella had known the newcomer's name without being introduced.

I guess they dropped us in Van Gilbert in case something went wrong, or in case it goes wrong, he thought. Jenny, Dwight, the bartender and the two hostiles in the bar weren't the most reliable witnesses individually, but collectively they made a good alibi. Hopefully, CCTV had also made it into town. *Just as long as Dwight wasn't the operator.*

Another thought hit him like a lightning bolt. He tapped Sandy on the shoulder.

"Do much gardening, Sandy?"

Pippa's eyes widened. The old man chuckled.

"Pete said you were sharp. I've been in the Garden Club for a long time. Keeps life interesting."

"But why are *we* here?" asked Pippa, not quite knowing if she felt surprised, angry or just plain curious.

"We don't normally run four vans," explained Twister, eyes fixed firmly on his smartphone. "This was a late addition when we heard Omar had arrived. We needed a van full of people we could trust; with one seat empty."

"Plus, it helps to have an international mix if we get stopped by a border patrol," added Amy, looking apologetic. "It muddies the waters."

"And we needed a courier for Omar's documents," said Sandy. "Everything happened so fast. Pete couldn't get them to me in time."

Pippa looked at her husband. "Pete knew you'd love to go storm chasing. And remember, he owed you for Ireland."

Sandy sniggered, then looked sheepish. "Sorry," he said. "Pete can be a sod. He's on a family holiday in Tenerife, but he said your *Path Finder* links might be useful if we run into trouble."

The van jerked slightly and almost ran off the road before Deke regained control.

"Apologies, folks," he said, risking a glance in his rearview mirror at his passengers. "You're involved in *Path Finder*, Simon?"

Pope shifted uncomfortably. "I know some people."

"Oh, it's a bit more than 'some people'," grinned Sandy. "If it weren't for this man here…"

"Haud yer wheesht, man." Except for Deke, who stayed commendably focused on the wet road, all eyes pivoted towards Omar, speaking in a broad Scottish accent. "Dinnae be a wee clip. This should stay clapped."

"Aye… aye… sorry Simon…" Sandy's face looked pale, despite the recent sun. "Where did you…"

Omar laughed at his companions' reaction, then switched to his more-natural English accent. "I did two years at Glasgow Med School after three in London."

The opening riff of AD/DC's *Thunderstruck* interrupted the conversation. Twister lifted his phone to his ear, answered the call with a quick "What's up?", listened for a minute then ended the call with a "Ten four" and checked their position on his laptop.

"There's a live checkpoint just south of the next settlement, about five miles away," he announced. "US Border Patrol and local support. We'll buy time with a toilet break when Deke finds a suitable spot, but you have about ten minutes to bring Mr and Mrs Pope up to speed with what they need to know."

The Checkpoint

Thanks to the heavy cloud, dusk arrived well before its estimated time of arrival. The rain came down sideways as the van, still streaked with dust and bugs but rapidly recovering its original colours, rattled towards the checkpoint, where two floodlights were warming up.

Orange cones, intended to funnel vehicles towards the border patrol, had long given up maintaining a straight line and rolled around randomly on their sides. The US flag on the hastily erected pole snapped one way, then the other, like a dog wanting to slip its leash and bolt across the desert.

"Uniformed personnel at the checkpoint," reported Deke. "The local boys are in vehicles a couple of hundred yards away on each side of the road. You can see the lights on their SUVs. Must be looking to intercept illegals trying to sneak by."

Three officers in Border Patrol uniforms huddled under a golf umbrella, which was fighting as hard as the flag for its freedom. A local militiaman in camouflage gear, a poncho and a Stetson held up a sodden hand to halt the van; the other hand resting on the butt of his rifle. The Border Patrol officer who had lost the game of rock, paper, scissors left the umbrella and trotted to the relative shelter of the side door, which Rob slid open.

"Afternoon all," he said. "Where are y'all headed and where've you come from?"

"Afternoon," replied Twister amicably. "We were at the Pesos Motel last night. The rest of our group is waiting for us at Big Bend. We had to divert to Van Gilbert to get our windshield repaired. Hail smashed it yesterday."

"Isn't this weather bad enough for you?"

Sandy cleared his throat and, in his best military broad Scots, launched into a rambling explanation involving mesocyclonic pressure drops, dodging the hook echo, pivoting over the dry line and a couple of other phrases he barely remembered from the briefing a few days earlier.

"Sir," interrupted the officer, "What the hell are you on about? And I'll have your passports, please folks, while I'm at it."

Omar leaned forward and handed over his passport. "My father-in-law is Scottish, officer," he explained in impeccable English. "He can be difficult to understand; believe me, I know. He's trying to tell you that the conditions around here are not right for the weather we're hoping to see, which is why we're heading north again."

The border guard flicked through the passport and looked hard at Omar's face.

"Have you been in America long, son?" he asked.

The others held their collective breath while Omar struggled not to swallow hard.

"With respect, sir, it's Doctor. America? Not as long as I'd like, but I'm enjoying my time here, even on a day like this. I'd like to say that your commitment to duty in this weather is highly commendable."

The officer grunted something about being the front line of America's defence, handed back the document and inspected the others while a second man asked Deke to open the van's rear door so he could check through the luggage.

Just as the check drew to a close, a red pickup truck pulled up behind and to the right, with its headlights on the side of the van. A man in a hooded waterproof emerged and walked to his superior, who was maintaining his vigil in front of the vehicle.

"Thank you, folks. Stay safe." The officer closed the side door and retreated to the umbrella as Deke secured the rear doors and climbed back into his seat. The driver gunned the engine into life and headed through the lights of the checkpoint as the militiamen stepped aside. Omar glanced through his rain-streaked window at the two men in conversation, just as the newcomer looked up and caught his eye. Omar looked away quickly, but not quickly enough.

"We have a problem," he announced, just as everyone in the van was relaxing. "The man who just arrived. He's in a Mexican gang. I think he recognised me."

"You sure about that?" asked Sandy.

"I'd recognise that eyepatch anywhere."

"A friend of yours?"

"No."

Deke checked his wing mirror and saw the two men still talking animatedly in the rain, one gesturing after the van, then running to talk to the Border Patrol, who were still fighting to control the umbrella.

"We need to move. Strap in," he ordered, then sped up as much as he could through the small town without raising suspicion, while Twister got on the phone.

Back at the checkpoint, Don talked to the officers while Patch watched the van's taillights disappear into the rain.

"My friend reckons the young guy in that van isn't a weather nerd. He's an Afghan who crossed the border just over a week ago."

The officer hitched up his trousers - a tricky task when hanging onto an umbrella - and shook his head.

"His paperwork said otherwise. He's a doctor from England, out here on holiday with his pa-in-law. Speaks perfect English. And he said we're doing a great job. When was the last time you met an illegal like that?"

Patch turned. "He's an Afghan; not a Brit. And dangerous. Got the drop on me and my friend. He's a threat."

"You got proof?"

"I've got a memory. Same thing."

The officer shook his head, spraying water from his cap all over his colleagues.

"Not in court, it ain't. Not yet, anyway."

Catch Up

Deke checked his wing mirror for the umpteenth time then turned his attention back to the treacherously wet asphalt in front. The town was long gone, and the road was still clear behind them, but his gut-feel was that it wouldn't be that way for long.

"A quick question," said Pippa, keen to break the nervous silence weighing down on them all like a wet fleece blanket. "How did you know? About the checkpoint?"

"We have a vanguard," stated Twister, without looking up from his laptop, but in a tone that suggested the topic was now closed for discussion. Unfortunately, Sandy didn't get the hint.

"We could do with a rearguard," he said. "Any thoughts?"

"We're on it."

"It's just that if you wanted to drop me off with a gun and a couple of grenades…"

"Good God, man," Twister snapped. "Where do you think you are?"

"Texas," came the calm answer. "And you have what I need underneath the back seat."

Finally, Twister shut the screen and turned around quickly, his eyes boring into the old man, who returned the stare with a smile on his face.

"Like I said, Sandy, we're on it."

The Scot shrugged, then nodded and turned his attention to Omar. "I'm betting this isn't the most dramatic thing that's happened to you recently, is it, son?" he asked. "Why don't you give us a couple of examples, just to pass the time?"

Omar hesitated a moment, then opened up. He explained how he had missed the flight from Kabul after leaving his family to help the injured in a nearby car explosion, only to be caught in a second blast.

He had avoided the Taliban by dressing in stolen medical clothing at the hospital and then kept ahead of them using his network of trusted friends and relatives for over a year, before establishing contact with a military connection and using their network to flee over the border.

He glossed over the details of the flights, simply calling that part of the journey 'stressful and boring in equal measure', then talked about his time near the border, in the Mission, and his encounter with Patch. By the time he talked about his crossing into Texas, he had the full attention of the van, except for the two up front.

There were no questions at the end; there was too much for everyone to absorb. Amy and Rob reflected on a couple of their own stories involving the newcomer, through which it became apparent that Rob's remit had involved more than simple logistics.

There were also anecdotes of their time in Afghanistan, where Omar had corrected Rob's mispronunciations of Pashto words, which had had his Afghan colleagues laughing uncontrollably, much to the American's puzzlement.

The rain had almost stopped, and the atmosphere in the van was just getting back to normal when Deke brought them all crashing back to earth.

"We have company," he announced. "Three vehicles, I think. Nobody look at them."

Everyone in the back of the van resisted the powerful temptation to stare out of the windows at their pursuers, relying instead on Deke's reports. Twister relayed his own commentary quietly into his mobile phone.

Sandy nudged Omar's elbow. "Don't you worry, son," he whispered. "You're going nowhere."

"Thank you, Kaka."

One of the vehicles - a black SUV with tinted windows - overtook the van and then settled in front of it, maintaining a steady pace.

"They're waiting for a flat stretch of ground, then they'll box us in so we have to pull over," said Deke, his words being echoed by Twister into his phone. As he spoke, another SUV pulled out and came up alongside them, revealing a red pickup truck, which moved up to prevent them slowing down or stopping and turning around. "That's the pickup from the Hernandez place," said Deke. "I saw it when we were replacing our windshield."

"We can't have Matty involved in this," said Twister. "Here's how we play it."

As he spoke, the hazard lights on the three militia vehicles flashed, and they slowed down. A variable message sign on the back of the vehicle in front flashed *Slow Down*, then *Follow Us*, followed by *STOP*.

Deke flashed his lights and pulled over, leaving a decent gap between his van and the lead SUV. Doors opened immediately on the chase vehicles, and six militiamen spilled out, wearing tactical gear and toting a selection of weapons. Once the group had fanned out around the storm chasers' van, the front passenger door of the lead vehicle opened. A tall man stepped out wearing similar gear to his team, but wearing sunglasses and a Stetson.

"Why was he wearing a hat in the car?" whispered Pippa.

"Maybe the sunroof stuck open," Amy giggled nervously.

The man, Don, strolled round to Twister's passenger window and knocked politely.

Twister rolled the window down and smiled a polite "Howdy."

Don touched his Stetson in reply.

"We're the local border militia, sir. We support the US Border Patrol and may carry out vehicle inspections within fifty miles of the Rio Grande."

"We passed through a Border Patrol checkpoint recently. Those officers inspected our paperwork and found everything to be in order."

"We don't think that's the case. One of my men believes he recognised one of your group from Santa Esperanza about ten days ago."

Omar felt movement on the other side of his window, but resisted the temptation to turn around. He didn't need to look.

"Twister. Ask that fine-looking cowboy if I can go for a quick pee while you sort this lot out. I take it I'm not the man you're after, sir?"

Don looked closely at the old Scotsman and shook his head.

"You're not the man in question, sir, and that's a fine accent. We're interested in the gentleman next to you."

Sandy looked at Omar, then laughed.

"My son-in-law?" he asked, then laughed again and moved towards the side door. "Maggie's never going to believe this when he gets home." He slid the door back, stepped outside carefully and stood up straight, looking into Don's eyes. "Maggie's my daughter," he explained. "She'll never let him forget this."

He patted Don on the arm as he walked past him, then limped slightly towards a thicket of spiny mesquite, shaking his head and chuckling to himself as he did so.

Don looked at Omar through the open side door.

"Sir, step out of the van and bring your documents."

"Not yet," laughed Omar, in an English accent so sharp it could cut through cacti. "First, provide me with proof of your authority to carry out this action. You forced us off the road, violating our civil rights. Any attempt to enter this vehicle will constitute trespass. Attempting to remove me physically will mean charges of kidnapping and assault."

Omar stopped a moment, partly because he wanted to give the militia leader time to process what he had said; partly because of the shouting, swearing and panel thumping he could hear just outside his window.

"I would also like to see proof that the person making this ridiculous accusation is a legitimate citizen of the United States of America. I can't see your authorities taking kindly to illegal immigrants being allowed into local militias, which I recognise do a great job supporting law enforcement. While you consider those points and in the spirit of cooperation, I'm happy to show you my documents."

Don tipped his Stetson back slightly and stared hard at the young man, buying time while he worked out what to do next. One of his men sidled up to him and whispered in his ear, throwing a thumb towards the bushes and pointing at the Popes. Simon recognised him first.

"Hello!" he said with a wave. "We met in the Garrison earlier, didn't we? Where's your friend?"

Another militiaman joined his mate and waved shyly.

"Great bar, the Garrison," Simon continued. "Look forward to going back there sometime. The burgers were excellent."

"They always taste better when the chef's drunk," grinned one man, before catching his leader's eye and slinking away.

Rob took the documents from Omar and passed them out of the door to Don.

He flicked through them as Patch marched around the van to his side and peered at the paperwork.

"This is fake," the cartel man snorted. "All fake."

"Looks legit to me. Entry stamp in the passport, plus stamps for other countries. Return portion of his flight ticket. Email confirmation and details for the storm chasing trip. I don't think he's your man."

"You're wrong." In a flash, Patch drew his gun and pointed it uncertainly through the open doorway towards Omar. Simon threw himself on top of Pippa, and Rob kicked at the door. It slid half shut, but the gun muzzle was still visible and the threat very much alive. Omar sat transfixed by the gun and the eye behind it. *So, it ends here*, he thought; then smiled; then laughed.

Patch's good eye widened in surprise and then he dropped his gun.

"That's better," murmured the Scottish burr. "Have I missed anything?"

Eyes turned to Sandy, who stood behind Patch with a handgun jammed against the gangster's head, but easily covering Don at the side of the Mexican. The militia raised their weapons but weren't sure what to do, with their boss and a teammate between them and the armed pensioner.

"Look what I nearly pissed on," Sandy said, although his eyes said something else entirely. "What happens next?"

"The endgame," said Deke, having caught a flash in his wing mirror. Before anyone could ask what the hell he was on about, a second Storm Snatchers van pulled off the road and crunched to a halt side-on to the pickup and the SUV at the rear of Van One.

The driver leaned out of his window, apparently oblivious to the militia team, which now found itself in the middle of a fast-developing situation, with no idea of what was to happen and unsure where to point their weapons.

"Afternoon," he smiled. "Twister, we need to catch up with the other vans north of Big Bend."

Twister turned towards Don and pointed north.

"Maybe we head that way to find some storms for these fine people; you head back towards the border with your Mexican friend; and we never speak of this again."

Patch spat on the ground. "We take the Afghan with us. They can't stop us. We have the guns."

"Not true," said Twister. "You don't have all of them."

As he spoke, six men in US Army combat gear and carrying automatic weapons emerged from the other side of the van and from behind the pickup and the SUV, each focused on a specific target.

"The photographers!" exclaimed Rob. "You can trust no one in that van!"

"That's harsh, logistics boy," grinned the nearest soldier, his eyes never shifting from his target. "Drop your weapons, gentlemen. I won't ask you a second time."

The militiamen did as they were told and stepped back from their guns with their hands behind their heads.

Simon lifted himself off his wife and checked she was okay.

"I'm fine, thank you, hero," she smiled, "But you have that look…"

"I'm okay."

He climbed out of the van and walked over to Patch, still being covered by Sandy.

"You threatened us. I'm going to make sure you never threaten us again." He raised his hand, and Patch flinched. "Activate your phone and give it to me."

Patch frowned, then slowly removed his phone from a pocket and handed it over. Thirty seconds later, Simon handed it back, then carried out the same process with the rest of the militia.

All the while, the low rumble from the south grew louder, developing into a thundering roar as Air Force One climbed into the sky above them. Van One's passengers tumbled out to get a better look, and the militiamen stared upwards as if they had never seen a plane before. Only the 'photographers' and Simon Pope remained focused on the situation on the ground. The soldiers picked up the militia weapons and removed the ammunition before placing the guns in the back of the pickup. Pope used his own phone to send a couple of messages and waited for the replies. By the time the second one arrived, the presidential jet was just a diminishing grumble emanating from the clouds above.

"Here's the deal," he said, looking each militiaman - especially Patch - in the eye. "I get very angry when people threaten my family and my friends. In the past, people have suffered terribly as a result." He paused, reflecting on what he was saying. "Many, many people."

Everybody within earshot believed him implicitly.

"Times have changed," he continued. "But I want to make sure that none of you even consider coming for any of us again. Ever. Check your phones." The militiamen checked.

"You have mobile banking. Some of you have debit and credit cards on your phones. Access them."

The militiamen did as they were told. At least, they tried to. The looks on their faces changed from puzzlement to consternation to realisation, then fear.

"We control your phones and everything you have on them," Pope explained. "Bank accounts. Emails. Messages. Photographs. We can review historical data; send it to the police, the FBI, the tax authorities. Anybody we want. We can write threatening or insulting messages and send them to your contacts under your name. We can spend your money or stop you from spending it. Do you understand?"

The looks on their faces gave him his answer.

He turned to Patch. "One wrong move, *amigo*. Just one tiny misjudgement..."

Patch sneered, but the tears welling in his good eye betrayed the bravado.

Pope shook his head, then waved his arms at his surroundings. "All of this," he said. "And for no good reason. Just a case of mistaken identity." He took a few thoughtful paces, winked at Pippa and then turned and looked once more at the downcast faces in front of him.

"We only have a few days left on this trip, and I'd like them to be good ones," he said. "Once we've left the USA, you will have control of your finances again, but if I ever hear of any threat or action against the friends I leave over here... Now, I suggest you get back to your vehicles and head back south."

The militiamen headed to their vehicles, apart from Don, who walked over to Simon.

"It's only a few days, but some of my guys earn very little," he said. "They'll struggle."

"Which is why I'll release your phone tomorrow. I look after my people. You look after yours. And think carefully before taking on another wild-goose chase."

The militiaman tipped his Stetson and strolled to his SUV. Nobody else moved until the three vehicles had turned around and headed back down the wet road. Sandy handed his gun back to Twister.

"I grabbed it from the compartment under the seat and jammed it down my trousers," he said. "Made walking naturally difficult."

"There was no ammunition in it."

"Aye," said the Scot. "I know. And the vanguard became the rearguard, did it?"

Twister looked across at the soldiers stowing their gear into their van and nodded.

"They were concealed behind an advertising hoarding. You were all listening to Omar as we drove past them. They were just about to follow when they spotted the SUVs and let us know. We figured letting things play out was the best option."

"Can you really do that?" Pope turned to see Rob and Amy staring at him. "Can you really control their phones?"

"Me? No. I wouldn't have a clue how to do it."

"But you didn't say 'me', did you, Simon?" Amy took a step forward. "You said 'we'."

"Yes, I did, didn't I?" Simon smiled at the 'married couple' in front of him. "I guess we all have our little secrets."

The Usual Stuff

Andrew Blackwell sat on his sofa wearing a wrinkled white t-shirt, a faded blue tartan dressing gown and a pair of underpants, staring at one smartphone, with a second lying on the coffee table in conference call mode. His canine houseguests lay on their beds near the television, keeping a close eye on any movement he made in case it showed breakfast was on the way.

"Any news?"

Fred and Ginger - the Popes' dogs - glanced at the coffee table, having never heard one talk before, never mind in an Irish accent.

"Not yet, Connor. Thanks for responding so quickly, especially at this time in the morning."

"Ah, the phones were easy to identify. They came in almost at the same time and from the same geolocation. Besides, you know me, Andy. I've been up since four. I can never wait to see how the numbers have changed overnight."

"Go on then." Blackwell knew the younger Kelly was bursting to tell somebody the latest figures, and he needed something to take his mind off his storm-chasing neighbours and whatever crisis they were facing. "Tell me what they are."

"Membership is up 98 million…"

Blackwell whistled. "That's doubled in just over a fortnight."

"*Trebled*, Andy. Membership is up *by* 98 million; not *to* 98 million. We're now at 146 and we have just under $2 billion in the bank, and counting. There was a massive increase from the USA. Can't say for sure, but there was a lot of media coverage of the president visiting a smashed-up town in Texas overnight our time. Apparently, *Path Finder* people were controlling the recovery operations."

"We don't have people anywhere."

"We have 146 million, all over the place."

Blackwell leaned back and stared out of the lounge window at the line of trees over the lane, blowing in the wind. He didn't know whether to feel delighted by Connor's news or worried. Taking responsibility and responding to those in need was one thing. Putting FEMA's nose out of joint and, by association, the US government's, was quite another. The vibration in his hand disturbed his train of thought.

"Crisis resolved," he reported after reading the text. "Keep those phones frozen for a week apart from one. I'll send you the details. Release that one tomorrow."

"Right you are. What was the craic?"

Andy flicked through the message from Pope.

"Border vigilantes...blah...road abduction...blah... photographers...blah...US special forces...blah...Air Force One...blah...old Scotsman with a handgun."

"Ah, right," said Connor. "The usual stuff then."

The Slip Up

In the medical facility aboard Air Force One, the President's physician looked at the x-rays of David D. Clampett's shoulder. He wondered yet again if the middle D actually stood for dumbass.

Demonstrating fitness and youthful vigour by running up mobile boarding stairs into an aircraft was one thing. Doing so after sheltering from a storm of biblical proportions for ninety minutes, then sprinting up the treacherous, slippery steps in the vain hope the rain wouldn't make your hair dye run was quite another.

Fortunately, the slip and trip had occurred on the penultimate step, causing Clampett to disappear as he fell awkwardly into the plane and slammed heavily onto the floor, causing damage to his arm.

The media had been as anxious as their leader to get out of the rain and had moved before he was even halfway up the stairs.

Now, they were settling down, tired and damp, while the flight attendants distributed coffee and biscuits. The pilot had given them an unusually long pre-flight briefing, slipping in a warning that the flight was being delayed to ensure the storm had moved away from the planned flight path. Nobody was going to object when their safety was at risk.

"Mister President, you dislocated your shoulder, sir," the doctor revealed. "There are no fractures, but I'm reluctant to attempt a closed reduction here. That could cause more damage to the joint and surrounding tissues. We'll get you to the hospital as soon as we land. In the meantime, I'm going to give you some local anaesthetic and will then immobilise your arm in a sling."

"I'll need painkillers, doc. Lots of 'em," Clampett winced, looking close to tears. He hadn't avoided the draft four times just to be struck down now that he was the most powerful man on earth. Life could be so unfair. The jet prepared for takeoff; the loud engines masking the president's screams. Once the stricken Clampett and his ashen-faced entourage had taken their seats in the forward cabin, the pilot and first officer taxied to the end of the runway, and requested permission to take off.

The air traffic controller picked up the radio receiver behind the counter of the airfield's café. "Hell, this is the back of beyond in Texas, boy. You can head off whenever you like."

The pilot's anxiety to escape between the weather formations on his reports, and the need to deliver the invalid back to Washington as quickly as possible outweighed his concern over the lack of control tower process. Sixty seconds later, the plane was in the air, much to the relief of everyone on board.

Jared Pfist gazed out of a window and shuddered as the plane flew over the path of destruction caused by the recent tornado. *You get a sense of the devastation when you're on the ground*, he thought, *but not the scale.*

The plane banked to the east and then headed northwards, following a highway back to civilisation and safety. He caught sight of a group of vehicles parked clumsily at the side of the road. "What's going on down there?" he asked the back of the seat in front of him.

Grace Hampton dragged her eyes from her mobile phone and took in the view. "Looks like a group of paintballers," she said, then returned to her phone. As long as they kept their guns pointed away from her plane, she didn't really care.

Jared watched the paintballers watching him until the trajectory and course of the jet meant they disappeared from view.

He took a sip of his coffee and relaxed, relishing every moment of peace until the seatbelt signs went out. Then he would have to feign concern for his ailing boss, and they'd all have to work out the significance or otherwise of this trip away from the office.

The Optics

The C-32A hummed happily along at 32,000 feet, basking in its identity for the day as Air Force One. The president sat reclined in his personal cabin, shoes off, tie askew, and high as a kite from the administered painkillers and self-administered alcohol.

His left arm rested awkwardly in the sling across his chest while his right hand picked individual cashews from a crystal bowl. A muted TV showed footage from the South Texas Falls visit on a loop - the president hugging children, nodding at rubble, and misnaming the Path Finder movement twice in one clip.

Grace Hampton stood in front of him, holding an electronic tablet. Jared Pfist hovered near the drinks cart, nursing a major headache, and a growing sense of unease.

"We're getting good cable pickup," Grace said. "Fox went with *Clampett Comforts Victims, Calls for Unity.* CNN ran it as *Tornado Unites Americans - Briefly.*"

"What about the social feed?" Clampett asked, flicking cashew crumbs off his windbreaker. Grace hesitated. Jared answered.

"Uh, mixed bag, sir. The hug photo is trending. That's good."

"Of course it is. I'm a terrific hugger."

"But so is she," Jared added. "The Path Finder. Carmen Vega."

Clampett squinted. "Does she have a TikTok?"

"Yes. And a name," Jared said. "Carmen's getting traction. There's a clip of her helping load medical supplies while you're talking about fridge symbolism."

"And who the hell came up with fridge symbolism again?" Clampett demanded, his anger diminished by the feeling he was floating at the top of the cabin, looking down on them all, including himself.

"That doesn't matter," Grace cut in briskly, before anyone else could say anything. "The net effect is... well, the optics are bifurcating."

Clampett blinked, feeling a little queasy with all the bumping against the ceiling. "The what are doing what now?"

"Sir," Grace sighed, "Your 'moment of unity' is being interpreted as her moment of leadership. You look like the federal guest star on Carmen's show."

He stared at the ceiling slightly too long, because others looked up as well, but he couldn't see himself anywhere, even though his mind could see them all from above. "She was supposed to be the damn backdrop."

Jared coughed. "Also, she's doing a livestream. Right now. With a kid translating her into sign language."

"Jesus," Clampett said. "That's emotional and inclusive."

"Yep," said Grace. "People love her."

The president sat forward, his feet firmly on the floor. "Do we have anything on her?"

"Nothing bad," Jared muttered. "Vegan, volunteers everywhere, no scandal, no unpaid parking tickets. She's not even a card-carrying member of Path Finder." He noticed the hope glimmer in his boss's eyes and added hastily, "But only because they don't issue cards to members."

"And she's not even running for anything?"

"If she ever does," Grace said, "We're screwed. Especially if the rest of them are like her."

There was a long silence, then the president spoke. "Alright. Fine. If this Path Finder outfit wants to get cute, let's invite her to Washington."

Jared's eyes narrowed, while Grace's started blinking unusually quickly. "Like... meet with her?"

"No," Clampett said. "Give her a medal or something; one of those things that says 'power has noticed you.' Then we - and the media - will forget about her by Thursday."

Grace didn't respond.

He looked up. "What?"

She spoke carefully. "Just... sometimes when you shine a spotlight on somebody, they don't fade. They grow stronger."

Clampett waved her off; the movement made him feel light-headed. "I've been in this business for years. I know how to bury a headline. People tell me I do it better than anybody else. Anybody."

The muted TV flicked to a new clip - Carmen Vega, handing out nappies to mothers, standing ankle-deep in mud and laughing as a child hugged her. The caption at the bottom of the screen read: *Community First: Path Finder Inspires Amid Crisis.*

"Turn that crap off," the president muttered and promptly threw up.

Jared let the doctor and nurse deal with the puke and turned off the news. The next segment was bound to cover the thunderstorm disaster and the major spoke inserted into the party's immigration wheel. The president didn't look as if he could remember any of that, so it could wait. As far as Jared was concerned, it could wait forever.

Realisation

Once the flight was safely on the ground at Joint Base Andrews, a pale-looking, one-armed president walked carefully down the moonlit forward steps, and straight into the waiting ambulance, along with the doctor and nurse.

The media stayed on the plane with the blinds down until he had gone. His deputy chief-of-staff waited until the ambulance moved, then jumped in the back seat of the presidential limousine to follow. Grace Hampton was already there, deep in conversation on her phone. The call wasn't going well. Grace's eyelids were a blur of motion as she struggled to remain calm and keep the incandescent fury out of her voice. By the time they arrived at the hospital, she was burning with rage, letting loose a string of invective that caused the embarrassed driver - a former marine - to blush.

Neither passenger attempted to leave the vehicle, even though their boss was being wheeled into the medical centre, surrounded by strangers and doped up to the eyeballs.

"She's not coming, is she?" Jared asked.

"There's too much to do in Texas. FEMA is struggling after the cuts. Path Finder has stumped up the required cash. Volunteers are flooding in to help. Our friend Carmen will manage operations on the ground until we get our act together, which could be never. We look helpless."

"She's turning down the chance to visit the White House, receive an award and meet the president? Path Finder will go nuts, missing out on that recognition."

"She says people and places come first, not honours or recognition."

Jared almost threw up, then looked inspired. "The media will flood down there. She'd be better keeping them out of the way by coming to Washington."

Grace shook her head. "I think Mindy Abbott has talked to the media. Mindy is a very smart cookie. She knows she has the story of the decade - maybe the century. You've seen the membership figures. I think all the key media are signed-up members of the club. They're holding off and will blackball any freelancer or social media outfit that goes for a scoop."

Jared looked incredulous. "Seriously? Why?"

"Time will tell, but if I were a gambler..." Grace looked pensive. "I think we could have a major problem on our hands. And if we do, then so does every government, political party, oligarch, religious leader, cult leader and anyone else who believes they hold the power."

"So who will hold the power? And what will they do with it?"

Grace's blinking slowed down purely because her eye muscles were exhausted.

"That, deputy chief of staff, is what we need to find out. But revolution is in the air."

The Mute Button

Andy and Mindy sat with their backs against one of the trees at the edge of the open field, enjoying the sunshine and watching the two dogs mooch around.

The UK's former prime minister was reminiscing yet again about his time 'on the run' - or hiding, as Mindy remembered it. Describing how two policemen who were part of the nationwide search operation intercepted and questioned Pope and himself as they left this very field, he was about to reach the part where the officers left without recognising him, when his phone rang.

"The White House," he announced, turning on the speakerphone. By the time the operator had checked she had the right person and put him through to the Oval Office, Mindy had placed her phone in record mode next to his, and both dogs had trotted over to see what the fuss was about, and whether it involved any treats.

"Andy! It's been a while."

"Mr President. Good to hear from you. I was sorry to hear about your accident. I hope you've recovered?"

Three and a half thousand miles away, David D. Clampett looked down at the sling. "I'm getting there, thanks," he said. "I hear I'm not the only one who's been busy lately. Aston Hail was telling me about your chat in Ireland."

So much for the non-disclosure agreement.

"In fact," continued the president, "We met up with one of your people down in Texas the other day. Carmen Vega. A very capable woman. She's doing a great job around South Texas Falls. You must be very proud of her."

Blackwell looked across at Mindy. She just shrugged. Neither had a clue who Carmen Vega was.

"I admire anyone trying to improve the situation down there, David. But I'm afraid I don't know Ms. Vega personally. We have no control over the individuals who have joined *Path Finder*. We're busy setting out the aims - or destinations - of the organisation, which we're encouraging individuals and groups to aim for, finding their own paths to get there. Sounds like Carmen and her team are ahead of the game."

"Andy," said Clampett, "Bear with me a minute, would you?" He muted the call and looked at his staff. "She's flying solo - raising the funds, organising the volunteers and running a *Path Finder* operation with no approval or recognition. She's a fraud. That's our story. And if Blackwell won't work with us to control *Path Finder* in our nation..."

"Then we'll take *Path Finder* down as well," Pfist smiled. "We can't have people running around doing good stuff that we should do and attracting others to their cause. There'll be anarchy; groups competing to do more good than other groups. Maybe even groups getting together to rise against the government and to change the system. That constitutes a threat to order, and we all know the love the American people have for the word 'constitution' - especially those who eat a lot of fast food."

"If they won't play nice, then we'll proscribe the group as a terrorist organisation, bent on destroying the fabric of our nation and others. We'll kill this thing before it's off the ground."

Clampett nodded. "We'll invite Andy over to talk about his baby. Then we'll put our cards on the table. If he plays nice, then we play nice."

Grace Hampton always got a little turned on when her boss went a little mafioso. "And if he doesn't, boss?"

"Then we feed him to the fishes. Let's get him back on the line... Andy? Sorry about that. Just needed to approve a shipment of weapons to somewhere. Listen. I'd like to hear what *Path Finder* offers and how the government of the United States of America can get involved. How are you fixed to fly over for a chat with me and my team sometime soon? We could arrange for Carmen to be here at the same time. Would be nice for you guys to meet up."

Pfist could barely stop himself from squealing in delight. *Genius!*

Blackwell was silent for a while as he absorbed the offer.

"I'm tied up for the next day or so, David," he said. "How about the weekend?"

"I'm supposed to be away golfing but... you know what... this is more important than golf. There! Something I never thought I'd say!"

Blackwell laughed politely, arranged for the White House people to talk to his people, then hung up. The greyhounds watched him expectantly, then wandered off when no treats were forthcoming. Mindy stopped the recording, checked it had worked by playing part of it, then backed it up by emailing the file to herself and her fiancé.

"Sounds like your weekend will be busy," she smiled.

"Oh, I'm sure it will."

"You're not going though, are you?"

"Hell no."

"And when are you going to tell him his mute button doesn't work?"

"I'm not sure I will."

The New Path Finder

The drive north turned into something of a marathon after Twister revisited his laptop and held a telephone conference call with the guides in the other vans.

"Today is a bust," he announced to Van One, "But tomorrow could turn into something special. The two vans at Big Bend are moving on to Midland, and we'll catch up with them there. We'll stop on the way, but I'd like to put some miles between ourselves and this place first, just in case."

Nobody objected. In fact, no-one spoke until the vans halted to refuel ninety minutes later and both sets of passengers headed for the restrooms and the food store. Rob, Amy and Twister had an intense conversation with the leader of Van Four, while everyone else mingled together, exchanging knowing smiles but without saying much in the busy building.

Simon and Pippa sat with a coffee and a burger before returning with extra supplies to the van, where Omar and Sandy were sitting on the back seat, in deep conversation.

"I have just learned two interesting facts," declared Sandy to the new arrivals. "Omar called me Kaka back there. Apparently, Kaka is Pashto for uncle. It's a mark of respect for older people, which is a relief, because the only other time I've heard the term was when an Israeli soldier swore at me."

"That's worth knowing," laughed Pippa. "What was the other one?"

"That young Omar here is a Path Finder."

"Really?"

Omar nodded, then recounted a tale that involved a shepherd in the mountains of Tajikistan, a lecture from a book salesman on the plane to Istanbul, eavesdropping a conversation between a mother and daughter on the way to Madrid and hearing a dog discuss *Path Finder* with a duck in a Glasgow pub. "Although I may have dreamt the dog and the duck. I was on a flight to Bogota."

Waiting for the Mission van to pick him up in Mexico City, Omar searched for *Path Finder* online, and signed up. "I figured if it appealed to all those people, it was worth a look, and might appeal to me," he explained. "I was right."

"Tell them the rest, laddie," urged Sandy.

Omar hesitated, concerned about how his next revelation was going to land.

"I accessed the site and joined using the browser on my phone," he said. "For the next couple of days, the phone was unusually slow. Messages seemed to arrive in batches. Web pages took an age to download. I worried about the people who had helped me escape, because I didn't hear from them and couldn't get in touch using the secure messaging app. Once I settled in Santa Esperanza, my phone was fine again. I put it down to signal strength and the local network..."

"But then we heard you putting the fear of God into those good ol' boys," interrupted Sandy. "You were very confident in your ability to control their mobiles, yet you only had each phone in your hands for a short time. Just long enough, I reckon, to access the *Path Finder* website..."

Pope looked at the old man, whose face was a picture of innocent curiosity, but whose eyes betrayed a more intense interest in the issue.

"Like you said earlier, Pete told you my links might be useful if we hit trouble. Fact is, there are millions of people who have signed up to *Path Finder*; not all of them with the best of intentions - some governments, intelligence agencies, hacker groups and so on. From the little I understand, the systems check out each source before allowing access to the site. That can cause minor, short-term issues for some users. Omar's travelling across the world would not have helped. If there's no obvious problem, it releases the machine, but it leaves a bit of code on each applicant's system as a safety mechanism. It monitors any potential threats to *Path Finder* and would take action to encourage individuals and organisations to leave it alone. That's what happened today."

"Isn't that illegal?"

"It's in the terms and conditions. They have to be accepted before you can apply for access to the site."

"But nobody ever reads them."

Simon shrugged.

"What software and systems does it use?"

Pippa jumped and turned to see Rob and Amy standing at the side door carrying bags of food and drink. At this rate, the van wouldn't need to stop for sustenance until it reached Alaska.

"I don't know," admitted Simon. "But it works - in fact you saw that today - and it's only used for protection and to guarantee the survival of *Path Finder* and its members. Nothing else."

"But it could be a powerful weapon in the hands of others," said Rob.

"So can a piece of paper," observed Sandy. "Sign it and start a war. Write on it and gain massive and undeserved influence. Or read what's on it and act on the lies."

"Who's for potato chips?" asked Amy to break the sombre silence that followed.

Heads Up

It was just after midnight when the vans finally arrived at a smart-looking hotel on the edge of Midland. The weary travellers dragged their bags off the vehicles and headed for reception, only to be interrupted by cheers and applause from the bar area, just off the lobby.

The rest of the tour had enjoyed an excellent day at Big Bend and had stayed up to welcome the stragglers. It was the first real time during the week that the guests had mixed properly, and Omar blended right in.

Nobody knew who he was and couldn't be sure they had seen him before, but that was the same with others on the trip and they were four pints into their evening, so who the hell cared?

Besides, his English was cute; although most of the women thought his father-in-law's Scottish brogue was more romantic, but sadly unintelligible.

At around one o'clock, Twister rang the bell on the bar to get everyone's attention.

"Thank you all for your patience today," he started. "Tomorrow, looking at the latest data, we have hot, dry air from New Mexico looking for a hot date with the warm, humid air surging northward from the Gulf." He waited for the wolf whistles to die down.

Rob placed his hand on Simon's shoulder and whispered excitedly, "This is going to be good. He never goes into detail… never encourages the T word… unless he's pretty sure…"

"It looks like a mid-level trough should swing in from the Four Corners region, which could provide the lift and wind shear we so desperately need," continued Twister.

Rob spotted Simon's frown. "Four Corners is the only point in the US where four states share a common boundary," he muttered. "Arizona, Colorado, New Mexico and Utah."

"Ah, a bit like in England where Lincolnshire, Rutland, Northamptonshire and Cambridgeshire meet near Stamford," Simon muttered back.

"Although there are some people who think there's a twenty-metre discrepancy," interjected Pippa.

Rob stared at his new friends and grinned. "You *are* geeks, after all. I just knew it. Amy owes me big time."

"With a fair wind," said Twister, allowing himself an awful pun that drew a few groans from his audience, "This setup should give us surface winds from the southeast with dew points in the upper 60s, and mid-level winds from the southwest with speeds of 50 knots, creating strong wind shear and the possibility of…?"

"Supercells!" shouted the crowd.

"Giving us a good chance of…?"

"Tornadoes!" they shrieked.

While he waited for the noise to die down, Twister caught sight of the two middle-aged female bartenders, who looked as if their shift should have finished at eleven and were desperate for the night to end.

"We leave at nine," he concluded. "Get to bed, but help these young ladies first by bringing your glasses and any trash back to the bar."

Decision Time

Mindy put down the phone and sighed. "They're being very persistent," she shouted through the kitchen door of their house.

Andy was next to the barbecue on the patio, basting chicken drumsticks in an oriental marinade and placing them on the grill. The hot charcoal beneath hissed as the sauce dripped onto it. The UK's former prime minister set a timer on his mobile phone, consulted the instructions he had printed out from a website, carried out the same process with the pork spare ribs and set a second alarm.

"Who are?" he asked, distracted by the challenge he'd set himself. There was no Simon Pope to rescue this project. Everything had to be perfect. Showing zero confidence in his skills as a chef, the two dogs lay on their beds in the kitchen and focused on Mindy as she prepared their tea.

"Clampett's people. Their boss is holding on to his tee time for Sunday, but he has a four-star general, a justice from the Supreme Court and a bishop in his four-ball. He doesn't want them turning up for no reason."

"That's bull. He's never going to play golf with that shoulder." The fat from the chicken skin had sparked the charcoal into blazing life again, so he grabbed the water gun and sprayed a fine mist to calm everything down.

"We need to give him an answer. If it isn't you, then who?"

"I put a call in to Ireland. Just waiting for a response."

"Martin and Mavis? They're shattered after hosting…"

"Connor."

The silence from the kitchen was deafening. Blackwell was busy turning the chicken when the quiet voice behind him made him jump.

"Connor? Have you gone mad? We can't let…"

"Not to go! I just want to find out how far *Path Finder* has made it into the White House. We know Clampett plans to play hardball if he can't get his way. I want to avoid that. We're about cooperation; not confrontation. If it's possible, I want to show him that the former is preferable for all of us, but especially for him."

He sprayed water again as pork fat dripped onto the charcoal and the flames rose once more.

"So, either we do a demo, or somebody goes over for a chat…"

Andy looked down as his phone started to flash and vibrate on the patio table.

"I guess we're about to find out," he said.

Debris On The Ground

By mid-afternoon the following day, towering cumulus had developed along the dryline and exploded into discrete supercells. One particularly well-organised storm had formed north of the Red River and was drifting northeast towards Oklahoma.

"That's our target," Twister broadcast to the occupants of the four vans parked up nose-to-tail alongside a rural highway in north Texas.

Each van's passengers craned their necks to see their driver's laptop showing the big high-precipitation supercell that was, in fact, plainly visible roughly six miles to the north and west of them. Heavy rain wrapped the storm's mesocyclone, but from the safety of their vantage point - and to Amy's delight - Rob reckoned he could make out some broad rotation.

Pippa leaned forward and pointed at some formations on the radar that were between them and the main event, looking like reluctant children on a walk with their parents.

"Outflow boundaries, also known as gust fronts," explained Deke. "They separate storm-cooled air from the surrounding air and act like mini cold fronts. They can trigger messy, less obvious storms, so we'll monitor the ones closest to us."

The opening bars of *Thunderstruck* filled Van One, and Twister took the brief call from a friendly chaser, positioned closer to the action.

"The storm's speeding up to the northeast," he said, getting confirmation of the report from the updated radar information on the laptop. "It'll cross the road network."

Deke started the van, turned it around onto the road and waited for the others to do the same, while Twister spoke into the radio handset.

"We're heading south for a few miles," he announced. "Then we'll cut east, get ahead of the supercell and intercept again in Oklahoma."

Deke glanced at the laptop. "Looks like we should avoid that gust front, but we might hit the trailing rain core," he said, pointing at the screen. "Free van wash!" He waited for the other vans to join the convoy, then headed off.

The excitement in the van was palpable, even more so as light rain hit the windscreen.

Even Omar - who could be forgiven for having more important things on his mind, and who had narrowly avoided a tornado only a week before - felt the thrill of the chase. For someone who had been the hunted for over a year, it made a welcome change.

As the wind increased and the miles sped by, the excitement diminished as the sky turned charcoal and the tidal wave of precipitation to their right swallowed up the furthest white turbines in a wind farm, then engulfed more as it forged a path towards them.

"Those of you on the right of the van," instructed Deke, driving as quickly as possible without risking immediate loss of control, "Grab a coat, a bag, anything you have and hold it against the window next to you, just in case that core plans to launch hail at us."

Twister focused on the radar picture.

"Hail might be the least of our problems," he muttered, before grabbing the radio once again. "Radar isn't showing it, but there may be a surprise in this storm," he said, forcing himself to keep as calm as possible.

As he spoke, sheets of water smashed hard against the windows of each vehicle. Even on max, the wipers couldn't cope, making it difficult to pick anything out other than the disappearance of the turbines in the looming and darkening grey mass.

"We're punching through, but brace for impact." Deke leaned forward to enhance visibility, his face illuminated by a ghostly greenish tinge in the sky.

Rob and Amy lifted their knees onto the back of the seats in front of them and wrapped their arms around both sides of their heads, clasping their hands at the back. Omar, petrified, held onto the seat in front of him and prayed that his adventure would not end so close to its conclusion. Sandy simply looked at peace. He sat with his arms folded and eyes closed, being rocked from side to side as Deke fought the buffeting winds. Simon followed Rob's lead and braced his knees against a seat back, one arm holding onto the same seat and the other around Pippa, who looked at him and smiled nervously.

"Next time I try to force you to take me on a trip, remind me of this moment," she said.

"You think I'm going anywhere else after this? You'll be lucky to get me out of the house."

Seconds later, just after a cry of "Debris on the ground!" over the radio coincided with Deke deciding it wasn't fun anymore and he should have stayed in the Marines, Van One punched through the far edge of the core.

The van no longer swerved from side to side. The rain eased, and silence replaced the roar they hadn't realised was there until it wasn't.

"Van One out. Van One out," Twister reported into the radio as the van cruised on for a couple of hundred yards before coming to a halt with its hazard lights flashing, alongside a small grain storage facility that gave some shelter from the wind-driven drizzle. Everyone stayed still, as if any movement might draw the attention of the heaving mass powering on behind them.

"Everyone okay?" asked Deke.

"Van Four out. Van Four out," interrupted the radio call. "We think Two and Three got hit. They just disappeared in front of us."

"Crap."

Van Four pulled up alongside and the passengers from both vehicles spilled out to watch the EF1 tornado barrel away from them over the fields on the other side of the road, throwing debris into the air like a drunk would the last, overlooked box of confetti at the end of a wedding reception.

"Load up!" shouted Twister. "We go back."

Just as the vans turned onto the road, the radio crackled into life.

"Van Three. We're okay. Bumps and bruises only, plus a couple of panel dents. Van Two is similar but has a broken radio aerial, a cracked side window and will need a tow from the field it's in."

A murmur of relief spread through both rescue vehicles before the radio crackled again.

"Man. We got hit by a twister and survived!" The whoops and hollers filtered through the speakers like a freezing fog. And just like that, the overriding sentiment in Vans One and Four switched from relief to something else. Envy.

"Do we really need to help?" came an anonymous voice from Van Four. "I hope you like smug, 'cause them folks'll be serving it by the gallon."

Sae Muckle Fun

The bar in the nondescript, but comfortable three-star hotel in Ardmore, Oklahoma was heaving with storm chasers sharing their stories of a tumultuous day.

None attracted attention more than the Storm Stalkers or, more specifically, those chasers from the two tornado-hit vans.

"We can barely see a thing when, suddenly, there's this whirling grey column that appears like a ghost out of the rain just ahead of us and then vanishes again. We're wondering what we saw, then the van lifts off its wheels on the nearside and slams down again, but by then we've lost control and smash into the rail guards by a culvert."

"One minute I'm on the road, driving through a waterfall, and the next minute all I can see is a field ahead of me and all kinds of things flying my way. I just dived to the floor."

"We just sat there holding on tight. The vans rocking violently, and not in a good way."

"I thought it was the end. I didn't pray; I was too busy crapping myself."

"I just sat there, wondering if the potato chips all over the floor were still edible, when Pete asked if we'd still get to see the big tornado and Zeke says, 'Bro, you *were* the big tornado.'"

Each of them was easily identifiable thanks to the *A twister hit me and I'm still standing!* t-shirts that were designed, printed and delivered to the hotel even before the survivors had arrived, thanks to an enterprising young woman in Van Three. And now, each of them was recouping the cost of their clothing by happily accepting drinks for selfies or for interviews that were appearing in real time online.

The rest of the tour sat in small groups at the far side of the bar, happy to deny any knowledge of the events of the day and to decompress. It had been a stressful 36 hours.

Simon glanced across at Twister and Omar, who were sitting with the photographers.

"Penny for your thoughts?" ventured Pippa.

"I was just about to make them the same offer."

Rob looked across and used his lip-reading skills.

"Wibble blob hotel the wheel me... That's all I got," he reported.

"Impressive," Amy snorted.

"Let's see you do better."

She fell silent for a minute as she sipped her gin and tonic and watched the small group at the far table. "No," she yawned, "I'm getting nothing and I'm tired. I need my sleep."

She finished her drink, then leaned over to hug Pippa as Rob downed his own drink and stood alongside her.

"Not sure I can take much more of that love-in over there," he smiled, nodding toward the large huddle of storm chasers. "See you guys tomorrow."

The couple strolled out of the bar, stopping for a brief word with Twister on the way.

"I guess it's time I turned in as well," said Sandy. "It's been a bit full-on, hasn't it?"

Pippa looked at the old man's pale face and realised he was exhausted. Even the sparkle in his eyes had dulled, although the smile on his face remained.

She thought back to two nights earlier and what she and Simon had overheard in Sandy's room.

"What do you think Morag would have made of the last couple of days, Sandy?" she asked, unsure why she'd said it. Simon sat with his beer halfway to his lips, not wanting to make a move that might impact what was going to happen next.

"Morag? Oh…" The Scot's chin dropped to his chest for a few seconds, then he lifted his head and the sparkle was back. "I think she'd have laughed at me using my accent for effect in the Garrison. She'd have whacked me around the head for waving an empty gun around yesterday and risking…" His chin dropped again, but his audience could see him blinking back the tears. "Her heart would have been in her mouth again today when we ploughed through that storm."

In for a penny, thought Pippa. "And if she were here now…?"

"She'd be sitting just there." He pointed to the chair vacated by Amy. "Shaking her head from side to side. Eyes wide open; mouth tight, trying not to laugh. '*Ya numpty*,' she'd say. '*Whit for be dowie when ye're having sae muckle fun?*'"

"Not just fun, Kaka."

The words made both Popes jump. Omar stood behind them; hands in his pockets.

"You saved my life as well. Why be down when you had so much fun *and* saved a life?"

"What on earth does tomorrow hold for Sandy Irvine?" laughed Pippa, tears in her own eyes.

"Hopefully more of the same," the Scotsman nodded and smiled, still gazing at the empty chair. "More of the same."

Great Minds

It was an incredibly rare occasion for Andrew Blackwell, former prime minister and First Lord of the Treasury, to be found sitting on a sofa in the middle of the day wearing only underpants and an old dressing gown, but recently, it was becoming something of a habit.

"Couldn't sleep," was his explanation to his fiancée, who had enjoyed a rare lie-in and had only just emerged from the bedroom. "Then I couldn't be bothered with climbing the stairs again to get dressed; plus I didn't want to put you off your attempt at the world record for snoring. Were you trying for frequency or loudness?"

He ducked as a cushion from an armchair flew towards his head.

"Some of us were busy yesterday, working hard until late into the night," Mindy announced, flouncing out. "Unlike others, who spent their evening drinking gin and discussing strategic options for the White House with a couple of greyhounds."

Andy looked up at the empty doorway. "That's not true," he told it. "Fred was asleep. I was only talking to Ginger."

On hearing their names, both dogs looked up hopefully from their beds, only to settle back down when it was obvious no treats were on offer.

"Not that you were much help," Andy muttered at the fawn dog. "Too busy licking your unmentionables."

"Did you come to any decisions?" Mindy called as the kettle boiled. Realising the noise would drown his reply, Andy got up and wandered into the kitchen.

"I think we need somebody in there to talk to him, face to face," he said. "We need to show our capabilities without revealing what they are, if that makes sense. But we also need to show him we're not a threat, unless he makes us one. And that *Path Finder* offers him as many opportunities as it does anyone else."

Mindy made a second coffee, then brought them both to the small kitchen table and sat down.

Neither of them spoke for a while; the only sounds came from the wall clock, gentle snores from the front room and the birds in the garden.

"I love the tranquility we have here," she sighed.

"Me too."

"It will not last though."

"No."

Both fell silent once more; their future now the focus of their thoughts. The soft pad of paws announced the arrival of Ginger, wondering where all the noise had gone. She walked to Mindy and gazed into her eyes until Mindy gave in and gave her a reassuring stroke.

"The Popes must be missing the dogs terribly," observed Andy. "I know I'll miss these two when they've gone, and they'll only be next door."

Mindy didn't reply; at least, not straightaway. Ginger's arrival followed by Andy's words had planted a seed of an idea, and she needed some time to let it grow.

"Actually," Andy continued, in one of those rare moments when he inadvertently proved to Mindy that he wasn't a total idiot, "Are you thinking what I'm thinking?"

Mindy smiled. The Popes' flight home was Saturday, arriving Sunday. Maybe a brief stopover in Washington D.C., a tour of the White House and a brief chat with the president would provide a fitting conclusion to a memorable break.

"You *are* thinking what I'm thinking!" grinned Andy. "We're getting a couple of dogs!"

Black Hawk

The military Black Hawk came in low, its dark silhouette emerging through the dawn's early light. As it drew close, the air filled with a heavy *whup-whup* roar, each blade cracking against the humid atmosphere. Dust and scraps of paper leapt from the waste ground as the downdraft hit, whipping grit into the air and forcing the group waiting by the nearby hotel to turn away until the helicopter settled onto the uneven earth with a reluctant bounce.

As soon as the skids bit into the dirt, the side doors slid open and a crew chief in dark overalls eased herself onto the ground and waved the passengers forward. Nine people ran from the edge of the lot, battling the rotor wash as they dragged small cases behind them, their shouts lost in the thrum of the blades. They ducked low, threw in their bags and clambered inside as if they had done this every day of their morning commute.

Within seconds, the last boot cleared the ground, the doors slammed shut; the engines surged with a deeper, urgent growl and the Black Hawk lifted straight up, the waste ground caught once again in a cyclone of noise and dust. With a tilt and a burst of acceleration, it streaked away, the fading *whup-whup* echoing off the walls of the nearby buildings.

Twister and Deke watched silently from the safety of the hotel lobby window. "I will never tire of that sight," Twister commented, "But I sure am glad I never have to get on one of those things ever again."

"You barely did anyway," murmured Deke. "You just told them where to go."

"Fair point," nodded Twister, as they headed towards the breakfast buffet bar, which was just opening. "Fair point."

In the Popes' room, the thrum of the departing rotor blades finally worked its way into Simon's slumber and woke him with a start. He sat bolt upright, wondering why memories from another lifetime had broken into his dreams.

His movement disturbed Pippa, who lifted her head from her pillow and frowned at her husband.

"Are you okay?"

"Yeah… There was a noise…" Simon swung his legs out of bed, stumbled towards the window and peered through the curtains. "Nothing…" he said. "I could have sworn… No… Nothing. Sorry."

He headed back to bed, kissing his wife on her forehead as she passed him on her way to the bathroom. He was almost asleep again when she returned and sat down on his side of the bed.

"We have a note pushed under the door," she announced, waving a sheet of folded notepaper in her husband's face. "It's from Amy. They've gone. Flown out with Omar and the photographers. She's given us some contact details. Rob and her are just friends. I knew it!"

"Black Hawk. That's what it was," Simon rubbed his eyes and yawned. "I heard a Black Hawk." He checked his watch and then, for the second time in two minutes, got out of bed.

"Breakfast time. We need to check on Sandy."

The Breakfast Proposition

The breakfast buffet had all the majesty of a community centre bake sale, crossed with the atmosphere of a funeral wake following the departure of the departed's close family and friends. There were glistening scrambled eggs that looked radioactive, sausages reclining in a thin film of grease as if waiting for the coroner, and a tray of waffles that smelt of cardboard. A juice dispenser hummed a death rattle in the corner, offering an orange-flavoured beverage from what appeared to be a municipal water pump. Fortunately, the coffee was hot and strong, and the fruit looked less than a week old.

At a small round table, Sandy sat alone, looking every inch like a man who would never be worried by dodgy-looking eggs. The widower's breakfast was modest: one banana, two sausages, and a pastry, which lay on a waffle because there were no clean cold plates left; just hot ones.

Pippa spotted him as soon as she walked in, having left her husband muttering into his phone in the hotel lobby. With a cheery "Morning!", she placed a glass of orange juice and a steaming Styrofoam cup of coffee on the table, then helped herself to the buffet - the most normal-looking of the eggs, a croissant that squeaked faintly like a dog's toy when pressed, and something claiming to be bacon.

She returned to Sandy and settled into the chair opposite.

"So then. Your fictitious son-in-law has flown the coop?"

The septuagenarian Scotsman nodded and cleared his throat. "Made sense. Every day on the tour was a risk. Yesterday proved that. It could have been our van that was hit. They flew him and the army boys out this morning. Leaves their van available for the folk who had no transport."

Pippa observed the old man carefully. "So. Mission accomplished. And mainly thanks to you."

Sandy sat up a little straighter. "We all did our bit, didn't we? Talking of which, where's Simmo? He didn't leave on the chopper, did he?"

"He took a call. He'll be here in a minute." She sipped her orange juice, grimaced, and opted for the coffee instead. "Forget Omar for a moment. Are you enjoying the trip?"

"I am," he said. "It's always difficult going away if you're by yourself and don't know anyone, but Rob, Amy and yourselves have been great. Plus, the adventure of the last few days has been brilliant. Dragged me out of myself a bit. Gave me a kick up the backside."

"Good!" she smiled, unaware her husband was heading for the table. "That's what I was hoping to hear. With a bit of luck, there'll be even more fun to follow."

"Good grief, Sandy," Simon laughed as he sat down. "Weren't recent events enough for you?"

"At my age, you need things to keep you going. You don't know how many recent events you've got left," smiled the old man.

"Interesting." Simon took a slurp of Pippa's orange drink, wondered briefly if it was safe to swallow, then unceremoniously let it fall from his mouth back into the glass, blithely ignoring the mix of humour and horror on his wife's face. "I think I have something that could be right up your street, my friend."

The Talking Dog

"He says he'll talk to Pippa and get back to me, but I don't think he's very keen."

Andy, now fully dressed and wearing a padded gilet to ward off the unseasonal chill, emerged from the kitchen and onto the patio.

Mindy sat at the table, close to the patio heater, typing up notes on her laptop. Seeing her focused on the task at hand, Andy took the dirty plates and the takeaway packaging from the table into the kitchen.

"They had one hell of a day yesterday," he called. "A small tornado hit two of the vans. No major casualties, fortunately, apart from one van. And a helicopter picked up some people from the tour first thing this morning and whisked them away. All sounds very dramatic. I think Simmo's had enough drama to last him a good while. I don't think he'll do it."

"Mmmmm."

Andy pulled a couple of beer bottles from the fridge, popped them open and brought them outside. He sat facing the garden and took a swig from one bottle. The lawn and plants were becoming established now, despite the best efforts of the dogs. He could barely make out the security cameras. Apart from the clicking of the keyboard, there wasn't a sound to be heard.

"Yes. One hell of a day," he said to himself, just to fill the silence. "An EF-1, apparently. Wind speeds between 86 and 110 miles per hour. Strong enough to flip cars."

"Mmmmm."

"They were lucky. Nobody needed the hospital. Apart from the van, of course. That's a bit of a wreck. Apparently the chopper was a Black Hawk."

"Mmmmm."

Andy gave up. He opened his mobile and selected the *PFAdmin* app. It never ceased to amaze him how the figures increased from day to day. Membership and revenues continued to grow and looked to be linked to relevant stories getting media coverage in specific countries. That had been the big surprise; the media's overwhelmingly positive response.

There had been no gathering of media experts in Ireland, because *Path Finder* didn't wish to be seen to be attempting to influence the media.

Make of us what you will had been the message to any requests for closer involvement made by global organisations, national broadcasters, podcasters and newspaper editors.

They received the information that most of the world could access directly, then made it their own by adding opinions and interviews from third parties, some of whom were experts in the field, others not so much.

That was all they got, and they loved it.

"You're treating us like responsible adults," a television titan had confided to Mindy. "You don't tell us what to say. In fact, you don't even try to. We can't find one word of spin in any news release or statement you make. It makes a refreshing change. We respect that trust and the responsibility that comes with it."

Mindy had nodded appreciatively, having spent most of her career spinning every single story that crossed her desk.

This was a hugely different approach and a big gamble, she had told the *PF* group, but it represented the openness and honesty *Path Finder* was all about. The media weren't idiots though, despite their frequent attempts to prove otherwise. They identified the opinion of their audience and then reflected it in their output, boosting their own popularity and commercial value.

The current opinion of *Path Finder* was sky high. The trick was to keep it there, and that depended on the effectiveness of the guides and the success of the projects they recommended for support.

Andy took another swig of his beer, vaguely hearing the tapping continuing behind him. *What needs to happen for Path Finder to work successfully without us?* he thought. *And how long will it take?*

Andy glanced to his right to see Ginger staring at him.

More success equals greater popularity. People oppose the status quo. When it goes, Path Finder not needed. Now, get my tea.

Andy stared back, amazed.

Did you just say that?

No, you idiot. You're asleep.

Andy woke with a start just as the bottle dropped from his hand, spilling beer onto the patio.

"Oh, crap," he said, hearing the tapping stop as he scrabbled for the remains of his drink. "Sorry."

"Your phone just beeped," Mindy said, still focused on the laptop screen.

Andy grabbed his phone before it slipped from his lap, then checked the message.

"Well, we have an answer from our friends in America," he reported.

"Good news or bad news?"

"I'm not sure, but beggars can't be choosers."

Home At Last

Inside the Black Hawk, Omar sat strapped to a seat between two of the 'photographers' and opposite two more.

Physically, they all looked much more intimidating than they did when wandering around carrying a tripod, with at least one camera swinging around their necks.

The cabin reeked of hydraulic fluid, gun oil, and a mysterious but familiar 'army smell' that could induce retching until you got used to it.

Maybe this is what all of America smells like, Omar thought. *Guns and sweat, with a hint of burger.*

The floor vibrated so hard, Omar thought his kidneys could jiggle loose.

Conversation was impossible, drowned out by the slap-slap-slap of the rotor and the occasional exchange of military hand signals that looked like a cross between sign language and an overly enthusiastic game of charades.

Omar wasn't frightened; just slightly uncomfortable. He'd spent years hitching rides on American helicopters over the valleys of Helmand.

He found it both absurd and yet reassuring that his journey to freedom was ending with him rattling over the southern states to Georgia in a flying tin can that had helped him avoid so many bullets in his home country.

When the bird banked sharply, a soldier gave him a thumbs up. Omar, deadpan, returned a thumbs down, which got him the first grin he'd seen since they had taken off.

The landing at Fort Blade was straight out of Hollywood. The Black Hawk flared, the wind from the rotors whipped up the red dirt, and Omar stepped into his new life. Waiting for him was Major Danny Hernandez, wearing casual civilian clothes, leaning on his walking cane, and wearing a grin that threatened to split his face.

They embraced like the old friends they were, Hernandez muttering, "You really couldn't just apply for a visa like a normal person, huh?"

"This way was faster," Omar replied. "Also, I like helicopters."

From there, Danny drove them to an administration block, where they walked into a debriefing room that looked exactly like every military debriefing room in existence: grey walls, a metal table and a jug of warm coffee. The welcome from the three people waiting for them was reminiscent of a disciplinary panel pulled together at short notice from a holiday weekend.

The team was mixed. The captain from the Intelligence unit squinted at Omar as if she were still in Afghanistan and about to interview a Taliban deserter, who could still wear an explosive vest. Captain Simmons, an Afghanistan veteran from Psychological Operations, already knew Omar's sense of humour and wisely ignored half of the answers to his questions.

The last member of the group - a late addition from Counterintelligence - clearly wasn't aware of Omar's record or the details of his journey to the USA and asked, "So, uh, how do we know you're not lying to us?"

Danny Hernandez rolled his eyes so hard he nearly fell over backwards.

After almost an hour answering predictable questions - "Yes, I crossed the border." "No, I did not smuggle drugs." "Yes, I still hate the Taliban." "No, I am not a terrorist and have never been a member of the Communist party." "No, I have never listened to drum 'n' bass." - Omar visited Human Resources, a department that military types feared more than the Counterintelligence team.

The HR officer wore a bored look and a green cardigan, which Omar found more intimidating than body armour.

"So, here's how it works," the officer said, with all the enthusiasm of a clerk describing how to renew a driver's licence. "You'll be fast-tracked for a green card. It usually takes five years, three notarised letters, and the blood of a sacrificed goat. But because you're a military asset, it'll take only six months, with no goat involved. Congratulations. You are now the property of the United States Army. Dental coverage starts in 90 days. Do not die before then."

Omar smiled. "Out of interest, what if I refused the job?"

The HR officer brightened up and tapped his folder.

"That would be fun!" he said. "We'll reclassify you as an 'undocumented agricultural labourer'. Within nanoseconds you're back in Mexico or in a holding pen, waiting for the next flight back to your country of origin. Your choice."

"Then I accept the translator position."

"Excellent. Leave everything to us. You are now a Pashto/ Dari translator in intelligence operations. Congratulations, you're both a refugee *and* an employee of the US military."

Finally, Danny drove Omar to his new accommodation, standard-issue base housing, apparently designed by the same architects who made Soviet apartment blocks, but with more beige.

"Your kit's already in there," he told him. "Get settled in and don't go off base until we sort out your ID. I'll see you in a couple of days."

He handed over a business card - "Call me if you need anything." - then drove off.

Omar watched the car disappear around a corner in the housing estate, then turned to look at his new home. The front door opened, and there they were.

His wife, Nooria, wearing fatigues with a badge that said *Interpreter*; her hair tied back, and tears in her eyes. His son was taller than he remembered, clutching a toy helicopter, and his daughter, clinging to her mother's leg, shy until she saw his face break into an enormous grin.

Fourteen months collapsed in a second. Omar fell to his knees, arms out, and the kids barrelled into him like human missiles. He laughed; he cried; he held them for what seemed like *an age* to both children. Finally, he stood, and his wife dragged him into a hug so tight he thought she had cracked his ribs.

"You took your time," she smiled. "I've missed you."

"Sorry I'm late," he smiled back. "I ran into a bit of trouble."

At that, even the kids laughed, although they did not know what he was talking about.

For the first time since Afghanistan, Omar felt like he was actually home.

In For A Penny

The Storm Stalker van pulled up at the airport's kerbside drop-off, its paintwork surprisingly clear of the Texas dirt and Oklahoma dust it had collected over the past week, thanks to the most recent storm-driven deluge. Chasing tornadoes, being hit by tornadoes, facing off against a local border patrol and rescuing an Afghan medic with perfect English had left its passengers looking as if they'd been tumble-dried on 'knackered', even after a peaceful night in a nearby Denver hotel.

Twister and Deke emerged from the driver's cab, Twister sliding the passenger door open while Deke strolled to the back doors and pulled out the luggage onto the sidewalk.

Simon, Pippa and Sandy spilled out of the van and looked around for a moment, getting their bearings. It felt strange watching the hurly-burly of the airport all around them; nobody knowing what the last few days had been like for them; no clue about what might happen over the next 24 hours.

Pippa had spent this last ride in the van working out how she was going to recount her adventure on social media. *We chased death, and it ran*, she thought, before realising death had chased them most of the time and she had never used her camera when it did.

Simon was a mix of exhilaration and nerves; delighted he and his wife had survived the week, successfully taken part in a Garden Club mission, met some special people and seen some amazing weather, but feeling very nervous for Sandy.

The old man didn't look nervous. He looked as if he hated airports; despised them with every atom of his very being. He heaved his canvas rucksack onto his shoulder as if it contained a still-warm corpse that needed shifting. Twister and Deke stood to attention and saluted him, and received a smart salute in return, followed by a wink and a smile. Then he led the Popes into Denver International's cavernous terminal; a building that didn't so much welcome travellers as make them feel like misplaced luggage.

The couple peeled off towards their check-in desk, trying to pull out the paperwork while keeping a watchful eye on their new old friend.

Sandy approached the counter for the Glasgow flight, presented his passport, and waited with the patience of a man who had once crawled through peat bogs for Queen and country. The attendant's expression softened into an apologetic smile.

"Sir, your itinerary has changed. Here are your new tickets."

Sandy squinted at the boarding passes. Business class to Washington, then - after twelve hours of what appeared to be sanctioned loitering - first class to Glasgow. *First class*. He hadn't flown first class in his life. He hadn't even *thought* of first class in his life.

Simon and Pippa came over, passports already in hand. Sandy gave a soldierly cough and shook their hands with a grip that implied this was definitely not goodbye, merely a tactical retreat.

"I won't be coming with you to the international gates," he said. "Whatever your people did, it's worked."

Pippa smiled as she blinked back the tears.

"On another adventure then," she said. "They're coming thick and fast."

"Aye, just as I like them."

"I wish we were coming with you."

Sandy laughed. "No, you don't. But you've no need to worry. I won't be on my own."

Simon shook his hand. "Let us know how you get on, Sandy. Best of luck."

"Don't you worry. You'll hear from me."

The Popes smiled, nodded, and walked off toward the train and concourse A, like sheep heading for the shearing shed.

Two hours later, having enjoyed at least a couple of malt whiskies in the business lounge, Sandy boarded his Washington flight, shoved his rucksack into the overhead compartment and settled into his plush seat. He had barely sat down before a tall man in a dark suit took the seat beside him.

"Mr. Irvine," the man said, flashing credentials that contained more eagles and holograms than strictly necessary, "I'm Agent Whitaker, sir. I'm your personal protection detail for the duration of this flight, through security, and onward to your meeting at the White House."

"The *what* house?" Sandy asked, peering over his bifocals. He had heard clearly enough, but he just wanted to hear it again.

"The White House, sir."

Agent Whitaker's voice was steady and reassuring, but with the forced confidence of someone following orders he didn't understand. Sandy grinned and shook the agent's hand. He hadn't expected being a recipient of the full-blown American state apparatus.

Still, he shrugged, buckling in. *In for a penny…*

"And what will happen once I'm at the White House, Agent Whitaker?"

"That's beyond my pay grade. I have one order, and that's making sure you get there in one piece."

Sandy gave the agent a sympathetic look.

"Son," he said. "I used to run a pub in Paisley. If I can survive the Friday nights before a local derby, I'm sure I can survive this trip."

The agent nodded respectfully, apparently mistaking the revelation for a coded military anecdote.

As the engines roared into life, Sandy leaned back and looked out of the window, while Agent Whitaker adjusted his tie and tried to look like a man who knew what he was doing. Somewhere in the bowels of a government server farm, a minor change to a travel itinerary was spiralling into a potential geopolitical event.

Sandy Irvine, ex-sheep drover, ex-commando, ex-publican, and inadvertent VIP, closed his eyes. If fate wanted to carry him to the White House, who was he to argue? He was in for the ride, with Morag alongside him.

The VIP

Washington, D.C. greeted Sandy with heat, humidity, and a convoy of three black SUVs he assumed were for someone else. They weren't.

"Sir, this way, please," Agent Whitaker murmured, as though Sandy was a visiting head of state rather than a pensioner in cargo pants. He ushered Sandy past queues, through security checks that treated him like delicate porcelain, and into the waiting motorcade. He sat in the back of a vehicle the size of a bungalow, gripping his rucksack like it was the nuclear football.

"D'you no think this is all a bit much?" he asked.

"Sir," Whitaker replied gravely, "There is no such thing as 'too much' when the President is involved."

Sandy wasn't sure the president *would be* involved - just his house - but the air-conditioning was lovely.

The White House loomed into view, its façade glowing smugly in the afternoon sun, bathing in the dubious admiration of the tourists pressed against the railings and mumbling disappointedly, "It looks tiny, doesn't it?"

To them, Sandy looked like yet another anonymous dignitary whisked through the gates.

Inside the building, aides either scrambled like caffeinated ants or ran around like chickens without heads.

"Who is he again?" whispered one staffer, peering at a computer screen in the lobby.

"Sandy Irvine. No idea of his status, but his clearance level is top secret," whispered another.

"And why's he here?"

"Don't know."

"And who's he seeing?"

"Ditto."

"So, where do we put him?"

"Hang on…" The second staffer typed on the keyboard and pressed 'return'. "The Oval Office."

"Does he have an appointment?"

"No… oh… wait… yes."

The conversation faded as movement through the formal entrance at the North Portico signalled the VIP's arrival.

Secret Service agents guided Sandy through the Grand Foyer, past security checkpoints and headed into the West Wing, leaving a trail of confused staffers behind them.

An assistant met the group and ushered Sandy into a waiting room, where he helped himself to a small tray of presidential sweets and a bottle of water, then settled onto a navy blue sofa.

Panic Stations

"Who the hell is he? How did he get in? And what does he want?" President David D. Clampett did not like surprises. No president did unless it involved wads of untraceable cash, a free holiday or a pretty girl.

Now, a foreign pensioner in cargo pants had flown into Washington, been transported to the White House and escorted through the building into the West Wing, where he now had an official appointment with the most powerful man in the country, all courtesy of the secret service. And Clampett knew nothing about it. Nobody did.

National Security Advisor Jeanette Lusstey swept in through the door from the adjoining office.

"I was in the Situation Room when I heard," she said. "Thought you might need some support."

Clampett stood behind his chair, his arm still in a sling.

"Do me a favour, would you? Check the guy out."

The NSA turned and left without a word, resisting the urge to smile. Walking down the quiet corridor, she stopped outside the waiting room and observed the stranger through the window.

Sandy was entertaining himself, admiring the paintings around the room, facing away from the door, throwing sweets into the air and trying to catch them in his mouth.

Jeanette knocked on the door and entered.

"Mr. Irvine? My name's Jeanette Lusstey. I'm on the president's senior team. He will see you shortly, but would you mind if we have a brief chat first?"

The old, wiry man smiled, wiped his hand on the side of his trousers, then half-walked, half-stumbled over to her and shook her hand.

The Message

Deputy chief of staff Jared Pfist took the thin file from his assistant and flicked through the two pages inside.

"Alexander Irvine, 72, born in Huntly, Scotland... Royal Marine Commando for 20 years... won the Military Medal... ran a pub after that with his wife... for fifteen years... she died fairly recently... landed in Denver eight days ago... his first time in the States... he's been storm chasing..."

"Harmless then," observed Grace Hampton, breathing a sigh of relief.

"Maybe." Clampett stared out of the window, hand in pocket just as his NSA re-entered the room. "The question is, how does a harmless British pensioner wander into the White House without so much as a by-your-leave, when he should be on his way home from Colorado?"

"Two words," answered Lusstey. *"Path Finder.* He says Andy Blackwell asked him to pop in and see you."

"Blackwell!" Clampett's jaw flexed. "Turns down a personal invitation from the President of the United States of America and sends a no-name geriatric instead?"

"A geriatric who breached our security protocols with no effort at all." Grace Hampton pointed out. "We should talk to him. He's not doing this for the hell of it. Blackwell's sending a message."

Clampett looked around the small group. Each gave him a slight nod.

"He's an ex-pub landlord from Scotland," POTUS ruminated. "We do this properly. Break out the bar."

As he reached the Oval Office accompanied by a uniformed Secret Service agent, Sandy could hear laughter and glasses clinking behind the closed door. For the first time since he had embarked on this adventure, he felt nervous. This room was pure history. The desegregation of schools, the Cuban missile crisis, presidential addresses; they had all happened in this room - as, indeed, had other less celebrated but memorable events. And now it was Sandy's turn.

The agent knocked on the door, opened it and stood to the side. Sandy straightened his spine and walked through. The first thing he noticed was the large, wooden Resolute Desk, presented to the USA by Queen Victoria in 1880, presumably when she was having a clear out at home. Behind the desk were three tall windows, framed by large heavy curtains.

"Mr. Irvine." Sandy swung to his right and saw four people looking at him with friendly smiles that didn't reach their eyes. One man loomed forward and extended a huge hand. "David D. Clampett. President of the United States of America. Welcome to the Oval Office. Drink? We're trying a bottle of 25-year-old malt. It's a gift from a distillery in your neck of the woods. I'd love the opinion of an expert."

"Mr. President. An honour and a privilege, sir." Sandy shook the president's hand, then accepted the tumbler offered by Jared Pfist, and sniffed its contents. "I'm getting cocoa, caramel and cinnamon with strawberry and peach," he announced, then took a sip. "It has a malty, cereal base, and there's definitely a hint of vanilla and perhaps coffee in the finish." He held the tumbler up to the light and examined it carefully, then brought it back to his mouth and downed the whisky in one before handing back his glass.

"I reckon it aged for over two decades in a blend of refill hogsheads and butts, but I imagine it also spent over a year in Oloroso Sherry casks. And I suspect I've just drunk about eighty dollars' worth."

Clampett laughed while the others looked either horrified or impressed.

"Come and sit down," he urged, plonking himself down in an armchair at the head of a coffee table, with two sofas facing each other across it. "We'll recharge our glasses, then you can tell me what I can do for you."

"Oh, I thought you wanted to see me," smiled Sandy. "The agent who flew here with me basically said the same thing, and that he'd got it from his boss."

While Pfist refilled the two glasses and the two men chatted about whisky, Grace Hampton left for the secretary's office, returned hastily two minutes later clutching a piece of paper and interrupted the conversation.

"Mr. President? The Director of the Secret Service believes you requested Mr. Irvine's presence here today in an email from this office two days ago. I have a copy here, sir."

"But that's impossible." The president's voice was still folksy, but he looked puzzled. "I've only recently learned of Mr. Irvine's existence."

Clampett reached for the paper, scanned its content and handed it to Jeanette Lusstey before heading for his desk and opening his laptop. Sandy stood and wandered over to view the paintings, busts and historic artefacts along the far wall, sipping his malt as he did so.

Looking over his boss's shoulder, Pfist pointed at a sent email on the screen.

"But I wasn't here that afternoon," protested Clampett. "I was at the Kennedy Centre watching a Russian opera company ruining Shakespeare. At least, I think it was Shakespeare..."

He pressed the intercom. "That NSC guy who was doing a Chicken Little impression in the West Wing this morning. Get him in here ASAP."

Within thirty seconds, a middle-aged man with rolled-up sleeves and an earpiece dangling from his neck walked through the door from the chief-of-staff's office.

"Remind me again why you're here today?" instructed the president.

The man rubbed his temple. "Sir, we discovered a breach yesterday, and I am trying to work out how many White House computers have been impacted. Although technically it's not a breach because we don't know where it came from and we don't know what it does. We just know it's there. At least, we think it is."

Jeanette kept her eye on Sandy. He seemed oblivious to the surrounding drama, just sipping his whisky and wandering around, soaking in the experience of being in the building.

"So, if it's not a technical breach - or *techeach* - what is it?" Clampett asked, dreading the answer.

The tech officer cleared his throat. "Sir, it's an autonomous, untraceable presence in the Executive Office mainframe. It's not doing anything, but we think it's aware."

"It's sentient code?" asked Jeanette, not sure what that was but remembering it from a discussion with her husband before they fell out and got divorced.

"Not sentient," replied the officer, amazed anybody apart from himself in this room could actually use that phrase in the right context. "Adaptive. It's seamless. Elegant. Like it was grown; not programmed."

The president swivelled his laptop towards the tech expert.

"Could it send emails like this one? I didn't send this. Wasn't even here at that time."

The officer read the email, frowned, and then nodded. He looked up at Clampett.

"Sir. Is there anything you have done with this computer - any site you may have visited, for example - that may…"

"Pfist and I took a peek at a website a couple of weeks ago." Clampett looked across at his NSA. "Just after we'd met up with Aston."

"Oh God," said Lusstey. "Tell me you didn't… Please tell me it was porn."

"I was bored!" whined the president. "It can be very boring, this job - it's a *bojob*. We accessed the *Path Finder* website from this machine."

The tech guy spent little time in the sun, but still went a few shades paler.

"We didn't do much," protested the deputy chief of staff. "We just registered, checked out some stuff and listened to the background music. They've got some banging tracks."

The tech guy took a few deep breaths and nodded.

"That music may also have been code, possibly embedded in a browser-native payload disguised as a background loop. It's elegant, invisible and completely undetectable by standard or even sophisticated firewalls." He opened his own laptop to reveal a screen share showing lines of shimmering code shaped like waveforms.

"This isn't malware," he whispered admiringly, sounding like the voiceover for a luxury food retailer. "It didn't *enter* the system; it *blended* into it, like it belonged here all along."

"So I need a new laptop?"

The tech guy laughed so hard he wheezed. After a couple of goes with his inhaler and a half tumbler of scotch, thoughtfully provided by Sandy when he sensed the man needed help, he tried again.

"Sir, any systems your laptop links to, and any systems those systems link to, and any systems *ad infinitum* are all potentially compromised. But we can't prove it. Any of it. It has copied no files. It hasn't moved or destroyed any data.

Unless it lights up and tells us where it is and what it is, we have no chance of finding it. The only sign we have of the potential threat is this email, sent from your office two days ago via a secure server."

The temperature in the room appeared to drop several degrees as most of those present worked through the implications of the NSC man's statement.

"Nothing about this leaves this room. If it does, whatever the source, every single one of you goes to Leavenworth for a considerable time; maybe even Guantanamo Bay depending on the mood I'm in." Clampett looked across at Sandy, sitting on a sofa once again with his back to the drama. "Thank you, everybody. I'd like a few minutes with Mr. Irvine, please. Someone arrange another bottle of this malt - there's a case of it somewhere - and a selection of food from the canteen."

Once his staff had left the office, Clampett picked up his glass, walked back to the sofas and sat down opposite his guest. He topped up both glasses and raised his in a toast. Sandy raised his in return. Both men took a sip, then sat and stared at each other for a while, neither willing to break the silence.

A knock on the door announced two trays of food and a second bottle of malt.

"How was the storm chasing?" Clampett asked as they loaded up a plate each with 'The Tastes of America' buffet.

"Intense. Boring mostly. Once, we were heading south when..."

"Yeah. Fascinating," interrupted the president, unable to contain himself any longer. "What's the message? What does Blackwell want?"

The timing wasn't perfect. Sandy had a mouthful of Maryland crab cake dipped in a sweet chilli sauce and took a while to finish it. He held up a hand in apology, swallowed, then washed the food down with another sip of malt.

"Andy and the rest of the team wish to be left alone to develop *Path Finder* along with the guide teams and the organisation's members," Sandy said, trying hard to make it not sound like something he had memorised word for word. "You feel threatened by its success so far. Andy urges you to use its progress to feed into your government's decisions for the people of America and the world beyond, for all our sakes, including your own."

"Nobody threatens the president…"

"*If he plays nice, then we play nice*, Mr. President. That's what you said to your staff when you were on the call to Andy the other day. You really should get that mute button on your phone fixed," Sandy took another sip of malt, enjoying the realisation dawn on Clampett's face. *All the critical calls to world leaders he must have made!* "And then, when someone asked what would happen if Andy didn't play ball, you said you were going to *feed him to the fishes*."

Clampett looked sick.

"So you are threatening me."

Sandy laughed. "Oh, dear me, laddie, I'm the least of your worries. I'm just filling in a bit of time before my plane leaves for Glasgow later tonight. There is no threat, honestly. Andy likes you. Andy plays nice, sir. He's very keen for you to remain the leader of the free world. He simply wants you to walk the walk."

"Then why compromise our systems?"

Sandy helped himself to a couple more crab cakes. "Because you threatened to compromise *Path Finder*'s existence, sir. It's an insurance policy that he hopes he will never use. And if it has to be used, he guarantees that the impact on the US government's ability to serve the American people will be zero."

The stuffed portobello mushroom balanced in mid-air on the president's fork.

"He's got nothing on me," he bluffed.

"Then nobody has anything to fear," Sandy beamed. "Although I need your assurance that you'll keep away from Carmen Vega."

Clampett snorted. "That woman is so busy being perfect, she wouldn't even fly up to meet your beloved leader this weekend. She's shiny. Not even the Texas mud sticks to her."

Sandy frowned. "Envy is not an admirable trait, sir, especially for a president. But it gives us an opportunity to learn more about ourselves and highlights areas for self-improvement. Leave Carmen alone, sir, but be as shiny as she is, for everybody's sake, including your own."

He checked his watch, then finished his whisky. "That's an excellent dram, sir, and that's from a man who knows a thing or two about drinking. Now, I must be away."

Despite himself and the whisky, Clampett felt his face redden more than it should, and he stood up.

"The president says when a meeting's finished."

"And so you have, sir. A pleasure to meet you. I appreciate your time."

A knock at the door broke the rising tension. Agent Whitaker entered with Sandy's rucksack and nodded.

"Mr. President. Agent Whitaker, sir. I'm here to escort Mr. Irvine back to the airport, as instructed."

Sandy rose, leaned towards the confused-looking president and shook his healthy hand.

"A word of advice, sir. Stop with the ridiculous *Clampisms*. *Bojob*? Really? Make a name for yourself that will last a long time, and for all the right reasons," he murmured, then smiled. "Oh, and check your email."

"Wait," said Clampett, taking a breath. "Give Andy my best wishes, next time you see him."

"Next time?" Sandy laughed. "You'd be quicker doing that yourself, sir. I've never talked to him, never mind met him."

He followed the special agent out of the Oval Office without looking back.

Clampett waited for the door to close, then stumbled back to his desk, opened his laptop and accessed sent emails.

"Well, goddamn, I *did* end the meeting," he muttered to himself.

Homeward Bound

Before today, Sandy had never been in an SUV with tinted windows, never mind a convoy of the things. Now he was in his second of the day, thundering down the freeway towards Dulles. Up front, black Suburbans parted the traffic like Moses did the Red Sea, but with no wooden staff or God at their side.

Sandy, wedged into a butter-soft leather seat, kept fiddling with the electric window button until Special Agent Whitaker finally snapped.

"Sir, could you *not?*"

Sandy replied with the breezy confidence of a man who'd been drinking whisky and eating Maryland crab cakes with the President of the United States only half an hour earlier, but was feeling slightly queasy in the swaying car. "Laddie, if I don't let the air in, we may both have a problem, and it'll probably be messy."

At the terminal, instead of the usual slog through check-in desks that smelled faintly of sweat and stale deodorant, Sandy marched through a private door. A big man in an equally big suit barely glanced at his passport or boarding pass.

Security was so cursory that Sandy's pocketful of presidential sweets avoided detection.

The X-ray operator did briefly consider calling in the drugs squad, before realising these suspicious items were actually leaving the country, so that was okay then.

Then came the lounge. Not the lounge he was used to, with a coffee urn, stale biscuits and a stack of local newspapers.

This one had leather armchairs a pensioner could get lost in, champagne flutes that refilled themselves when you looked away, and a buffet table glittering with many intriguing foodstuffs, including sushi. Sandy piled his plate with mysterious, glistening rolls.

"They're raw fish," explained Whitaker.

"Oh," said Sandy, chewing thoughtfully, "Well, where's the air fryer?"

When boarding commenced, it was not a scrum. There was no stampede of flip-flops, crying children and duty-free bags.

Instead, Sandy bade farewell to his escort, then a discreet woman in pearls and a matching two-piece led Sandy through a velvet-roped corridor straight onto the jet bridge, in full view of a line of economy passengers glaring at him with the resentment of medieval peasants watching nobility ride past.

He ignored them, as nobility was wont to do in the olden days when 'wont to do' was a far more common phrase.

First class was less a seat and more a private lair. His 'chair' reclined into a bed longer than his own at home. There was a menu that required an online search engine to interpret.

The steward addressed him as "Mr. Irvine" in a tone usually reserved for royalty or high-value celebrities. He accepted slippers, a hot towel, and a glass of something fizzy before the safety demonstration even started.

As the engines roared and the runway lights streaked past, Sandy lifted his champagne and toasted his own reflection in the window.

"To *Path Finder*," he murmured, "The most exciting adventure I've been on in the last two days."

Then the aircraft heaved itself skyward, leaving Washington, Whitaker, a flummoxed president and the last of Sandy's sobriety far below.

Back Again

Once the plane levelled off, Sandy made a vow; not a wink of sleep. The seat must have cost the price of a small semi-detached in Paisley, and he was determined to wring every penny out of it.

He attacked the dinner menu like a man on Death Row opting for a taste of everything for his last meal on Earth. When the steward asked if he'd like a digestif, Sandy grimaced and said he didn't know what one was, but could he have a pint, please.

Every hour brought a new indulgence: champagne replenished before the glass even looked half-empty; a constant conveyor belt of snacks; and tiny bottles of condiments, which he pocketed discreetly for later.

Sleep was for tomorrow. He wanted his money's worth, even if technically it wasn't his money. When the lights dimmed and the other first-class passengers slid gracefully into sweet oblivion, Sandy cackled quietly to himself while starting up yet another film. *Nine hours of champagne and all the legroom a man could ever want? They'll no' break me.*

On landing, he looked like a man who had lost a bare-knuckle fight with a soft toy. His hair stood on end, his eyes twitched, and his skin glowed faintly pink from the repeated application of complimentary face mist.

But he strode off that plane feeling like Caesar returning to Rome after the battle of Zela, even though he looked like a zombie on a catwalk.

The steward - not looking that good himself after joining his VIP for a couple of drinks and a lengthy debate on the benefits of the haggis - shook his hand as he departed, then whispered "Legend" to the other cabin crew just loud enough for the pensioner to hear it.

Vene, vidi, vici indeed!

In Glasgow, he made it through a priority channel so quickly that he hardly registered he was back until the baggage carousel spat out his rucksack first, tagged with a lurid red sticker that practically screamed *Important Person.*

He walked tall and gave a regal nod to the weary travellers watching him go, as if he were doing them a favour by existing in their presence.

And then - bang. The VIP handler peeled away, the sliding doors hissed open, and the glamour evaporated instantly.

Outside, the icy rain slapped him across the face. The long-stay car park stretched ahead of him, and the chill, early-morning wind seemed intent on impeding him every step of the way, whatever his direction. Sandy trudged through the puddles on the uneven pavement, his windblown rucksack wobbling this way and that on his back, the leather slippers he'd 'forgotten' to return already soaking through.

His faithful hatchback sat waiting: 2004, colour once silver but now closer to lichen green, pigeon droppings clumsily stippled across the bonnet. The trip had been first-class, but the finale? Not so much.

He unlocked the car manually; the fob had died sometime three governments ago - and shoved the rucksack into the boot.

Inside, the familiar smell of wet dog greeted him, although Sandy had never owned a pet.

He sat down, the suspension wheezing in protest, and pulled the door closed against the rain.

He took a moment to catch his breath and laughed to himself, a long, wheezy chuckle that steamed up the windscreen.

For one magnificent night he had drunk with a president in the Oval Office, dined like a king, and flown like an oil sheikh.

Now, with a hangover brewing and the disintegrating wipers smearing rain across the windscreen, he was back where he belonged: alone, damp, and coaxing old Molly onto the M8.

I'm back, he thought. *But life will never be the same.* Not that he could tell the neighbours much of what he'd been up to over the last week or so. *And even if I could, they'd no' believe a word of it.*

The Invisible Threat

Connor Kelly had never meant to start a revolution. He only wanted to build a website that worked better than any other site in the world; a site as secure as the Clonbrinny local site, but offering hope and inspiration to whoever visited, wherever they were. But people had flocked to it in numbers he hadn't envisaged: millions at first, then tens of millions.

The *Path Finder* platform was now the nerve centre of a dynamic global movement. People around the world demanded that governments serve humanity and the planet, not themselves.

Connor had told no one he was behind it. He'd promised Declan that he wouldn't, but why would he? He lived quietly in one of the refurbished cottages by the small lough, saw his brother and his friends virtually every day and coded late into the night.

His brother was the brains behind the Kelly Industries Group, fuelling the local economy and making an impact across the country. Connor was just "good with computers", as he would say to anybody who asked - a phrase that was guaranteed to see the conversation change rapidly to another topic.

But Connor also knew governments and intelligence agencies were desperate to find the site's architect.

He knew because of the comments on social media, because of the warnings the *Path Finder* group received from its membership, and because he could monitor activity on any system that had even attempted to access or hack the site.

Some mornings, his first thought was whether this would be the day they knocked on his door. And that thought was becoming more frequent as the success of *Path Finder* continued to rocket.

Connor's second biggest concern was shopping; especially for clothes. The lights were too bright, the music too loud and the shoppers too many. But his trousers were fraying, and his mother had always talked about 'looking respectable', so he stood awkwardly in a menswear shop in the middle of Dublin, staring at a mannequin.

The T-shirt on display read: "Today, Not Tomorrow."

Connor's breath caught.

"Do you think that suits you?" smiled the shop assistant. "I could see if we have your size."

Connor stared at her, wondering if this was a warning. *They're on their way. Now. Are they coming for you?*

"I'll just take these, please," he said, handing over two pairs of chinos and a jumper.

At the till, his debit card refused to work. The assistant smiled and said, "Oh, the machine's playing up today."

Connor stared at the screen: *AUTHENTICATION FAILED.* A message relayed by *his* website to every attempted visit from a bad actor. Was it being thrown back in his face? Were they watching now?

"Are you okay, mate?" Stuart Morris, a former British police sergeant who had delayed retirement for a part-time role as Connor's companion, walked over from the front door where he'd been trying on caps.

"Not sure." Connor's eyes scanned the store, looking for anybody looking at him.

Morris watched him carefully, then saw the sales assistant removing the card from the machine.

"Here," he smiled, producing his own Kelly Industries Group credit card and handing it to her, "See if you have more luck with this one." She did. Morris accepted the bag and the receipt, then guided Connor through the crowd and out of the store. The younger Kelly's face looked pale and strained.

"We need to get out of here, Stu."

Morris knew the signs. "Of course, mate. Come on."

They hurried across the road and through a large shopping centre, retracing their steps twice when a column or a corner covered the action, and eventually leaving from a rear exit close to the car park. Neither said a word until they were back in the car. By then, Connor's face had regained its colour and his breathing was calmer.

"We've got half an hour before your date," Morris said calmly. "Fancy going early? We can have a coffee while we're waiting for Kara."

"I might need something stronger, Stu."

"No problem." Morris started the car and headed off. Once outside the car park exit, he sped up the road and then turned into a small side street just around a bend, pulling in by the pavement. Both men swung around in their seats and stared out of the back window. Two minutes passed, with no vehicles anywhere to be seen, never mind a van full of secret agents armed to the teeth.

"You can relax, Connor. We're fine." Morris turned the car around and headed to the small café. Despite their early arrival, Kara Walsh was already there, typing on her laptop with a half-full cappuccino on the table.

She looked up when she heard the door open and waved as the two men entered. Morris raised his eyebrows as he waved back.

"I'll see you later, Connor," he said. "Kara will bring you back home at three." He saw the concern in the younger man's eyes. "Don't worry, mate. I'll stay outside for a while."

Connor smiled and headed for Kara's table. Behind him, Morris shook his head slightly. The female police detective - a close member of the extended Kelly family - clocked the move and gave a slight nod of acknowledgement.

Kara was one of the few people who could talk Connor out of his head. She filled silences, laughed readily, and made sure he ate.

"You look pale," she said, having ordered the lunch special for two and a couple more cappuccinos.

Connor shrugged, eyes darting to the window. Two men stood across the street, laughing together while they enjoyed a cigarette. They weren't looking at the café. Not obviously.

Kara went on. "I hope your day's been better than mine."

"Why? What's happened? What's gone wrong?" The urgency in Connor's voice, bordering on panic, told her all she needed to know.

"Nothing's gone wrong," she reassured him. "We just had a couple of unexpected international inquiries dropped on us by the SDU. As if we didn't have enough paperwork."

Connor gulped and looked suspiciously around the room, half-expecting other diners to be standing up, brandishing Special Detective Unit ID cards of Ireland's counter-terrorism force.

"Not about me?" he asked.

She frowned. "What? Of course not... unless you've been laundering money for Russia's FSB by running several kebab shops in Great Britain."

She smiled and Connor laughed, but his thoughts tangled, even in the reassuring company of his closest friend.

Coincidences were never coincidences.

The Blue SUV

The motorway out of Dublin felt longer than normal to Connor. He drove fast, then slowed, then fast again, switching between lanes and using the vehicles around him as hiding places.

Try as he might, he couldn't slip the blue SUV he'd noticed just after leaving the centre of the city.

Kara sat quietly in the front passenger seat, regretting her decision to give him the keys, but needing to finish a couple of emails regarding the SDU inquiries before she could call it a day as far as work was concerned.

The man she was thinking of as more than a loving elder brother wasn't driving recklessly.

In fact, it was only after she had sent the emails and closed her laptop that she noticed the unnecessary weaving through the traffic.

Connor gripped the wheel so tightly his hands ached. His eyes seemed to spend more time on the rearview mirror than they did on the road ahead. Kara shifted the passenger wing mirror to get a better view of the problem, but couldn't see one. Connor spotted the surreptitious move.

"I think that blue SUV in the middle lane is following us," he said, as calmly as possible given he wanted to scream it at the top of his voice. "Watch."

He indicated right and moved from the inside lane into the middle, then accelerated and overtook a lorry using the outside lane before pulling across into the inside lane once more and slowing down. The SUV followed him past the lorry, then slipped back into the middle lane and reduced its speed.

"You see?" Connor almost shouted.

Kara didn't, but determined to sort the situation out preferably before the lunatic next to her did irreparable damage to her car or, more importantly, to her.

"Okay," she said. "There's an exit half a mile ahead. Come off there, and we'll see what happens. Do it normally, though. Indicate early."

Connor sped up in the inside lane, and the SUV dropped in the space created behind him.

"You see?" he said. "You see?"

One hundred yards from the junction, he indicated, then decelerated as he turned down the slip road. The blue SUV continued on the motorway, the driver probably whispering a quiet prayer of thanks that the drunk guy in the hatchback had finally gone.

Connor pulled into a lay-by just off the junction roundabout and switched off the engine, his chest heaving.

Both of them sat where they were for the best part of ten minutes; Kara sat without commenting, working out what she would need to tell Uncle Declan.

Connor's eyes flicked from window to mirrors and back again, while he whispered encryption keys under his breath like prayers.

Proof

Friday nights at the Fallen Hero were big nights, because Friday nights were quiz nights. They were also the only night off for Orla Brennan, owner of the hotel and bar and girlfriend of Stuart Morris, which was why both of them were sitting with friends, forming one of the quiz teams, at the far end of the bar, near to the quizmaster.

Unusually, Connor Kelly had turned down the opportunity to take part, but had agreed to head into Clonbrinny with the giant that was Brendan Dunne for a couple of drinks and to witness the proceedings. The quiz nights were always good craic and, as his brother had told him, he needed a break from his work on *Path Finder*.

They sat in the near corner of the pub, close to the main entrance, with two pints between them and the fire crackling. Others from the region who wanted to see the legendary Clonbrinny for themselves, plus the handful of tourists who were staying at the hotel, had boosted the usual crowd of locals in recent months.

This really was home, Connor thought. He knew almost everyone in the bar, and they knew him.

He felt safe, surrounded by folk who had proven that they would fight hard for their town and each other, plus he was with Brendan; his brother in all but blood.

It was the accent that caught his attention. Two Americans sitting in the residents' dining area, having a conversation with Margaret and Jimmy Doyle, who regularly used the room for an evening meal and a few drinks.

The general noise level as the crowd prepared for the quiz made listening to the conversation difficult, but Connor caught some fragments.

"…so how do you make that kind of money in this day and age?"

"…passed a row of beautiful cottages just outside town…"

"…can't be a lot that you locals don't know about the family…"

The younger Kelly's blood ran cold.

"They're asking about us," he whispered.

Brendan followed his gaze. "They're just nosy Yanks with too much Guinness in them. Margaret's telling them the tale."

"No," Connor insisted. "It's all connected. The store… the SUV… the men outside the café…They're here for me."

"Connor." Brendan put a heavy, powerful hand on his shoulder. "If the Russians or the CIA wanted you, they wouldn't send eavesdroppers to the local pub. They'd just take you. Relax."

Connor nodded and sipped his pint. But when one stranger glanced casually in his direction, it was proof enough.

The net was tightening.

Things Get Serious

The cottages by the lough looked stunningly picturesque. From across the water, they seemed like something from an old postcard; six neat little houses huddled together, their whitewashed walls and slate roofs dwarfed by the sweep of the surrounding hills.

Up close, however, a keener eye would see the neat trickery of the renovation - the way each pair of cottages had become one home.

Neither Declan nor Connor had really wanted to abandon the location that had meant so much to their family and especially their mother.

A brief discussion after Clodagh's funeral, triggered by the lament written and sung at the wake by Orla's daughter Sinead, had resulted in a tremendous challenge for the Kelly Industry Group's design and construction arm.

The architects and builders had completed the refurbishment and reconstruction of the properties in record time, due in part to the cooperation of the local council planning department, but mostly to the loyalty of the workforce and their determination to provide Clodagh with a lasting memorial.

The six cottages still looked like six cottages, but inside, the contrast was startling.

The old stone walls concealed vast, airy rooms with polished floors and ceilings latticed with beams fitted discreetly with modern lighting. What had once been narrow kitchens and draughty parlours were now open-plan spaces, with underfloor heating, hidden speakers, and windows that drank in the changing light off the water. Each space was furnished with a blend of handmade pieces and subtle luxuries.

Even the technology, no matter how advanced, was unobtrusive, hidden in the old bones of the cottages so that the place felt both rooted and forward-looking.

From nearby Clonbrinny, the cottages seemed a world away, tucked into their own quiet hollow by the water's edge, with the hills standing guard behind them. They looked secluded, but with one property for use by the Kellys and Brendan Dunne and the other two prepared for visitors, they carried with them the ongoing possibility of company and community, as though they had always been waiting for a return to life.

The road outside the houses was rarely used, meaning nighttime was very quiet, the only sounds being the wind, the occasional bird call and the gentle lapping of the water on the shore.

Brendan loved the tranquility. Every opportunity he had, he would forego his apartment in Dublin and head out to the peace and the solitude provided by the cottage.

With Declan away on business, tonight offered one of those opportunities. He headed for bed around eleven, leaving Connor focused on the back office workings of the *Path Finder* website as usual.

The lad loved working quietly, without distractions. Brendan obliged by going to sleep as soon as his head hit the pillow. It was the crash and the shout that woke him three hours later.

He tapped the security app on his phone, but nothing happened. The property seemed quiet and secure, but all the lights were off.

Dunne slipped on a sweatshirt, picked up his gun from the bedside cabinet and headed onto the landing. A sound in the darkened lounge caught his attention.

He crept down the first four stairs and saw Connor peering out of the front window. Then he watched him hurry through the hallway and into the unlit kitchen, where he looked out onto the back garden.

"Connor? Everything okay, pal?" he asked quietly.

The younger Kelly swung around. Brendan's heart stopped briefly when he saw the handgun. Connor never held a gun. Brendan didn't even know he had one. He was just relieved it wasn't pointing at him.

Connor headed to the computer room, picked up his chair and pointed at the three blank screens on the desk.

"They've found me, Bren," he whispered, in tears.

The Connor Bombshell

"We have a major issue, and I hold myself to blame," an ashen-faced Declan announced on the secure video link. "What we have created is becoming too big, too quickly. It's seriously affecting Connor's mental health. Frankly, the pressure on him is enormous. The more we're taken seriously, the more people expect from us. Add to that the amount of effort needed to fend off the attacks and hacks we're taking… mentally and physically it's all too much. I'm worried about him."

Andy Blackwell sat at one end of his dining table alongside Mindy, facing the large screen at the other.

The display showed four different camera shots - Declan by himself in the cottage, Isaac Delemos at his company headquarters, Martin and Mavis, who were currently at Peace Castle, and his own pairing in the Midlands.

All apart from Declan tried hard to keep their poker faces, despite the bombshell start to what Andy had thought would be a comfortable update on recent progress.

Connor was out of the way, at the zoo with Brendan and Kara; two of his favourite people at one of his favourite places and one of only two locations where he felt comfortable being stared at - the other being aquariums.

"Oh, poor Connor," said Mavis. "What's happened?"

"He's getting stressed with the workload. Plus, there have been events over the last month that have concerned him. The last one was a power cut in the middle of the night. It took down his IT before the backup generator could kick in. Each event has been totally innocuous in itself, but they've all fed into his paranoia. He believes that government agencies are intent on destroying *Path Finder* by destroying him. Well... all of us, actually. He wants us to start *Fortress* in Clonbrinny, but I've talked him out of it."

Andy raised his hand. "I guess we're not high on any government's popularity list, but Connor can't think they'd go after him, surely? There are higher-profile individuals in the group. We said we'd keep the two of you out of it, and that's what we're doing."

"Brendan found him in the kitchen at two o'clock this morning, carrying a loaded handgun. Neither of us knew he had one. And governments may not know he's the key to protecting everything we're trying to build here, but we know that's a fact. If something happens to him... deliberate or not..."

Mindy stood and walked out of the room. Andy noticed the general look of consternation on the screen.

"Oh, don't worry about her," he said. "She'll be pacing the garden. Helps her think."

Everyone fell silent, their eyes shifting from the screen, as there's only so long one can stare at others before it becomes socially unacceptable. Some looked downwards; others gazed at the ceiling, or off to the side. To the relief of all of them, it was only a few minutes before Mindy came back, her return heralded by the opening of the fridge door and the clinking of bottles. She handed one to her fiancé as she sat back down. Others on the call took it as their cue to get their own refreshments, which delayed things by a couple more minutes.

Once all settled down again, Mindy started the discussion.

"We have two obvious choices," she announced. "Stop what we're doing, announce we've achieved our goal of starting a debate, distribute the revenues to the guide groups or good causes and shut up shop. We'd take a lot of flak, but nobody could argue against that position. After all, Andy's already walked away from the UK prime minister job, so it's probably expected anyway."

She waited a few moments, secretly pleased to see the smirks on the screen and her fiancé's sigh of exasperation. *Hopefully, that's lightened the mood a little.*

"Alternatively, we carry on with what we have, but without Connor's help, and hope that we can create critical momentum while the systems hold up against hacks. Opinions welcome."

First up was Martin. "Declan. Are you proposing Connor drops out now, or are you thinking he may still be involved for a period while we implement whatever we decide to do? And will you still continue to be involved?"

The elder Kelly shrugged.

"Peace Castle is yours whenever you need it. So is Clonbrinny. I'll still be around, but it'll depend on how the lad's doing. If anything happened to him..."

"I had a lovely chat with Connor after the funeral." Mavis rarely spoke at these meetings. "Obviously it was a sad day, especially for him, but he talked about the debt recovery calls he does with Brendan. He really... *enthused* about them. I got the feeling he loves every one of them."

Declan nodded warily in agreement.

"My point," said Mavis, "Is that his work for *Path Finder* is reactive. Something happens - an attempted hack, for instance - and he has to respond to it and to respond well. Every single time. If he fails, we have a problem. That's a lot of weight on his shoulders."

"But that's how we operate," Andy interrupted. "We float an idea or a principle; wait for people to respond and then react from there. We're not challenging or confrontational. That's the point - to work in harmony. We're not a threat to anybody…"

"But we are. Many out there want us dead in the water so they can maintain the status quo," said Mindy, then hesitated a moment. "We're being too nice. We're playing rope-a-dope; absorbing attacks in the hope we can withstand them until we're too big to mess with and they go away."

"Mavis has a point," admitted Declan. "Connor gets a kick out of persuading businesses they'd be better off playing nice and paying up. He's good at defence, but he prefers offence."

Mindy started scribbling on a notepad. "And if we get it right, he'll feel empowered. The danger he feels will disappear as the threats fade away, and we'll end up in a far stronger position."

Andy frowned. "What about how we're perceived? How will *no more Mr. Nice Guy* go down with our members?"

"They'll never know."

"How can you be sure?"

Mindy looked up at the screen. Martin noted the look on his protégé's face - a look he'd seen many times before - and nodded. Isaac shrugged a *why not?* shrug. Declan looked thoughtful and appeared to be about to say something, then thought better of it and opted for an uncertain smile instead.

"I guess you'll just have to trust me," said Mindy.

"We need to get governments involved without being seen to do so," said Declan, having had second and then third thoughts about saying something. "The original plan was to galvanise the public; to make them the catalyst for change. But we need a response from governments at some stage. If they're slow to react, that could cause public frustration and trigger conflict…"

"Which would encourage violence and repression, neither of which is good for *Path Finder*'s future," concluded Andy.

Martin broke the subsequent brief silence.

"We need to find a balance where those in power are realistic enough to recognise the need for change, who share in the excitement being generated and who are pragmatic enough to adapt and adopt," he said. "We need to convey the potential threats to those who don't get on board, and the exciting opportunities for those who do..."

"By persuading them it is very much in their interest to work alongside us, rather than against us," agreed Isaac.

"I'm glad we're all agreed," beamed Mindy. "Quietly, under the radar, without implicating us, we'll make them an offer they can't refuse."

All eyes turned to Declan.

"Connor will love it," he grinned. "It's his debt recovery gig, but on a grander scale. Just one thing, though. No Godfather-style horse's head in beds. He loves his animals."

"Oh, I'm pretty sure we can come up with a suitable alternative," Mindy smiled. "And I reckon the alternative will be equally terrifying."

The Uninvited Guest

The parade had been long, loud, and satisfyingly theatrical. From the balcony of Tiananmen, the Chinese president had smiled until his cheeks ached, waving at the columns of troops whose synchronised goose-stepping inspired awe rather than orthopaedic sympathy.

Behind the ceremonial smiles, however, the three leaders - the host from Beijing and his guests of honour, the visiting Russian president, and the Indian prime minister - were already exhausted. The parade was not for them after all. It was for television, for the archives, and for history books that would describe things only as they were meant to be remembered.

Now, in the comfort of a private reception room overlooking the square and guarded by several echelons of security, they finally relaxed. The Russian loosened his tie, undid his top button while he could still breathe and poured himself a large vodka.

The Indian prime minister helped himself to pakoras, slumped onto a sofa and murmured a prayer of thanks, though whether to a deity or to the kitchen staff remained unclear. Meanwhile, China's leader nursed a porcelain teacup, wondering how long he needed to stay until he could excuse himself and phone his advisors.

Nobody spoke, preferring to enjoy the tranquility after the racket outside, each rehearsing the speeches they would soon deliver in the Great Hall of the People, each of them already tired of ceremony.

That was when Carol Pitcher wandered in through the enormous door, without ceremony or security clearance.

She looked spectacularly wrong, like a middle-aged British tourist who had wandered off from a package tour, perhaps in search of a bathroom, sporting a red silk qipao, sensible shoes - the kind sold in discount shops with slogans like *Food for the Sole* - and hair that had given up resisting the Beijing humidity.

She had the brisk, yet unhurried gait of a woman who had once infiltrated paramilitary groups for MI6, but now stacked discount beans in a Midlands supermarket. Both roles were, in fact, on her résumé.

She hummed to herself as she ignored the confused leaders and plucked a dumpling from the buffet.

The Chinese president froze, then his hand twitched towards a switch on the wall.

"Please don't bother. I passed four security points on the way in," the woman said with the unflappable tone of someone accustomed to calming stressed-out supermarket managers late on Christmas Eve. "I'm here with a message for you all on behalf of *Path Finder*."

The three leaders stiffened.

The Russian spoke first, his voice laced with vodka and disdain. "Never heard of it."

The Indian added politely, "Nor have I."

The Chinese president gave a small, bitter chuckle. "I'm sorry. Am I meant to be impressed by that?"

"Are you impressed that I have found my way in here and am talking to you in one of the most secure buildings in China?"

Each of them felt his guts tighten. *Path Finder.* The name they never spoke out loud. A network their advisors swore was *a harmless bunch of idealistic do-gooders.* The movement that was not a government, nor an army, but something far worse; millions of ordinary citizens quietly connecting, sharing information, aligning their will.

The termite colony beneath the palace foundations.

The leaders had all received the reports: the leaked proposals submitted to the *Path Finder* guides; the national manifestos circulating on supposedly encrypted forums; the whispers of webs of connections inside banks, ministries, police forces and even intelligence services.

And they all knew, without admitting it, that if *Path Finder* ever turned its attention to toppling governments, there was a serious risk that none of them would last three months.

The woman popped the dumpling in her mouth, chewed thoughtfully as she poured herself a cup of tea, and continued.

"Impressive show today. Tanks, hypersonic missiles, underwater drones and robot dogs. Half of it fake, of course - the fibreglass shells, the repainted prototypes. The other half genuine enough, but so terribly expensive. Imagine what you could do with that money if it weren't being wasted on keeping up appearances."

She gave a polite little cough.

"*Path Finder* has other ideas. Useful ideas. Governments redirect those billions into things people actually want— health, schools, a liveable planet. Buy into that and you'll not only survive, you'll prosper. Because the people will finally *trust you.*"

The Russian narrowed his eyes. "Ideas cost nothing. Power costs billions."

"Power," she replied, "Is easily lost. It can slip through your fingers like water unless you adapt."

She placed her plate carefully on the table, then turned and smiled winningly, as though she were about to begin a presentation at the local parent-teachers association or, more likely, to a disgruntled team of shelf-stackers, called in on their night off.

"We want little. Just a public commitment to support the *Path Finder* initiative. To work with our people in your country and your regions. To redirect resources to building, not destroying. And create a better tomorrow for your people; a better tomorrow for humanity. That's the only way you stay in office, gentlemen."

The Indian cleared his throat. "And if we decline?"

Her smile was as soft as it was lethal.

"You do not know how deep we have penetrated into your governments. For example, how about your domestic arrangements in India that would not stand the disinfectant of daylight, Mr. Booty Call?"

She turned to the Russian. "How about the FSB billions stashed in secret accounts in Switzerland or invested in Vegas casinos for a rainy day? The Swiss money you can't touch for now, because we've temporarily frozen the relevant accounts. We can bankrupt the casinos any time we like by flipping your algorithm and creating many, many lucky winners within a few hours." The Russian paled and knocked back his tumbler of vodka.

"We also have accessed the so-called 'Chinese' technologies, acquired illegally overseas. We've scrambled the key data in the core documents on your high-security cloud database, which makes them worthless, and have deleted any versions we could find on any related system. Those that were auctioned off to other countries and organisations have all been traced, along with the names of the government officials who sold them."

The silence lingered longer than was socially acceptable.

The three men avoided each other's gaze, each wondering how much the others already suspected, and how much this absurd British tourist was bluffing, or whether she really knew.

The Russian shifted first, pouring himself a drink. "Blackmail, then."

"Insurance," Carol corrected him. "You all now know each other's secrets. If any of your governments tries to damage or destroy any element of Path Finder, you will fall from a great height, and the other two will fall with you. Look at it as an updated version of mutually assured destruction. Each of you has an incentive to make sure the others do nothing other than support what we're trying to do in their respective nations."

The Chinese president's teacup trembled slightly as he set it down. The Indian prime minister suddenly found himself chewing a samosa that had turned to ash in his mouth.

Carol ignored her pounding heart, wiped her fingers on a napkin and smiled, like a schoolteacher to recalcitrant boys.

"Look, you're not weakening your positions by supporting us. You're strengthening them, because here's the thing: every other government is getting the same message. If you're seen to resist while your rivals work alongside us, who looks backward? Who looks paranoid?"

She picked up half a dozen samosas, wrapped them in a napkin and stowed them in her handbag.

"It's your choice. I don't need an answer today. Just a hint. A line in your speech at the Great Hall. A promise of cooperation. Something the cameras will record. Say nothing, and we will assume you've chosen the old way - secrecy, suspicion, self-destruction. Say something - anything - that hints at cooperation, and you secure your future. At least for now. Your choice. "

She glanced towards the door.

"Thank you for the food. Lovely dumplings, though the ginger is heavy." And with that, she walked out as serenely as she had walked in.

The leaders of three of the world's great superpowers sat frozen in their chairs, each calculating in silence.

Each already knew the others would say very little in public. But each also knew that *Path Finder* had just walked into the most secure area in China, uninvited, and left them holding their futures like fragile china teacups.

And, somewhere down the corridor, Carol Pitcher was probably looking for the gift shop.

Paths

The Great Hall of the People was crammed with delegates, cameras, and enough microphones to bug the entire solar system.

Red banners draped the balconies. The air smelled faintly of lacquer, testosterone and ambition.

The three leaders stood in the wings, waiting their turn. Each replayed Carol Pitcher's words in his head like a cursed ringtone.

The Chinese president stepped to the podium first, the picture of composure. His granite smile held as the applause thundered, carefully measured in length by party officials.

Say something, just a hint, he thought. *But not too much. Must look strong. Stronger than the others.*

He began in his usual cadence.

"Today we have witnessed the strength and unity of our great nation, whose history stretches back five thousand years..."

The speech went smoothly until he reached the improvised section, where his eye twitched.

"...and in this modern age, true strength comes not only from weapons, but from... er... paths. Yes. Finding fresh paths. Paths that lead to peace, development, and mutual respect."

He paused. The hall rustled. Some delegates nodded solemnly; others scribbled furiously, wondering if this was a new ideological slogan.

Satisfied, he pressed on.

Somewhere in a Beijing hotel room, Carol Pitcher was watching it all on television, sipping jasmine tea and writing notes on her smartphone.

Next, the Russian strode to the podium. He exuded confidence, but his thoughts were less composed.

He gripped the podium like a tank commander feeling queasy on rough terrain.

"The world today is filled with danger. But also... opportunity. True power is not measured only by rockets or tanks, but by... by cooperation." He spat the word as if it tasted sour. "Cooperation on new directions. On finding the path... forward."

His aides winced, knowing newsrooms would immediately clip this straying from the published remarks and transmit it around the world.

He added quickly: "Of course, we will continue to defend ourselves with unmatched strength."

He banged on the podium. "But strength is nothing without... vision."

The audience applauded nervously, unsure whether this was a threat or a confession.

Finally, the Indian leader ascended the stage, prayer beads still clutched in one hand. His mind churned, but he beamed at the crowd.

"India believes in peace. India believes in progress. And India believes in walking together on the great journey of humanity."

He let the phrase hang in the air like incense.

"Some call it destiny. Some call it dharma. But truly it is... the path we must find together."

The words echoed, syrupy and grand. The tumultuous response in the hall left none of them in any doubt that the message had struck home.

Backstage, the three men avoided each other's eyes. Outside the hall, the press swarmed with excitement. Commentators dissected the sudden obsession with 'paths' and 'finding'. Was this a new trilateral initiative? A secret agreement? A coded warning?

Carol watched the footage as the three men retreated from the hall.

"Good boys," she smiled. "I'm very proud of you."

Then she celebrated with another samosa, cold from the minibar fridge, and sent the report she had prepared on her phone. Before the acknowledgement was received, a key in the door signalled the safe return of her mission partner from his chat with representatives from two former Soviet republics and the North Korean foreign minister.

"You took your time," she observed as he threw the key on the sideboard.

"What can I say?" said Sandy Irvine. "We got involved in a drinking game."

"Who won?"

The Scot looked smug for a moment, then collapsed on the bed, where he'd remain for the next 24 hours.

The Great Vanishing Act

It began, as history often does, with something that looked like a clerical error.

At precisely 7:00 a.m. Eastern Daylight Time, the President of the United States failed to appear for his daily sweaty waddle around the South Lawn of the White House. His security detail, unnerved, found only a discarded tracksuit outside his bedroom door and a note reading: *Back in two days. Don't start any wars without me.*

His national security advisor took the phone call from the panicking head of the secret service, replied with the vocal equivalent of shrugging her shoulders - *"Meh"* - then turned over and went back to sleep.

In London, the prime minister's convoy gathered outside Number 10, then set off for a pretty average photo-op at a pretty average sewage farm. It was only after they arrived that the shit hit the fan - literally *and* figuratively. The PM's chauffeur opened the back door to find the rear seat empty. A phone call to Downing Street and a quick sweep of the building confirmed the PM had *'done a Blackwell'*, as the staff referred to Andy's disappearance over a year earlier.

In Tokyo, the prime minister's schedule cleared abruptly and without comment. The German chancellor's office declared a two-day holiday - but only for the chancellor.

In Paris, word got out that the president's croissant had gone uneaten. For the French, that was the true scandal and, to nobody's surprise, was the catalyst for a protest involving tractors, bakers and cow manure across the capital.

For those who were counting, twenty world leaders disappeared into thin air. Within hours, every major government had convened an emergency committee. The scenes were unsurprisingly similar: shock, confusion, anger, hysteria and panic, followed by the liberal distribution of tranquillisers, primarily benzodiazepines, washed down by alcohol. The exception was the Italian cabinet, which agreed unanimously to break for a long lunch and never to reconvene.

By mid-afternoon, most governments had issued a similarly worded statement along the lines of *Our leader is currently unavailable. There is no need to worry. Please continue paying your taxes.* All except the British where the Downing Street press office, with rare - if not unique - candour, admitted they had "no earthly idea" where their prime minister was, but advised the public not to worry as "he did little anyway, and the market functions perfectly well without national leadership."

Having talked to Mindy, the global press bit its communal tongue and followed the government line, which the public believed with the same faith they normally showed in diet tips or the promise of affordable housing.

The internet was less restrained. Speculation included alien abductions, the lizards finally shedding their human form, wind farms and the world's royal families.

The more popular *#WheresMyLeader* memes featured the Russian president on a surfboard in Hawaii; the Brazilian president squashed into a suitcase with a *Please look after this president* label on its handle; and the head of China leading a yoga retreat for penguins.

The truth was far stranger.

On the foggy west coast of Ireland, eight sleek jets landed at a private airstrip. The leaders filed discreetly into black vans, which were driven along a winding forest road to a clifftop hotel, an exclusive establishment designed for oligarchs who liked their privacy, their whiskey neat and their wine expensive. Even the local sheep were subject to non-disclosure agreements.

Once inside, the leaders gathered awkwardly in a ballroom decorated with images of genuine human, animal and environmental suffering on large, wall-mounted visual display units, which presented the images as classical oil paintings. "This is how we see our history," the gallery seemed to convey. "Do you want this to be your legacy?"

President Clampett broke the silence.

"Welcome everybody. Thank you all for coming."

The German chancellor adjusted her glasses. "Did we have a choice?" she asked, although they all knew the answer.

"Not if we want to keep one step ahead of developments," replied the US president. "We have two days to work out how to keep our heads… sorry… help save the planet and everything on it - apart from, maybe, the tech bros."

"We have to get this right," sniffed the French president. "Our very survival is at stake, never mind everyone else's."

The Indian prime minister thumped a nearby table, almost disguising the consequent pain he felt in his hand, but not quite. "Then let's begin before the tabloids declare we are being probed by Martians… again."

And so the top-secret Global Reset Conference began. Sitting in Peace Castle's security control room, where digital recording units faithfully saved every image and sound from the ballroom for posterity, Martin and Mavis exchanged a hopeful glance over the top of their champagne flutes.

Game time.

The Great Reappearance

By the end of the second day, twenty well-fed and hungover world leaders struggled up the steps onto their respective aircraft.

Twelve of them turned like robots on the top step and waved to the media, even though no media were present and the audience comprised four black vans that were already leaving the airfield and three sheep who couldn't tell anybody what they had witnessed.

Martin and Mavis stood in the control tower, sniggered at the useless waving, and watched the departures, reflecting silently on the potential enormity of the last 48 hours.

Day one had been mostly acrimony, serious division and two fights that the toss of a coin had resolved rather than risking violence. World leaders weren't so brave when there were no armies around to do their fighting for them.

A sumptuous dinner and copious amounts of alcohol had worked their magic though, and the leaders had reached a rare consensus before heading to bed or for a skinny dip at the foot of the cliffs, in the Atlantic.

They had signed a draft agreement promising to put humanity and the environment at the centre of a global policy for a new world order.

As expected, there had been compromises.

The French president, for example, demanded an exception clause for wine production, and the Australian PM made a big thing about retaining barbecue rights. But they emerged from the conference invigorated, united, and smelling faintly of peated whiskey, with a statement of intent to put to their respective governments and to the United Nations for further debate.

Nobody mentioned Path Finder during the conference, and even the statement failed to reference the organisation. History was being made and, as their egos demanded, the kudos was to remain with the leaders who made it.

As the final jet took off, Martin hugged his wife, who had a huge smile on her face, then shook hands with Mr. Widdock, who had added air traffic control to his list of careers. Even Widdock allowed himself a slight grin. He was part of history, but could tell no-one about it, and even if he could, he knew they wouldn't believe him.

Over the next twelve hours, the leaders quietly reappeared in their capitals. Official statements insisted they had been on routine business, but the public, whipped into a frenzy by two days of unchallenged conspiracy theories, refused to believe them.

"Global cooperation?" sneered the host of a political TV show in America. "For the planet? For humanity? Isn't that just what the lizard people want us to think?"

The White House spokesperson sighed. "Nigel. We're fed up with your crap. We're actually trying to save the world and everyone in it this time, even the Russians. Even you, you sad, despicable little man."

The host looked slightly taken aback, then leaned in, eyes glinting. "Exactly what an alien impostor would say."

The spokesperson decided she'd had enough. "No, what *you* just said is what an alien imposter who didn't want to be identified would say."

And so it continued, and television did what television does - draw the public's attention away from what really matters - and the leaders returned to business as usual, although this time, it would not be as usual as the public expected.

"The agreement is so radical that none of them dare publish it until they're all ready nationally; then they'll do it together at the UN," Martin reported to the group. "I suspect it may change during the internal discussions, but the central points will remain: that humanity and sustaining the planet will be the objectives of government."

"And we're not implicated?" asked Andy.

"Not a chance. They want the credit for themselves."

"Excellent. Well done, both of you. Anything else? Mavis?"

Mavis Barnwell took another sip of her gin while she considered what she wanted to say.

"Just a personal observation," she said. "The world coped with the disappearance of its leaders for forty-eight hours with no ill effect. Actually, it improved things. Fewer wars were declared, fewer absurd speeches delivered, and there was a huge reduction in motorcades blocking traffic."

She stopped briefly for a large gulp of her drink.

"I think our leaders should vanish more often - quarterly, at least. Eventually, maybe perpetually."

"We'll stick it on the list," laughed Andy. "Many thanks."

"You see?" Mindy put her arms around her fiancé. "You were a groundbreaker after all."

The Global Dignity Agreement

Media leaks from across the world suggested governments were moving in the right direction. There were whispers of more openness, a greater responsibility to do the right thing, primarily for the country, but also taking the global situation into consideration.

Interviews with senior people hinted at the same; reinforced in opinion articles written by political editors.

Even the political sketch writers, whose job was to hold those in power to account by ridiculing them, referred in slightly more respectful tones to the prospective changes.

Government spokespersons still refused to mention the *PF* words, even when specifically asked about the organisation by the media, and that was fine by *Path Finder*. Its aim was to inspire, encourage and galvanise the people into demanding change, which meant working with the people, not cosying up to the institutions that kept them in check.

The political scene was changing, and now the finance industry felt the pressure.

The men and women behind the markets were used to keeping their own business private while sticking their noses into everyone else's.

But times were changing; they didn't like it, and the world seemed to love it.

"We need to know what's happening, so we can defend our current positions and create new ones," said one chief executive on the video conference call.

"How can we make money if we don't know where to invest?" moaned another.

"We need to drag this *PF* crap into the mud. Get everything back to normal," said a third. "Otherwise, we're the ones taking the risks. I wanna leave that to the suckers."

"We should show we're trying, as tiresome as that sounds," suggested a fourth. She suggested they organise a jolly where they could produce some fanciful paths of their own. "When *Path Finder* rejects them, we'll declare the entire project fanciful and not worth investment. That'll drag their membership back from the dark side. Normality will return."

It was the jolly that created the enthusiasm, which is why fifty bankers, economists, venture capitalists and pension providers attended an unsurprisingly expensive week-long retreat in the Swiss Alps.

According to three delegates who were also *Path Finder* members, the week started like a frat party, degenerated into a drug-laced seance involving two priests and four ambulances, then - to everyone's astonishment - emerged from that hell with a shared epiphany.

"Someone came up with a crazy idea just after we realised there had been magic mushrooms in the fondue," explained one self-identified *PF dude*. "She said what if we made the economy work for people, rather than the other way round? And we were like... just blown away... boom... so we had some more fondue and stayed up all night working on it. Even the priests got involved, which was wild..."

The Global Dignity Agreement was an absurdly ambitious, partly plausible, occasionally hilarious economic overhaul, designed to ensure everyone had financial security, or at least enough to take a nap without worrying about money.

"It's coming your way, but here's the lowdown so you can be ready," warned the dude.

The Agreement listed several global initiatives for financial security.

Universal basic dividends for every human, with a monthly dividend drawn from the global profits on natural resources, taxes on automation that denied people a job and a billionaire wealth siphon.

Public banks of joy, or PBJs, would be non-profit banks focused on wellbeing and local return on investment by offering 0% loans for housing, education, green projects and 'fun stuff'.

An automated global wealth tracking system - proposed by a very bitter forensic accountant - would link to AI taxation systems that automatically detect hidden assets, tax evasion and suspect behaviour.

"We think billionaires will be very keen on philanthropy after this," confided the dude. "And more about this planet rather than the others. Public opinion will see to that."

"There are more proposals, like happiness-adjusted GDP, where economic success is based on public health, leisure time, income equality, and collective mood," Mindy reported back to the group. "We'll get more detail in due course, but it looks like finance is on board."

"Any negatives?" asked Declan.

"Some stomach pumping and a police investigation into who supplied the mushrooms," said Mindy. "And one economist stormed out saying if we eliminate financial insecurity, we risk eliminating ambition, anxiety, and the despair that makes capitalism fun."

She smiled at the huffing and the shaking of heads on the video conference call. One economist wasn't a problem. They had the markets on side, as well as the politicians and the media, without being directly associated with any of them.

Path Finder would gain credibility from that and would lose nothing in return because of the distance it maintained.

It remained to be seen whether the proposed changes in the financial model held or collapsed under the weight of their own optimism, but that was the same with *Path Finder.*

Unless you tried it, you'd never know.

Where It Started

Omar had learned through what seemed a lifetime of wars, both declared and undeclared, that survival was less about courage and more about organisation. Now a translator in the U.S. military - an occupation that sounded respectable until you realised it mostly meant explaining American slang to confused allies - he found himself once again in Santa Esperanza on the Mexican side of the border, sipping burnt coffee from his favourite kiosk half a mile from the crossing point with the man who had once nearly ended his story.

Patch, the one-eyed gangster whose résumé included cocaine distribution and attempted homicide, leaned across the table with the twitchy energy of someone who considered social interaction a form of violence. For a moment, it seemed the reunion would end with blood on the patio tiles, but then two discreet red dots danced across Patch's chest like laser pointers wielded by overenthusiastic cat tormentors. He stiffened, suddenly aware that Omar was not here on a nostalgia trip, or by himself, for that matter.

Omar explained his proposition in the tone of a man negotiating broadband packages for the umpteenth time today. He didn't want drugs, or guns, or revenge. He wanted to do business - names of Afghans trying to make the same desperate crossing he had.

If Patch supplied those names and some background, Omar could identify those who might be useful to the U.S. military machine. It was a vetting service, with the potential to turn refugees into assets and to get them safe access into the States. Payment would follow, the reputation of Patch and his cartel would grow, and nobody had to dig shallow graves behind taco stands. On the other hand, news of Patch's double dealing could reach his bosses. Being paid to get people across the border, then taking bounty money on the other side to ensure they were caught and sent back again, may not go down that well with the cartel.

Patch considered his options, chewing on the irony that he was now subcontracting to the same empire he targeted with smuggled narcotics and people. The two men talked, and to their mild surprise, discovered a common philosophy: survival was the only currency that never devalued. They bridged the moral canyon between them with a cautious handshake.

When the car pulled up to ferry Omar and his team back across the line, he stood and placed something on the table with a soft clink: the bullets he'd once taken from Patch, gleaming like pocket change.

It was a gesture of reconciliation or the world's most passive-aggressive tip. Patch chuckled, picked them up, and slipped them into his pocket, the unspoken message clear - every debt could be recycled into the next transaction.

On the way back to the crossing, Omar diverted to the Mission. The former church still looked battered but proud. The bell-less bell tower tottered even more than nine months earlier, but remained upright. Just. Leaving the vehicle and his support team outside, Omar pulled a couple of cases from the trunk and carried them up the steps and through the main entrance into the dimly lit hall beyond, where he stopped.

Had it really been almost a year? Looking at the desperate crowd of humanity crammed into the cots or wandering around wrapped in whatever they could find, it could have been yesterday.

Two figures walked towards him. Sister Theresa, in her uniform of jeans and t-shirt, and Chucho, looking smaller than the last time, but with a broad smile on his face.

"They kicked you out then, *hermano*?"

"Only for a couple of hours. Can we talk?"

The nun led them into a small office and closed the door behind them. Omar set both cases on the table.

"This is for you, sister. We had a collection at the base."

Theresa opened the case to reveal six new t-shirts and six sweatshirts, each bearing the logo of the Mexican Red Cross, but the main gift was underneath the clothing: wads of US currency totalling $20,000, to be used however the sister wanted to use it.

The stunned nun crossed herself. "This will do so much good," she said, cupping Omar's face in her hands and planting a kiss on his forehead, before counting the cash to check it was all there. This was a Mexican border city after all, where old habits die hard.

Omar pushed the other case towards the man who had made his crossing possible. "It's everything you lent me, Chucho, paid back in full, with some interest."

"*Gracias, amigo.*" The wily old mongrel didn't even move towards the case. He had no intention of revealing anything of his stash to the nun, no matter how much he thought of her.

"There's this as well," said Omar, handing over a padded envelope. "It's a Mexican bank debit card, fully loaded. And a US debit card, fully loaded. With my thanks."

"Thank you. I'm grateful," said the former coyote, "But the US card…"

"It's for when you decide you'd like to see how the other half live, my friend. You call me, and I'll sort the paperwork. Come for a vacation, an extended vacation or if you want a change of lifestyle. Your choice."

The older man was visibly shocked.

"You once told me I deserved a chance; that I had proven my worth by making it here," Omar felt the emotion in his own voice. "But you made it here as well, *muchacho*, and you deserve a chance of your own."

Chucho's eyes moistened, but the look he exchanged with Sister Theresa told Omar that the third choice wasn't an option, and the Afghan could not have been happier.

Conflict Resolution

Uncertain of its involvement in the fast-changing new world order, the paranoid in the United Nations held a brainstorm for any staff member who could make it to a downtown New York bar, ensuring a ready supply of drink and fatty foods and determining to stay there for as long as it took... whatever 'it' was.

The theme was conflict resolution, based on the submission received from the Path Finder peace campaigners' conference as its starting point.

Fourteen hours later, the survivors staggered out, waving a sheet of paper and blabbering to anybody who would listen about the Global Conflict Reformation Proposal.

"The proposal removes the need for warfare when resolving international conflicts," Martin reported, having received information from a contact in the NYPD, who had talked to the brainstormers before they entered a drunk tank to sober up and save whatever brain cells they had left.

"All the proposed global changes mean that armed conflict will be unnecessary anyway - at least until the aliens arrive. In the meantime, the UN wants nations to agree that war is obsolete. Every nation will re-channel military aggression into serving humanity in entirely different, less explosive ways."

The UN suggested resolving conflicts through the use of live-streamed Battle Arenas, involving games, debates, and video game tournaments. Petty national grievances like border disputes or trade squabbles were to be settled through televised competitions involving speed knitting, competitive gardening and the like; 'the like' being something wacky and never witnessed in public before.

Countries with serious national grievances would use their native comedians and mime artists to first acknowledge all their own historical wrongdoings before listing their grievances with the other. But all participants would do so after inhaling from a helium-filled balloon.

"The aim is no bloodshed, national pride preserved, honour satisfied, small egos, high empathy and nobody gets drone-bombed," Martin summed up.

Andy had spent the last couple of minutes staring at the ceiling in Peace Castle's boathouse.

"It's really happening, isn't it?" he asked no-one in particular. "Our baby's growing up without us." He coughed to hide the catch in his voice as he spoke. "So, what will the armed forces do?"

"What they've always done, I imagine," shrugged Mavis. "Disasters, pandemics, fires, floods, and infrastructural collapse - but resolving, rather than creating them."

"They could work in post-conflict zones, remote regions, or developing countries," mused Isaac. "Military deployment could mean installing bridges, hospitals, and solar grids in high-need areas. Maybe factories and warehouses as well."

"And military cyber units could protect the global internet infrastructure rather than attacking it. They would prevent digital sabotage, and stop teenage hackers from triggering thermonuclear explosions," offered Connor. "They could also provide tech support to the elderly, so they don't do something similar accidentally."

"Maybe veterans could train new recruits in peacekeeping, mental health, and emotional wellbeing," suggested Sandy, whose exploits in America, the Far East and elsewhere had resulted in an invitation to the inner sanctum via a video link.

"I could run a military boot camp including yoga, non-violent communication, and a four-week stint as a kindergarten teacher. That'd sort the men from the boys. I'll need something to do, now there are no more world leaders to surprise."

"Don't you worry, old man." The group was stunned to see a woman dressed in a red silk qipao walk behind the veteran, stroke his hair, then wander out of shot. "I'll find something for you to do."

Sandy blushed, then reached towards his laptop. The screen went dead.

It was Declan who broke the stunned silence.

"Barbecue time," he announced.

Barbecue Time

The grand, castle-like mansion of Caisleán Síocháin, or 'Peace Castle', still sat proudly on the high promontory overlooking the spectacular coastline of County Clare.

On the opposite side of the building to the main entrance, an outside dining area had provided unrivalled views of the Atlantic Ocean for hundreds of years.

During the period the mansion had played host to famous Irish poets, playwrights, and artists, guests had also witnessed fisticuffs between their emotionally charged peers and the occasional lovelorn swallow dive off the clifftop onto the rocks below.

Today, the location doubled as an occasional helicopter landing pad, as well as being a useful barbecue area.

The barbecue itself was a stainless-steel monstrosity the size of a small cargo container, fitted with unnecessary but impressive add-ons, including a rotisserie capable of handling a whole cow, and a baker's oven to ensure the optimal freshness of any complementary bread products.

Guests gathered here for sausages and sunburn with the same reverence once reserved for philosophical debate. Today, arguments weren't about the finer points of Romanticism, but whether ketchup had any place on an expensive artisan bratwurst.

The smoke that drifted lazily across the cliff edge now bore less of the romantic, peat-fuelled aroma of old Ireland and more of the acrid tang of overcooked burgers, sacrificed on the altar of 'alfresco dining'.

The mansion staff usually watched the antics discreetly from the building's windows, enjoying the sight of posh people in linen shorts and deck shoes wrestling with patio umbrellas, and speculating on which wrestler would fall over first while the Atlantic winds reminded them all that nature remained firmly in charge.

Not this evening, though.

The *Path Finder* team had given the staff the night off and sorted themselves out with the 'sumptuous special' from the Limerick Smokehouse.

Andy's culinary expertise had preceded him, and the Kellys firmly declined his generous offer to cook, which was why the rest of the group was now unpacking the food delivery while he sulked near the cliff edge.

Mindy walked across the grass to join him, and handed over one of the two large glasses of wine. Both gazed at the waves tumbling contentedly onto the shore below them, and soaked in a moment's peace as the sun sank below the horizon.

"Do you know it's almost a year since we first sat down there?" Mindy pointed at the flat boulder, resting close to a rocky outcrop halfway up the beach. Her fiancé nodded, although he hadn't realised how quickly time had passed.

From a scrap of a concept to 180 million members and the world's leaders scrambling to get on board, and all in less than twelve months, he thought. *Martin and Mavis with a new part-time role as global ambassadors and mine hosts of this wonderful place. Declan and Connor with the chance to make a new life for themselves as well as honouring their mother's memory. Mindy and himself finally making a real difference.*

They turned and watched as former strangers, who were now their friends, laughed and joked as they set out the food on the dining table.

Declan chatted with Martin and Mavis, casting an occasional glance their way, as if they were the topic of conversation. Kara and Connor giggled together as they arranged the cutlery and glasses, while Brendan Dunne and billionaire Isaac Delemos brought out a couple more chairs from the main dining room.

Andy sighed. "And where do we go from here?"

"Well, Carmen and Jeanette are flying in tomorrow to begin their assimilation, although I'm pretty sure they already know what they need to know. Then there's our guides' conference, and on the tails of that is your UN General Assembly speech, followed by the G20 in Brazil."

"They'll make a great team." Andy thought of Carmen's recent successful appearance on a late-night talk show, where the other guests had, coincidentally, included the USA's national security advisor. "Carmen will speak the people's language and Jeanette will knock heads together."

"And they'll have us for support if they need it. Martin and Mavis will be here. Isaac and Declan at the end of a phone and Connor at the end of his laptop, if he can take his eyes off Kara."

The UK's former prime minister jumped, as if hit by a lightning bolt. "I wonder what would have happened if we'd turned down Aston's invitation, or if Simmo and Co had gone somewhere else for their break?" he mused.

"Something very different." Mindy sipped her wine as she watched the sun's late rays bouncing off the windows.

"It might have taken longer to get where we are, and the route would have been longer and trickier, but I can tell you one thing." She linked her arm through his and rested her head on his shoulder.

"It would still have happened."

"I'm not sure I'd have been up for the hassle. I might have run off again. Done my disappearing act."

"Maybe. We'll never know, and do you know why we need never talk of this again?"

"Because I chose the right path?"

"Because *we* chose the right path."

Thank You

The vibration of the phone on the bedside cupboard didn't make too much of a racket, but it was enough to disturb the two greyhounds, who took it as an alarm call - more specifically, a breakfast call - even though the room was still very dark. Simmo scrabbled for the phone and checked the caller ID while Pippa roused herself and tried to calm the dogs, who were already downstairs and looking expectantly at the closed kitchen door.

"It's three o'clock," he grumbled, having left his late shift only five hours earlier, "And I might have guessed."

"Hello, Storm Boy!" bellowed a voice that would have disturbed the next-door neighbour if he had been in. As luck would have it, he was on the other end of the phone, on a beach in Ireland and trying to talk over the noise of crashing waves, but not sound too drunk at the same time.

"Do you have any idea what the time is?"

"No. But I have a very important message for you. TWO. I have TWO important messages for you, but I have to be quick because the police are coming."

Oh God. Now what?

"First, I'll be back later on tomorrow and would like us to have a game of golf the day after, followed by a splendid meal at the clubhouse."

"No chance. I'm working. Why are the police coming?"

"They're not. I just wanted to make sure you're wide awake for the second message."

Pope closed his eyes and counted to ten, as Pippa returned to the room with two unhappy dogs in tow.

"Come on, Simmo. Hurry and finish counting," pleaded Andy Blackwell. "I'm drunk, it's cold and I need the loo."

Pope added another ten seconds to the count, purely out of spite.

"What?"

"I just wanted to say thank you. We have done something that might give us all a better future. And it's all down to you, Simon Pope. Thank you. You are my hero and a genuine friend."

"What did I do?"

Now it was Andy Blackwell's turn to be silent. All Simmo could hear were the waves thudding onto the beach, then the crackle as the water drew back into the ocean through the pebbles.

"Do you know... I can't remember," confessed the UK's former prime minister, then promptly threw up.

The Oval Office was unusually quiet for a Monday morning. No reporters. No aides bustling with coffee or crisis briefings. Just three men, shut off from the rest of the world.

President David D. Clampett, still hungover from the weekend, hunched over the Resolute Desk and stared at his laptop as *Path Finder*'s membership figures continued ticking upwards with monotonous regularity.

"One hundred and eighty million," he muttered, unable to take his eyes off the screen like a car driver stuck on a railway crossing fixates on the approaching train, hoping against hope that it's going to stop. "They'll be up to one-ninety by the end of the week. Two-twenty by the end of the month."

Across from him, newly appointed National Security Advisor Jarod Pfist adjusted his tie and cleared his throat with all the enthusiasm of a police officer preparing to give bad news to the family of the car driver on the railway crossing.

"It's not just the members, sir," he said. "It's the data they've collected. They know things. About us. About... offshore accounts in..."

Clampett's look dared Pfist to continue the sentence, and the NSA leapt instead to a swift conclusion.

"We're in trouble."

"And so are they." Leaning casually against a century-old cabinet, billionaire tech magnate Aston Hail twirled a silver *Path Finder* lapel badge between his fingers like a magician about to make it disappear forever.

He was the only man in the room who looked relaxed and happy to be there, having returned to the inner sanctum as soon as his ex-wife had left the White House building. The beleaguered Clampett had made the call himself. He needed all the friends he could get.

Even if one was Aston Hail.

"My people reckon they're in trouble; they just don't know it yet," Hail said, flashing his trademark smile, "And it's going to get worse."

Clampett rubbed his forehead, wanting to believe, but not quite having the required faith.

"They'll have members arguing about everything," Hail continued. "Everyone will have their own opinion on climate targets, education reform, economic models, whether mindfulness for cows is a thing. There'll be groups pushing to be prioritised. Governments will engulf the guides with proposals and will press for fast approvals before their electorates boot them out of office."

Pfist nodded.

"*Path Finder* wanted nations to interpret its objectives to match their national interests, but we're not sure they're prepared for the complexity and confusion that's created. Imagine it's a religion. Now think of the massive issues that various interpretations of the same religion have created over the centuries."

Hail chuckled softly. "And yet the founders insist everyone 'finds their own path'. It's a charming notion, but idealistic, unrealistic and completely unscalable."

Clampett looked up, a glimmer of hope in his otherwise-dull eyes. "Can we control it?"

"Control?" Hail mused. "You can't control what you don't know. The founders are pretty superficial now that the organisation has critical mass. The system behind it is the key to its ongoing success. We thought we'd traced the tech genius behind the technology... in Ireland, of all places. We had him under surveillance for a while. Turned out to be some guy who needs carers and has a bit-part role collecting debts for his brother's business. A dead end. But we know that, eventually, the excrement *will* hit the air conditioning. We should be there for *Path Finder* in that moment; help them overcome their teething problems. Offer support... possibly some infrastructure..."

"So, we turn the world's biggest grassroots movement into something we can steer?"

Pfist hesitated. "With respect, sir, if they find out we're trying that..."

"They won't," Hail said confidently. "And they *will* need help. Why shouldn't it be us?"

For the first time that morning, President Clampett smiled. It was not a comforting sight.

"At the rate they're growing, a path won't be big enough or strong enough. Let's offer to help them build their road," he said, clasping his hands. "And make sure it goes through Washington."

Hail nodded, inwardly elated to be a vital part of the team once more, and equally delighted to have the chance of payback against Blackwell and his ex-wife.

Somewhere beyond the White House lawn, distant rumblings announced a storm starting to gather.

The wind was changing again. And nobody knew which way it would blow.

First of all, special thanks to my wife Clare and to Simon Burn, who read through the draft and went to great lengths to ensure I hadn't made any huge errors.

I also appreciate the help of my storm chasing buddy - and awesome storm photographer - Nate Nelson, who cast his eye over the Tornado Alley sections in the novel. Keep chasing and shooting, Nate!

To you, my reader, a sincere thank you for checking out *Where The Winds Blow*. I hope you enjoyed reading the novel as much as I enjoyed writing it.

If that's the case, please consider leaving a rating and review on your preferred book retailer website and any relevant social media groups. There are plenty of book-related pages and groups out there!

All three books in the *Path Finder* series have been blessed to find a readership that 'gets' the humour, appreciates the satire, relates to the characters and responds positively to the optimism and hope in each story.

Some may say the idea of *Path Finder* is great in theory, but would never work in practice because too much in the world would need to change.

I don't have any issues with that viewpoint. The book is, after all, fiction! However...

We're led to believe that great people and great ideas make history. But if you look closely, on many important occasions, it's usually made by someone having a terrible day - a monk who got annoyed with his boss, for example; or a baker who left the oven on; or a chauffeur who took a wrong turn.

Time and again, the grand machinery of civilisation is set in motion by a series of unfortunate - or fortunate - events.

When the German monk Martin Luther nailed a few complaints to a church door, he didn't plan to split Christianity in two; he was just venting on what may have been the medieval equivalent of social media.

In 1618, Czech Protestants objected to the Holy Roman Emperor trying to close their churches and threw two Catholic governors out of a high window in Prague Castle. It was a local issue - the governors landed in a heap of horse dung and survived - but it grew into the Thirty Years' War, which killed millions and ultimately reshaped the political map of Europe. A tantrum became a continental apocalypse.

When a baker's oven caught fire in Pudding Lane in 1666, London burned down. From the ashes came new methods of city planning and sanitation.

In 1893, a young lawyer called Mohandas Gandhi was thrown off a train in South Africa for refusing to move from a 'whites-only' carriage. That petty act of discrimination sparked a philosophy of justice, resistance, and dignity that reshaped the world.

In 1914, Archduke Franz Ferdinand's driver took a wrong turn in Sarajevo and stopped right in front of a man with a gun and a grudge. The result was World War I - a war so catastrophic it needed a sequel.

And in 2019, a curious incident, possibly involving a bat or a similar mammal in Wuhan (or maybe a laboratory leak - you decide), shut down the world, upended economies, and turned toilet rolls into the currency of choice for millions.

Whether it was a Petri dish of bacteria left open in a lab over a vacation period, angry colonists throwing a shipment of tea into a harbour or Albert Einstein daydreaming in the Swiss patent office, the world is far more open to change than many imagine.

Minor acts, accidents, incidents and overreactions can alter everything. History isn't a steady march forward; it's a series of stumbles.

So, if you ever feel insignificant, remember this: the revolt that marked the beginning of the end of feudalism in England, started when a tax collector assaulted a peasant's daughter. The catalyst for the Russian Revolution was a group of women in Petrograd - now St. Petersburg - demanding bread.

The next significant shift might begin with you - perhaps over tea, a train ticket, or an especially bad email. Maybe it will start when a world leader decides they've had enough, disappears during an official visit somewhere and ends up in the garage of someone who doesn't particularly like him. Who knows?

Once again, I appreciate your interest in my work.

If you'd like to stay in touch, then please visit my website **www.philrennett.com** where you'll find my blog and other bits and pieces, plus a free subscription to the very occasional *Path Finder* newsletter.

Registering will also give you exclusive free access to a series of short pieces, where I'll reveal more about the characters you've already met.

I look forward to seeing you there!

Best wishes.

Phil

Author's Books

<u>The Path Finder Series</u>

Paths Not Yet Taken
"The setup is hilarious, the pacing sharp… the satire
thoughtful without being harsh… even with all the chaos, it is
grounded in real emotional moments… clever, light on its
feet, and refreshingly hopeful, which is rare in political
fiction."

Good For The Soul
"A brilliantly chaotic and fiercely intelligent satire that
doesn't just entertain but bites with purpose… full of intrigue
and razor-edged wit… absurd, revealing, and surprisingly
hopeful… the blend of suspense, humour, and commentary
gives this book a pulse that's rare and unforgettable."

Where The Winds Blow
Your turn. After all, you just read the book!